Prolog : Chassidy

I spotted the 9mm handgun in the center of the floor. I knew if I even so much as attempted to move in that direction, every hair on my naturally curly head would be ripped from my scalp. His grip was just that strong on my bush. *Fuck it*, I thought. *There's some wigs in my closet I've been dying to wear.* I had to make a move or I was going to die in there. I kicked my foot backwards, my stiletto pump landing directly between his legs, causing him to wince in pain. I scurried from beneath his grasp as he loosened his grip and he dropped to the floor appearing to be hurt while I scrambled towards the middle of the room. For the first time in a long time I was glad I took my ex-husband's advice to have a handgun in my office. "We're living in an evil world with lots of weirdos out there; It's better to be safe than sorry," he said one night before he kissed me on my forehead and left me to go be with his new family. I was left feeling sick, two months into my pregnancy with nowhere to go. I opted out of mentioning it to him, not wanting to be one of those women that used a baby as a desperate attempt to keep a man from leaving. Now what stupid son of a bitch that went and broke into the office tonight, clasping their OJ Simpson glove all over my mouth, preventing me from screaming was beyond me. Suddenly, I felt heavy and tired, as if I'd been drugged. My adrenaline seemed to be the only thing keeping me alive at this point. I thought about the baby. Was it even alive? My first time being pregnant, I couldn't decipher between fetal movement or nervous butterflies fluttering in my stomach. If in fact I had been drugged, I wondered if the drug I'd been given was too strong for the fetus. Or was it the champagne? All I knew was if something happened to my unborn child, whoever was behind this had better kill me or they were a dead man walking. I'd do anything to protect myself and mine. I finally got a hold of the glock and picked it up with both hands in an attempt to control my shaking. I had never held a gun, let alone, used one so I was trembling, nervous as hell. I aimed it at the perpetrators head and their eyes grew wide as they slowly stood up. I, on the other hand, felt like I was going to pass out. Not only was my vision blurring, but I was getting dizzy. "Don't make another fucking move," I instructed him. Something wasn't right with this though; the masked man seemed to be looking past me. He was being distracted by something behind me. That's when I noticed the shifting shadows on the dimly lit hallway walls and I realized we were not alone. I had seen enough scary movies to know that if whoever it was were there to help me, they would've said so by now. This was real life and I had to do whatever I had to do to save my child's life and mine. I spoke with my eyes never leaving the attacker. "I don't know who either of you are but if you make another move I will blow your brains out with no remorse. I'm the one with the gun." That's when I heard the shifting shadow say, "Your clip is empty and I have the bullets bitch." Then *WHAMM!* All I could think about as I dropped to the floor was my unborn child. As I laid there it was like pictures of my life flashing before my eyes and I thought about the events that lead to this point. I was almost certain I knew who my attackers were after hearing that voice, so this was no robbery. This was personal. Lately everything has been happening so fast. As I felt the blood trickle from my head, past my nose, and to my lips I pondered, *"Where did it all go wrong?"*

Chapter 1: *Chassidy*

Squats my ass, I thought cynically, in reference to Mercedez Jackson's noticeably plump behind on her petite frame. She claimed to have got that way doing squats to tighten and lift her booty but I was almost positive she had gotten a Brazilian butt lift. I continued to gaze at her from afar thinking, *Ain't no way no squats turned that flatty into a phatty.* I smirked at my own cynicism. Was I hating on the beautiful bronze skinned girl that had the shape of a swimsuit model? Sure, I mean, I wasn't a hater or anything but it was just easy to envy a girl like Mercedez. Out of jealousy I often joked and called her "Olive Oyl" from the classic cartoon *Popeye the Sailor Man*. *Olive Oyl* was Popye's extremely skinny girlfriend. Although Mercedez didn't resemble the character at all it was just funny to ruffle her feathers a little bit. Whether I was hating on her or not, either way I was convinced that when she went to California for six months during the pandemic, she took a detour to Florida and went to see *Dr. Miami* and got that work done. I had to admit, she looked Hollywood good. She had naturally hazel, almond shaped eyes with long eyelashes. She always looked so wide eyed and innocent but you never knew what the bitch was really thinking. All I knew was she could go from zero to a hundred real quick, so I tried to stay on her good side. If you can't beat them, join them. I didn't trust her as far as I could throw her though. Mercedez stayed scheming. I had been hearing rumors about her, like she was on some scam artist type shit. Once she came back from Cali her name kept coming up in all the PUA and SBA fraud schemes. I heard about how she was getting people forgivable loans that ranged from ten to two-hundred and fifty thousand dollars by obtaining fake EIN and tax i.d numbers. Suddenly everybody in the hood had a business. The counters at the Arahb stores were covered with colorful business cards from people who weren't qualified to work at a company, let alone own a business. I wish I was bold enough to defraud the government but I'd probably be the first one to get caught. Then, I'd end up in jail doing whatever time they gave me because I definitely wasn't a snitch. My momma always used to say, "Snitches get stitches and wind up ditches" and who was I to test that theory?

    I continued to stare at Mercedez, mesmerized by her beauty. I had to admit, she was a 10, meaning she was the full package. She had beauty, body, and brains. Mercedez caught my eye through the lens of my bifocals so I logged off the kiosk I was charting on and made my way over to speak. I leaned over the nurses station where Mercedez had been standing there talking to Dr, Candace Raye, who was also a fucking ten. This bitch was drop dead gorgeous and swimming in dough and it showed. She was always dressed to kill, dripping in the latest designer wear, and she rocked the Rihanna cut that complimented her Halle Berry look alike face. Never dressed in scrubs, she was the flyest medical doctor in the south. She could've easily been on one of those reality television shows like *The Doctors* or *Married to Medicine* or something like that. The killer part was that as beautiful as she was, she remained humble, down to earth, gracious, and kind. I felt honored to even be in her presence; that's how you know you've reached black queen status and that, she was. She waved bye to both Mercedez and me and disappeared down the long corridor.

"What you finna do?" Mercedez asked, popping her pink bubble gum while she talked. What she really meant was, "I'm about to ask you to do something".

"Huh?" I asked, although I had heard her the first time, I just needed more time to get my lie together. She always caught me off guard with that question, often throwing it in the middle of a conversation about all things irrelevant to work. Mercedez was just all over the place like that. "I've got to give nine-teen her meds," I said, referring to the resident who occupied room 19, Mrs. Katherine."

"Oh Kathy can wait," she dismissed me with a waive of her hand. "Come help me with Miss Diana real quick." She started walking towards room twelve as if I had said yes. *I'm way too nice*, I thought as I followed her.

I said, "Now you know nothing is quick when dealing with the princess," which is what we called Miss Diana amongst ourselves because of her diva tendencies. "What you gotta do?" I asked pointlessly because I knew I was going to help her regardless. I wasn't one of those nurses that thought I was too good to help the nurse aids.

"A damn bath," Mercedez grumbled.

"Yeah, you take the phrase 'real quick' totally out of context," I said jokingly. I was really serious though and she knew it. She just didn;t give a fuck.

I pushed the stand-lift, a device used to move patients from one resting spot to another, and I slapped the red stop sign on the door that read PATIENT CARE. I had decided to help my co-worker out, despite the fact that I really didn't feel like it and I had my own work to do. This wasn't the first time Mercedez took advantage of the fact that I rarely spoke up for myself. "So, what's been up with you? I asked, making small talk while we tended to caring for the resident. It made the time go by faster. "Anything interesting happen on your three day break?" It was Tuesday morning and I hadn't seen her since we last worked together on friday. Whenever we returned to work after our days off, Mercedez always had a funny story to tell about whatever she endeavored while she wasn't at work. My life seemed so dull compared to hers, I sometimes made up stories just to keep from looking so lame.

Mercedez pulled the blue, elastic, hospital gloves over her rich caramel skin, then flipped her long honey-blonde hair behind her shoulders. There was no way I'd ever be bold enough to wear that hair color against my dark, chocolate skin. I didn't even understand how Mercedez could even stand to wear her hair down to her butt while she constantly had to wipe old people's butt; I'd be afraid of getting shit in my hair or one of these combative patients pilling my wig off! That's why I rocked natural hair, but to each their own. "Girl, how about my baby's daddy done got out of jail," she was saying. "And he didn't even call, he just decided he was gone pop up on a bitch."

I chuckled, looking at her dramatic hand motions and asked, "Oh my God, are you serious?"

"Girl, hell yeah," she said as she massaged Miss Diana's scalp roughly with shampoo. Only a diva would think to get her hair done while lying in the bed. And believe me, it was almost as impossible as it sounds.

"You can just place the bucket under my he-a-d," Miss Diana instructed us with a strong, southern drawl. When I tell you this woman was 'Gone With the Wind' fabulous! I wondered if her royalty treatment she demanded had anything to do with the fact that her son owned a small share in the company.

As she rinsed Miss Diana's hair, Mercedez went on to explain how Solo, her baby daddy who had been in jail for nine months (which was longer than the semi-annual bid he usually did in the county), was about to become the ex factor. She claimed this time she was on the brink of leaving him because she was tired of him putting her and her six kids (three from him and three from her ex-husband) through the drama of him being in and out of their lives, and she thought it'd be best to just move on. Of course she always said that every time Solo went on his government funded vacation and I couldn't help but wonder if she was using being "fed up" as an excuse to do her while he was temporarily out of the picture. I knew that as soon as Solo came home, she'd take him back. It had been that way for the past two years and I found myself pondering over which one of them was dumb for taking the other one back. I guessed both of them were just fools for love, I was glad I didn't have them problems. *Better her than me*, I thought. I did, however, have my own man problems, minus the kids and the drama. I was recently divorced from an asshole that I'm convinced had no heart whatsoever. I mean, who would serve someone divorce papers on their job? I'll never forget that rainy day. Mercedez, seeing what happened, pulled me outside to her Hummer so I could smoke a cigarette to calm my nerves. Mercedez opted for weed instead.

"Look," she said, inhaling a thick cloud of smoke and then blowing it out. "We can go slide on dat ma'fucka if you want to G". I laughed at that, knowing that she was dead serious. She must've inhaled too much of the smoke because she started coughing violently; I thought she was going to throw up. But when she caught her breath she smiled and said, "This some good shit." I laughed, amused at the fact that she could smoke weed like she was a nigga or somethin, and could probably out-smoke them all too. I personally had never been a fan of marijuana, although I did vote yes on initiative sixty-five which was a ballad to allow medicinal marijuana in the state of Mississippi. I was all for non-recreational medical use for those who actually needed it because it did help patients in many ways such as vision, depression, and poor appetite. I understood the positive attribute of the drug. I just wasn't a user. It made me nervous and jittery and took my anxiety from zero to a hundred real quick. Nevertheless, medicinal marijuana was a step towards total legalization, which would eventually stop so many minorities from being targeted, set up, and imprisoned for either using, selling, or trafficking the drug. Mercedez had better got out and voted because a bill like that would stop her man from going to jail so many times. Then again, he'd probably end up behind bars for laying hands on her anyway. She never talked about it but we all knew. In a small town like Hattiesburg, it was impossible not to know everybody and their mama's business. Especially if you were as popular as Mercedez. They had been the talk of the town quite a few times for either fighting and acting a damn fool, or some gang related shit Solo was involved in. People also loved to gossip about who Mercedez was seeing while Solo did time and, as a result, who Solo was cheating on Mercedez with when he came home.

After we had gotten her dried and dressed, we lowered the lift and Miss Diana squirmed in the wheelchair in an unaccomplished attempt to get comfortable. "I don't feel like I'm in here qui-i-i-te ri-i-ght," she said in that annoying country accent of hers. It was like she was singing every syllable.

"How's that?" Mercedez asked, pulling her further back into the seat by the back of her pants.

"That's go-od," she said, seemingly satisfied for the time being. I knew I was about to get up out of there before Princess Diana started barking out orders and asking me to do a million things at once as if her aid for the day was not even present in the room. Although I was the nurse and Mercedez was my CNA, I think I was Ms. Diana's favorite because I was more attentive while Mindy was always distracted by her phone. I wondered if Solo would call her a dozen times a day while he was free like he did when he was locked up. *Probably not* I assumed. Niggaz will be niggaz. But I did have to admit, at times Solo seemed to be head over heels for Mercedez. The way he catered to her every need and beckoned to her every call was something that I never experienced and wished I would. My ex-husband never even paid me much attention at all. Suddenly a heat wave felt like it came over me and I felt hot and nauseous at the same time.

"Are you okay?" Mercedez asked, eyeing me curiously but I assured her everything was fine. I waved bye to Miss Diana and closed the door behind me. *Speak of the devil,* I thought humorously as I spotted Solo at the nurse's station. He was holding a bouquet of flowers, looking good as ever. He looked bigger than the last time I saw him, like he picked up a few pounds. Light skinned men weren't my thing though; I preferred a chocolate brother like Morris Chestnut or Taye Diggs. There was something about a strong black man that made me feel safe. Solo looked more like Chris Brown. I stood there, eyeing him then suddenly my nausea heightened. I needed some promethazine for my stomach and some codeine for my nerves. Mercedez called that duo kesha, after the hit song *Wokesha* by the famous rapper, Moneybagg Yo. When the coast was clear I was going to poor me a big cup and all my problems would disappear. "You've been pumping Iron, I see," I said, playfully punching Solo's large, muscular arms. His skin was bright so his tattoos stood out on his chiseled body, so much that I counted Mercedez on him at least three times. He wore a black muscle shirt that made his muscles pop and rocked a bald fade with green eyes. I had to stop myself from staring. The nigga was fine.

Solo ignored my comment and said, "Yeah, my boy told me how you played him to the left like you had a husband or some shit," My smile quickly faded and he said, "It's all good, you don't have to explain it to me but you should definitely holla at him though." His boy he was referring to was Tragic, another inmate and another member of the crips. Tragic was in jail for first degree murder. Did I believe he was a murderer? No, I didn't. I believed him when he said it was self defense. The story was he had just gotten out of jail for a bank robbery six years ago when he found himself back in trouble with the law again, He didn't actually rob the bank, he was just with the nigga that did. He gave him a ride from the motel and the guy asked him to stop by the bank so he could pay Tragic gas money. What he didn't know was that the nigga was about to rob the bank. It didn't dawn on him until the man jumped in and yelled, "Go nigga! DRIVE!". They ended up on a high speed chase because Tragic had too many bricks

of pure cocaine to get caught by the cops. He had just re'd up and instantly regretted giving the man a ride. Of course they were caught and the judge showed him no mercy with a twenty year sentence, being eligible for parole after five years, which he made with good behavior. Now there was a girl named Kalasia or *Lady K* who was also in the gang and had been keeping in touch with Tragic the entire time he was incarcerated. So naturally, when he came home, she was the first person he sought out to see. He used his sister's car to pick up Kalasia and they ended up driving to a bar, *Mugshots,* where they had several drinks. Seeing he was too drunk to drive home Lady K took his keys but instead of driving him home, she drove to her own apartment, beckoning him to come in and smoke a blunt with her. Fucked up and not in his right mind, he gave in to her, against his better judgment. He knew she was married but he was blindsided by the pussy and devoured every inch of her in her Queen sized bed. In his intoxicated state of mind he didn't even feel bad; he wasn't the one breaking any vowels, she was. He fucked her hard, punishing her for giving away his pussy to another man, because in

All actuality, he had hit it first. She had been his ole lady when he went in and as soon as he was out of the picture, she had let another man into her heart. A dopefiend at that. Dude had a reputation of getting high off his own supply, breaking the number one rule as a hustler. Her husband was a meth head and was no comparison to Tragic. He didn't hold a candle to him on Tragic's worst day. Kalasia knew this and she missed Tragic in the worst way. But she had lost him so she figured that after he had got the pussy, he would be gone. What she didn't know was that Tragic had matured a lot in prison and he was a stand-up guy; he had no intention of hitting it and quitting it; he was there to get his woman back and claim what was his. Had she not slipped the xanax in his drink after they had made love all night, he would have had the chance to tell her just how he felt.

Not knowing this, when he smacked her on the ass after round three and told her to go fix him something to drink, she'd crushed the pills to dust and stirred it in his tequila. She just wanted one night with him before he walked out of her life not knowing that he was about to profess his love for her. He had downed the drink so fast she wanted to tell him to slow down but there was no use. Tragic was carefree and before he knew it, he was out for the count. When Tragic finally came to, he awoke to a steel blade beneath his chin. "Man what the fuck," he managed to say through gritted teeth, his jaws clenching so hard he thought they would break. Who the fuck was this man standing over him with a knife pointed beneath his chin? He tried to piece together the events of the night but came up with nothing. "You thought Kalasia was just gone snap back into the role of Lady K just cause yo ass got out of prison?" the man asked with a menacing glare. The mention of her name made the events of that night rush in like a flood and putting two and two together it hit him like a ton of bricks when he realized what was happening. He had been caught red handed sleeping with another man's wife in *their* bed. They hadn't even thought to lock the door, remembering Kalasia saying how she had changed the locks during their last break up. She had told him the man had been gone for days on a drug binge like a junkie, so she had changed her locks so he wouldn't come in and steal her shit. He cursed himself for being so careless because being the tactful guy he usually was, this was uncharacteristically sloppy of him. He didn't know what had gotten into him, it was almost as if he wasn't himself that night.

"I come to my house lookin for my wife and imagine my surprise when I see you," the man was saying. "I'm gonna gut your ass just like i did that stinkin' bitch." It was in that moment that Tragic turned his head slightly and was mortified to witness Kalacia's lifeless naked body lying in a pool of blood. She had been murdered in cold

blood, all while Tragic lay passed out next to her. "If you gone murder me nigga do it

like a man and let me put some fuckin drawers on," Tragic said, glaring up at the man

with contempt. "Be a man about it," he tested the man's ego. He knew he had gotten to

him because he began to lower his weapon while Tragic reached for his drawers *after*

he pulled a .22 pistol from beneath his pillow. In one swift movement he knocked the

knife from his attacker's hands and pistol whipped him so hard the man instantly hit the

floor. Tragic put his boxers on and fired two shots to the man's dome. "You should've

murked me when you had the chance bitch ass nigga," he spat on him. He knew the

shots rang loud into the night but because they were in the hood, the police weren't called right away and once they were, it still took them a while to get there. This gave Tragic time to flee the scene. However, a few anonymous tips that promised cash rewards led them to Tragic's sister's door step in no time and just like that he found hisself at the mercy of the court again. He went down for both murders. That was nine years ago. He was set to be released in one year. He marveled at the fact that he got a tougher sentence for selling drugs than he did for so called murder. The justice system was all fucked up and served

no justice at all. I had a brother in prison once so I understood how a man could get lonely in there with no one to write, call, or see, so when Solo introduced us via video phone one day when I was over Mercedez's house, I was happy to become his pen pal. My husband paid me little to no mind so it was nice to have someone to talk to, so it worked out for the both of us. Now Tragic was fine. I mean, fine fine. I'm talkin 6'2" of brown skin, light brown eyes, and long dreadlocks that he kept neatly twisted with his sides at a low fade. He had a body out of this world and a perfect set of white teeth in his mouth and not a full grill like most of the hood niggas she knew, just a small diamond embeded two front teeth. He was the type that would have money and still not be flashy about it in the streets. *That would be drawing too much attention to yourself,* he explained to me. Tragic and I actually hit it off pretty good, at first. He was a good listener when I needed someone to vent to. It never occurred to me that he had nothing but time on his hands anyway. He often video called me, showing off his chiseled chest and it not once crossed my mind that there was nothing to do in jail besides work out all day anyway. He even sent me poems and love letters, unbeknownst to me guys passed around and traded letters with each other, all sending them same tired ass lines to several girls. None of it had been original. Yet, those were the things that attracted me to him in the first place. He was giving me everything my husband wasn't. I was suffocating in my marriage and Tragic was like a breath of fresh air. Before I knew, i was all in. It's no wonder how my ex husband was able to have an affair right up under my nose when I was out here wide open, trying to hold down somebody that was locked down. I was sending illicit photographs of me in lingerie and I would make soft porn for him via video call. I didn't hold nothing back, It didn't matter when or where; from the bedroom to the bathroom stalls at work; I could've been a damn porn star. I had got so good at performing and I became so comfortable with my body that I decided to start an *Only Fan*'s page, a website that people could pay to see you explore your sexuality. Tragic had convinced me to do it so it was only right that I started sending him money. It hadn't dawned on me that I wa letting a nigga basically pimp me out from jail and I was blind to the bull shit as i fed on his lies and hung on to promises that would never come true. Tragic had used me in the worst way and after sending him money through *Cash App*, paying for video chats and phone calls, and putting money on his books, it wasn't long before i was broke, looking busted and disgusted. Once the divorce was settled, I was left with nothing thanks to my dumb ass signing a prenuptial agreement that stated if I initiated the divorce or was a partaker in infidelity, I would leave with nothing but my name and of course when he found out about Tragic I had basically given him a golden ticket out. It was a cruel punishment, especially considering that *he* had been unfaithful to *me* first; I was just the one careless enough to get caught, and leave a paper trail at that. Every credit card statement was filled with payments to *Global Telling* and *citi telecon*, the companies that allowed collect calls for inmates. My ex husband's attorney had even been cruel enough to enter the nude photos into evidence. I was so embarrassed and ashamed as the judge looked through each picture. His face was flushed and it was obvious he had grown uncomfortable, probably getting an erection as he went through the exhibit. When he had seen enough, I couldn't even bring myself to make eye contact with the judge. He had made his decision. Those photos were just nails in the coffin. I walked out of there a divorced, broke bitch and I had nowhere to turn. Tragic had stopped calling after the money stopped and I felt like a fool for allowing him to ruin my fucking marriage, just for him to jump ship and abandon me in the end. Then he had the audacity to act like I played him? In all actuality, the only one that got played was me. I snapped back to reality when Solo gave me a light punch on the arm and I expressed to him how I felt used by his homeboy. "But that's your friend," I said at the end. "That's the type of company you keep."

"Whoa, whoa," solo laughed, throwing his hands up and inching backward. "It ain't like I put a gun to ya head and made you fuck wit' the nigga. And I never said that was my friend; I told you that was my homeboy."

I just looked at him like he was crazy. Friend, homeboy; what the fuck was the difference? As if reading my mind, a voice said behind me, "A friend means yall been kickin it since the sand box." It was Mercedez. "A homeboy is a simple implication of two dudes in the same gang." She took the roses from Solo and hugged him before giving him a quick peck on the cheek.

I shifted my weight from one foot to the other and folded my arms stubbornly. "Sounds like the same thing to me," I huffed. I was genuinely pissed off that Solo had hooked me up with such a foul ass nigga.

Solo wrapped one arm around Mercedez's shoulders and moved his hands as he spoke. "Nah, my nigga, they not the same thing at all. To break it down in simplest terms; being from the same set is like being in the same family. You don't have a say in who's in it ."

Mercedez grabbed the hand he had wrapped around her shoulder and spun around. "You guys like literally have a say so of who's in it," she said and we all laughed.

The cordless phone began to ring behind us and I reached behind the nurse's station to answer. "Brooksdale Health and Rehabilitation center, how may I direct your call?"

"Aye, what's good love?" a voice boomed on the other end. "Can I holla at Mercedez real quick?" I cupped the phone with my hand and told Mercedez and Solo I would give them some privacy, then I hurriedly walked away, waiting till I was out of ear shot before I spoke. "Mercedez is unavailable at the moment but I can take a message."

"Well where she at? She told me to meet her up here on her lunch break now her phone going straight to voicemail."
Damn, I thought, shaking my head. She had blocked that nigga with the quickness! I had to give it to her; the bitch was fast on her toes. "Yeah, well her phone's been

acting up," I lied, not wanting to tell the truth and be the bearer of bad news. I wasn't as good of a liar as Mercedez though so I wanted to hurry up and end the call before he sniffed out my bullshit.

"Yeah, well just tell her I'm gone man, I can't be sitting up here like this. She know my money be callin me and I got plays to make," he was rambling. "Just tell her I came up here like she said bruh but she gone get a nigga jammed up! I'mma just get up with her later man. Thank you um-"

"Chassidy," I offered, slightly amused. Mercedez had the poor guy all over the place.

"Yeah, Chassidy, I knew that already, my bad man. It's been a long day already."

"Yes, it has," I murmured, keeping my eye on Solo and simultaneously looking back and forth out the glass doors to make sure Justin had pulled off. Once he hung up and I saw his tail lights disappear as he peeled out of the parking lot, I breathed a heavy sigh of relief, glad to have helped my friend. It almost felt as if I was the one who dodged a bullet when it was actually Mercedez who just dodged what could have possibly been a real one. If Solo would've seen Justin up here, that would've gone a whole other way. Justin's paranoid ass probably would've shot Solo to keep from getting beat the fuck up. My friend would've jumped in the middle and took the bullet for Solo because she loved that nigga that much. They was on some real thug passion type shit. For a moment, I envied my friend, because I had yet to experience a love like theirs.

I saw the two hug and when I was certain Solo was in the parking lot, I rushed over to Mercedez. "Girl, that was Justin calling here looking for you!" I exclaimed. "You must've blocked him?"

"And ain't finna unblock him, She said matter of factly, "He'll get tired of calling and eventually move on to the next pretty bitch willing to give him some pussy." My mouth dropped open. "How you just gone do Justin like that when yall been fuckin around heavy for the past five or six months now?" That was just wrong. I wasn't about to say that to Mercedez though.

"Justin aint' my man," she explained. He's just a man I like to hang out with when my man is away. He's not even a side piece. He know how the game go, ain't no loyalties." We headed towards the cafeteria for lunch. "On top of that, he got an ole lady and her name ain't Mercedez.

I looked at her in astonishment. "You mean to tell me this nigga thats up in this parking lot every damn day; the nigga you go on dates with, the nigga that be trippin when he can't be around you, has a *girlfriend?* " I found that hard to believe. How did he even manage to have time for a girl when he beckoned to Mercedez's every call? "So who is she? Because whoever she is she has to be dumb as fuck to let a nigga straight play her like that."

"Some German bitch with blonde hair and blue eyes," Mercedez stated, seething. She could try to sound as casual as she wanted to but I could practically hear the envy rolling off her tongue. "They live together and everything." She picked up a green apple and examined it , then she put it back down. I made a mental note to steer clear of the fresh fruit on the buffet line from now on.

"I don't understand," I started. "How does she not know about you when you've been to his house and in his bed?" I would sniff another woman out instantly if she was rolling around in my sheets.

"I sure have," she answered, nonchalantly. "While she was at work, or out running some random errand he'd give her to get her out of the house long enough for him to slide in this wet wet," she giggled. "And besides, he's a fuckin drug dealer. If she ever were to come home and I was there, I'd just fake like I'm trying to buy something." We placed our trays on the conveyor belt, paid for our food, then found a small table by the entrance to eat our lunch. "Shit, we even did it while the bitch was there one night, upstairs sleeping. She has great taste in bathroom accessories," she grinned, devilishly. I was truly in shock. And slightly offended. My husband had done the same thing to me. Yet there I was, listening to my so-called friend brag about doing the same shit to the next chic. I shook my head, not knowing who I was disgusted with more, me or her?

How well do I really know this girl? I began to ponder, then came to the conclusion that I really didn't know much about her at all. I heard her talking with food in her mouth but I wasn't really listening. Instead I wondered why the good girls always ended up with lousy men and vice versa. I didn't know Solo that well but at that moment, I felt sorry for him. He had a real sociopath on his hands and he just didn't seem like the type of man who deserved such a bich of a girlfriend. Who would commit such heinous acts and feel absolutely no remorse? She and Justin deserved each other because I was almost sure that if karma did exist then the both of them would be getting what's coming to them much sooner than later. It was at that moment I decided to fall back a little on our friendship because when the lightening finally did strike I didn't want to be anywhere near her. Mercedez was in way over her head but I kept my mouth shut. She was a grown ass woman and none of this was my business. I didn't take too well to drama so I was planning on keeping her at arms length. Girls like her always came with plenty of baggage and a big load of bullshit behind them and Mercedez was airing her dirty laundry. I planned to avoid her bad karma having ass as much as possible because when the shit hit the fan, I wanted no parts of it.

Chapter 2 : *Mercedez*

I make sure to put my phone on mute before I walk out of Miss Diana's room to meet Solo, just in case Justin gets smart and tries to call me from another number. He won't be able to reach me even if he calls restricted because I blocked restricted calls from coming through too. I know once he realizes it, he's going to try to call me from his homeboy's phone which is funny because them thirsty ass niggas been waiting to get my number. I know for a fact that ain't none of them niggas around him really his friend because they had all tried to shoot their shot at me one by one as soon as Justin turned his back. Them niggas is grimy and I hope Justin isn't careless enough to dial me out on another niggas phone. That would be just one more nigga I have to stop from calling me now that Solo was home.

    I approach my man from behind and overhear him trying to explain the difference between a friend and a homeboy to Chassidy's bird brain ass. "Homeboy is an implication they're in the same gang," I make my presence known. I hug my man and give him a quick kiss on the cheek, not wanting to make a PDA scene at work. The roses already have everyone staring and it feels like all eyes are on us as we post up at the nurse's station. I know the homeboy Chassidy is referring to is Tragic, the nigga Solo helped scam Chassidy out of all her money a couple months ago. Maxed out all her credit cards, poor thing, She had told me she was just working on repairing her credit too. Niggas ain't shit. Oh well, better her than me. I know the game and I play it well, that's why my nigga sends me money from jail and not the other way around. My nigga is a bonified hustler, ain't no prison walls gone stop him from providing for me and making sure I'm straight. *Cash App* was a game changer for niggas sending and receiving money in jail.

When I hear the phone ring, I cringe, knowing it's probably Justin. However, I can't afford to flinch an inch in front of Solo. Our connection is so strong and our bodies are so in tune with each other, he'll probably feel the tension in my body if I felt some type of way so I break free from his embrace, just in case. "So what are you doing here?" I ask after Chassidy excuses herself from the conversation. I watch him as he watches her walk away and I swear if Chassidy wasn't so not his type I would've gotten jealous just that quick. But, I know that I'm a bad bitch and the only thing Chassidy has on me is a naturally fat ass. A man is going to look at ass off of instincts, period. "You can't just be popping up, my boss be trippin and shit," I tell him. "I'm glad that bitch finna quit," I say, placing the roses on the counter.

"I saw her mean lookin ass on my way in. She smiled at a nigga, probably thiinking I'm a patient's fine ass grandson or something," he boasts, sticking his chest out and flexing his arms. "A nigga done got big while I was in the pen. I look good don't I," he asks and to stroke his ego, I tell him yes, even though I hate when he fishes for compliments. That conceited shit turns me off. However, I plan to keep up the small talk until I feel like Justin's ass is out the parking lot. I know he came because I had told him to come but that was before I got a surprise visit from my boyfriend. So now, I need Justin to leave. I won't have to hold Solo here for much longer I know because Justin has zero patience and won't wait around for long.

"Whose car are you in?" I ask Solo curiously. I know he's not in any of our whips because I have all the keys. "Don't tell me you got your big little sister to bring you up here to my job," I say referring to Solo's younger sibling. "You know I don't fuck with her." Jessica is what we call an overweight yet pretty girl in the south; a "Big Doll". She's fresh out of high school with two kids and one on the way. Jessica might be cute in the face but inside she's just another miserable big bitch. To say she is messy would be an understatement. Messy people start a lot of shit. Jessica stays in a lot of shit. I don't see how her baby daddy put up with her shit after all these years. He has to really live up to his name, Psycho, to put up with her drama because she would have driven a sane man crazy a long time ago. Psycho is a big time dope boy that runs with Solo and his crew. He got his name honest because he is known for fuckin a mothafucka up and going loco about his paper. He even skinned a mothafucka alive one time for fuckin with his money. He wanted dude to be an example to any and everybody that even thought about stealing from him or not paying him. And that shit worked. Niggas respected that big, black, dreadhead goldmouthed mothafucka. You either respected him or feared him. It was no secret that Psycho was at the top of the food chain but he made sure everybody ate. I never understood how a King could pick a hood rat like Jessica to share his throne with. She and Psycho were in different leagues, ran in different circles but at the end of the day I suppose it was their differences that made their shit work. Hey, if they like it, I love it; I ain't never been no hating ass bitch and I'm not about to pick today to start. In fact, Jessica and I used to be cool. She was Solo's baby sister; that alone was enough for me to put in a little effort to get along with her. We were actually starting to get close but that came to an abrupt halt when Jessica's sticky fingers landed on my laptop. Her intentions were to sell it to the pawn shop so imagine her surprise when she went to delete everything on it, including my google photo album and she saw *her* man on *my* PC. The shit was actually an innocent situation. If i wanted to fuck her nigga I sure wouldn't leave the evidence laying around in my boyfriend's car. What jessica had seen was a picture of her babydaddy and me, hugged up at an out of town night club and she instantly jumped to conclusions and assumed we were fucking around. If I wanted to fuck the nigga I could have effortlessly done so but we we'rent even on no shit like that. We had run into each other coincidentally that night when Solo was in jail and Jessica was in Atlanta, Georgia, on a boosting spree. Her nigga had enough money to buy her anything she desired yet she would still be up in stores stealing her ass off like some project hood rat. You can take a hoe out the hood but you can't take the hood out of a hoe. The night Psycho and I ran into each other we were at a nightclub in Biloxi. As a matter of fact, Psycho was already in the club when I got there. I just happened to bump into him, literally.

"Damn, ma, my bad," he had apologized even though I was the one that almost caused him to spill his drink, trying to hurry up and get in. He was on his way out.

"Psycho?" I peered through my green contact lenses, squinting to see through my long, dark eyelashes. "What's up bro?"

When he finally recognized who I was he started grinning from ear to ear, showing a mouth full of gold. "Oh shit, what you doing out here?" he asked.

"Shit, I'm tryna see Young Boy like everybody else but the bouncer dude is trippin," I said, sucking my teeth. "Normally I'd be flattered but tonight I'm fuckin freezing and I'll be damned if I wait in this long ass line again just to go grab my

I.D. out the car,"

"Oh is my man Tim giving you a hard time," Psycho asked, throwing his head in the bouncer's direction. "Yo my man, let her in," he told Tim with authority. "She's with me," he said pointedly. And just like that, without saying a word, the tall, muscular *Debo* looking mothafucka unlatched the velvet rope and waited for me to enter the huge yet over crowded night club.

Psycho walked back in behind me and I said to him, "Thanks for the hook up big bro but weren't you just leaving?"

"Yeah, but I think I got a reason to stay now," here said, rubbing his hands together while grinning.

"Buy me a drink?" I offered, yelling over the music blaring through the speakers all around us in the VIP section. The nigga was balling out of control so I was at the right plce at the right time. There was some business concerning him I'd wanted to get squared away with anyway and while he was being generous it seemed like the right time to pitch my idea. I waited for the young, big booty waitress that was serving us to walk away after taking our drink orders before I started to speak. I was ready to talk cash money shit. I leaned in on him. "Let's talk business." From what I'd heard, Psycho was the coke connect for all of southern Mississippi and he even had west Mississippi on lock. I was jobless at the time and to be frank, I wanted a piece of the pie. But, I didn't have time to be on corners selling rocks; politics had shown me that the trickle down effect doesn't work. I wanted to move weight. I had no job and mouths to feed and Solo had spoiled me so much with the fast life and easy money that I couldn't see myself working a nine to five at some dead end job. I mean sure, I had planned on going back to school but even that required money that was intangible to me at that time. Too proud to start stripping, the only other option was to hustle. I could quadruple my money in less than half the time it'd take working. The plan was, I would pay for college and get back into nursing like I had planned before I started having children. Then once I had enough money saved, I would leave the game for good. At least that was what I told myself.

"How much work you need?" Psycho asked and it was like music to my ears. "I can give you a few cookies to make you a lil' money on da crack side."

"Cookies?" I grunted and sat back against the red leather seat. *What kind of small-time hustler did he think I was? I'm not no fuckin corner boy and I'm not Solo,* I thought incredulously. Sure, the only reason Solo even dealt crack was because he had all the time in the world to catch every play since he was in the hood all day anyway but I, on the other hand, wasn't no hood chick so I couldn't do anything with crack. I needed a couple of bricks of raw cocaine.

Psycho sat his Cognac down and looked me in my eyes as if he were searching for something. Finally, after a brief moment of silence he clasped his hands together and said, "So, you want me to front you two kilos of raw cocaine and I don't even know the people you'll be dealing with?" before I could respond he said "I'd prefer to know who it is I'm getting in bed with. Especially when you request my services on consignment."

"I can vouch for them," I say, confidently.

Psycho laughed, then with a serious face he said, "You can vouch for no one. Always remember that. When a nigga facing twenty-five to life it ain't hard for a nigga to start singing. A bitch nigga knowledge is a loyalty battle between his family and the streets. And if he ain't self made, the pussy hold the power. All you can vouch for is *you*."

"If a nigga turned state on me then the only one he can snitch on is me because he will never meet you. That way they'll always need me to eat, therefore I'll always have a seat at the table and you'll be safe," I say with a smile.

"I see Solo taught you well," Psycho commended me.

"Nah, he didn't teach me shit, at least he didn't try to. I was just always paying attention. I'm very observant," I said eyeing him sexily with an arched brow and biting my lip. "Fuck with me," I said seductiivley drawing circles around his ankles with the tip of my red bottom pumps. "I promise you won't regret it." I knew his mind was no longer on business and I smiled inwardly, knowing I would end up having my way as long as he thought he was having his. He was right, pussy did hold the power. He wanted to fuck me and I knew it. He was probably having all kinds of dirty thoughts between those two ears as he appeared to be undressing me with his eyes. I knew I was stringing him along like a puppet and unfortunately for him, sex wasn't a part of my plan at all. Under no circumstances was I sleeping with a nigga for drugs or money like some crack whore. Besides, if I had to do something for it, the shit wouldn't be called a *front*. Unbeknownst to him I had zero intentions of being obligated to his sexual advances. He was my *baby daddy*'s *baby sister*'s *baby daddy*. The shit would get messier than it sounded so that potential entanglement was off the table. I just didn't get down like that. But if Solo wasn't his brother-n-law I'd take his ass down through there. I knew him first so my loyalties weren't with Jessica, I just respected Solo enough to not smash the homie. Jessica needed to be thanking me that I wouldn't because if I wanted to i'd fuck her man. When and wherever I felt like it. I could see the lust in his dark brown eyes and it was written all over his face. Although it would never happen I didn't see any harm in entertaining the idea, especially if it meant I could walk away from that table having got exactly what I wanted. I was young and fearless and thought I could have whatever I wanted. I wasn't seasoned and cautious because I hadn't gone through enough shit yet. Wisdom wasn't something that was acquired according to age, it was according to *experience*. Solo wasn't there to do everything for me anymore; it was time to jump off the porch and get my feet wet.

I reached in my purple Louis Vuitton clutch and pulled out a *Newport* short. Psycho reached across the round table and flicked his blue *BIC* lighter and held the flame up to my cigarette. He said, "I don't usually play with fire because I can't risk getting burned. Before I play with fire and get burned I'll put the fire out at the first sign of smoke." He released his thumb and the flame disappeared. I took a long drag off the nicotine as I let his words sink in. "Well lucky for you," I said through a thick cloud of smoke, "I don't play at all." He nodded his head as we both understood the coded words spoken. He wanted me to know that if I tried to burn him by running off with his money or product or showed any sign of shadiness, he wouldn't hesitate to use a burner to smoke my ass. He would hurt me, if not kill me, and the family ties wouldn't save me. Little did he know, I wasn't afraid of him. I knew his reputation and the repercussions for crossing him before I sat down at the table. I had no intention of getting out on him so I had no fear in my heart. I knew I was one hundred. If I said I could do something that's because I was confident I would deliver because I was more than capable of getting the job done. So neither one of us had anything to worry about. I was about to make us both a whole lot of cash and he knew it because just like I heard about him, he had heard about me and when it came to the hustle i was a beast. Shit most people had to go to school for what came to me naturally because I was a shark when it came to them numbers. In a perfect world, I wouldv'e dreamed bigger and been an accountant at my own finance company or some shit like that but I had dropped out of college because I was afraid to dream big. I didn't know what I was more afraid of, success or failure. With success came the pressure of responsibilities and expectations and with failure came disappointment and humiliation. Unfortunately in life we are limited to what we are exposed to and I dumbed myself down trying to fit in. As an adolescent, I was teased for being smart so by the time I was a teenager, school had gotten boring to me while the streets seemed enticing. I had been exposed to the street life at such a young age because my dad was a kingpin drug dealer. My father was getting so much money in the drug game, my momma was treated like the queen of the hood so i definitely came from street royalty and naturally wanted to be just like her. When my dad got locked up, business didn't stop because my mother picked up right where my father left off. She kept dealing with the Italians and moved weight from New York to Baltimore and eventually the trafficking expanded down south from Atlanta to New Orleans. I watched the way she moved even when she thought i wasn't paying attention so I knew how to handle a nigga when I needed to. Even from behind bars my dad ruled with an iron fist and made sure I kept my head in the books but once I'd graduated high school and moved out of my parents house my ambitions had been reduced from the college life to being a hood nigga's babymomma.

When the waitress asked if we wanted a picture, I put my cigarette out and pulled out my new *Galaxy* phone and handed it to the girl. I then scooted over to Psycho's side and raised my flute champagne glass. He lifted his glass as well and we made a toast with huge smiles plastered on our faces while posing for the picture, with Psycho throwing up his gang sign with his free hand and me holding up my middle finger with mine. I liked to make memorable moments obtainable in places other than my own unreliable mind and surely that was a night to remember. It was the beginning of the come up. "You guys look good together," the waitress said, handing me back my phone. We both stumbled over our words trying to explain that we weren't a couple then we burst out laughing as she walked away. I studied the image on the phone. We were sitting pretty close in that booth and we were both cheesing looking like we were good and fucked up. Without explanation, I can see why the photo made Jessica's insecure ass mad, but had she been woman enough to ask me instead of making a big deal out of it to Solo, I could have told her what was up. And it was so funny because I distinctly remember saying to Psycho that night, "I'm not gone post us on facebook cause I don't wanna make yo girl jumping to conclusions but baby we on instagram straight flexin!" He laughed, shrugging his shoulders. "Fuck it." I decided to post it on IG instead of FB because Solo and his sister didn't follow me and my account was private. I didn't want my crazy ass baby daddy tripping on me. The last thing I needed was for him to think that I was out doing me while he was locked in a cell when I was really trying to make money moves for us. Sure, we were technically broken up at the time but we agreed not to see other people. Deciding not to let thoughts of Solo bring me down I pulled Psycho to the dance floor. It was time to turn up. The night had officially turned into a celebration for me and my new business partner and I felt like dancing. We danced until the sound of shots being fired brought the night to a halt and we instinctively dropped and the music stopped. The lights came on but I was still afraid to come from beneath the table as I watched people get trampled over each other in a panic. People were literally piled up in the exit, stepping on each other in an attempt to get out of the building. It was pure pandemonium and I thanked God when Psycho snatched me up and led me to a back door in the VIP room we had been sitting in. The bouncer put in the code to let us out and Psycho covered me like a human shield and got me safely to his car where his driver was waiting with the engine running. To my surprise he put me in and closed the door. "You're not coming?" I was confused.

"Nah, give me ya keys, I'ma make sure you and yo whip both get home safe." I don't know why I felt disappointed but I handed him my keys and he promised he would drop my car off at my house as soon as he could get out of the club traffic. I knew he was right and just trying to make sure I made it home safe so I didn't protest and left him standing there as we pulled off and weaved in and out of traffic. Moments later my phone was ringing in my hand. The words on the screen read "incoming call from Psycho".

"What's up?" I answered immediately. "Did you find my car?" "Yeah, I'm in it now, I'ma go to the gas station and fill ya whip up," he said. "Can't have you out here riding on e shorty."

"Thanks," I said, embarrassed.

"It's nothing," he said reassuringly. I was about to tell him I didn't want to go straight home when he beat me to the punch. "Yo, you sure you wanna ride back to

Hattiesburg tonight? I'm sayin, I got a suite up the street, we could get something to eat at the hotel bar and sleep this liquor off. Then you can just drive yaself back after you sober up because to tell you the truth I'm fucked up," he chuckled. I agreed because I didn't want him driving my car drunk. Or at least that's why I told myself I agreed. Fifteen minutes later we were pulling up at the *Hilton Garden Inn*. I was disappointed at the events of the night and how everything unfolded at the end. Needless to say, NBA YoungBoy didn't show up that night and who could blame him? A fucking shoot out? Those clubs on the coast were just as ratchet as the ones in Hattiesburg and if it hadn't been for me wanting to see my favorite rapper, I would've never been there in the first place. Honestly, I grew out of clubbing when I was in college. I had been sneaking into night clubs since I was thirteen so the club scene wasn't exactly enticing to me. I no longer was excited about getting dressed up just to hear the loud music, dodge the thirsty niggas and fight the hatin ass hoes and now to avoid mass shootings. Besides, I realized early that at the club everybody was looking for somebody and everybody wasn't shit so, I was cool on that. I had other things to worry about, like getting money.

    As I followed Psycho to his room I knew he wanted to do more than conduct business because there was nothing else to discuss. We had sealed our fate with a simple handshake at the club. For some reason I trusted him enough to know that he wouldn't try anything or apply pressure, trying to get me to do something I didn't want to do. Once we made it to the room, he went into the night stand and pulled out some *swisher sweet* cigars and a big bag of sticky,purple weed or what we called "loud". I smiled and kicked my shoes off thinking, *now this is my type of party.* I loved to get high. When I smoked, it was like all my pain went away and I became numb to the bullshit of day by day drama. Everything was just fuckin funny and I was smashng any food in sight because I always got the munchies. I knew Psycho only smoked the best kush so it seemed like it would be a good night. We ended up smoking three blunts back to back, passing the blunt back and forth as we talked about any and everything till the sun came up. I don't think I'd ever laughed so hard in my life! The nigga was super funny and when room service delivered our food, my night had officially turned to perfect. Psycho had managed to make me forget about

the shooting at the club that had me so rattled earlier. Surprisingly, he had not once asked me about nor try to initiate sex. We just kicked it like we were homies and I had to admit I was enjoying myself. I really appreciated his company and was grateful I had time to sober up before the long drive home. I would have stayed there with him longer but the sun was rising and I knew my kids would be awake soon and I didn't like the idea of them waking up and I wasn't there. While I was putting my shoes on, Psycho's phone rang. He answered it on speaker.

"Jessica done went to Atlanta and got her thieving ass arrested again," Jance's loud, obnoxious voice blared through the phone. Janice was Solo's ghetto, overbearing and slightly overweight mother. I paused at the door, nosily, to hear the rest of the conversation and her next words hit me like a ton of bricks. "Solo got out last night, now she go in; this don't make no damn sense!"

That was my que to go. If what Janice was saying was true and Solo really was out of jail, the fact that he had not been blowing my phone up all night meant that he had come home to someone else and I didn't know how I felt about that, despite the fact that we were broken up at the time. It was like I didn't want him but I didn't want no one else to have him either. I hated to admit that Janice was right about that much and that was saying a lot because she and I rarely agreed on anything. I didn't know what it was about country ass women and the relationship they had with their sons but it was weird, like on some real life *lifetime movie* type shit. Some of these women down here were obsessed with their sons. Or at least the ones I've run across. They acted like they were dating them instead of having raised them. It was sickening how jealous and immature grown ass women could act when their sons would bring another girl around. It was such a turn off because like for real, who wanted to be in competition with somebody's mother?

A whole three weeks went by before I saw Solo that time. Just as I suspected, he had been staying with Janice and back fucking around with his babymomma. I bet Janice would've washed that hoe's dirty drawers if it meant keeping him away from me. I never knew exactly what her problem was with me but I know she was always bringing his son up like Solo was a bad father to his own child by fathering mine. Just because he had been living with me and taking care of my children didn't mean I was causing him to neglect his own child. That didn't have shit to do with me. I just knew that regardless of what kids he may or may not have had outside my house, as long as he was living under *my* roof, he was going to provide for me *and* mine. Maybe that's what prompted Janice to urge his baby's mother to put him on child support. I couldn't be mad at that though being that my ex-husband had been on child support for all three of our boys before the divorce was even final.

In the three weeks Solo and I were apart, Psycho and I had made so much money that I was able to move out of my mother's house into a condo downtown. Business was good and my plush condo was definitely an upgrade from the project apartment I was kicked out of. Apparently too much "foot trafficking" was grounds for eviction; I didn't even know foot trafficking was a thing. But yes, there were a lot of people in and out of our apartment because Solo had been selling drugs. That wasn't the only thing that got me evicted though. All of the 911 calls from the neighbors reporting domestic violence contributed to the situation also. I would say a lot of it contributed to the drugs because we got high and caused hell. Ironically, it was the times we were sober that the worst fights occurred. It's like as long as we were high we were happy. I had a real prescription pill problem back then and whenever Solo would do coke, I would hit a line or two. It made the sex better. Whether we were fighting or fucking we were still disturbing the peace but we didn't give a fuck about the neighbors hearing us fight; we had bond money. We were so dysfunctional back then.

When Solo heard about the condominium his ass wanted to come back all of a sudden and I can't lie, I missed my man. It was the small things, the intimacy that I couldn't feel with another man like his affectionate kisses or him stroking his fingers through my hair. As a matter of fact, besides my ex-husband, Solo was the only man I'd let see me with my lace front off. I wasn't bald-headed or nothing, as a matter of fact, my hair was long and thick but the humidity of the south made it hard to manage so I kept it braided to the back and wore a wig. I could be myself around him because I felt safe. I missed his protection and the safety I felt in his arms. Nomatter what we went through i knew he wouldn't let a mothafuka fuck with me, not while he was still breathing. Plus, he promised that he had stopped fucking with that bitch, so I allowed him to move into the condo. It was hard to say no to him. How could you deny the person you were used to spending 99% of your time with? I spent more time with Solo than I had ever spent with any man, including Desmond, whom I was married to for years. I think I had been with Solo the entirety of my marriage to Desmond because Desmond had spent the first three years in prison. We were legally separated at the time but by the time i had met Solo, it had been past due time for a divorce. Truth be told, the only reason I agreed to marry Desmond was because we had made three kids and I didn't want to settle for being someone's babymomma; I wanted to be a wife. Des was my best friend so he went along with whatever made me happy at the time. It was as if I was wearing the pants in our marriage and to be honest, it was a turn-off. That's why when Solo came along and told me to "sit the fuck down" or "shut the fuck up", it was quite refreshing. He taught me how to be submissive, something Des hadn't been able to accomplish. Of course his mom and i didn't get along either, in fact, I think part of the reason I said "I Do" was to piss her off and let her know the best woman had won. Looking back, I have to really question my mental stability if I made a life changing decision in an attempt to hurt somebody's feelings. It was that and the fact that I didn't want to have all these kids and no husband. We ended up getting married at the courthouse in downtown Hattiesburg on April 27th and by June 29th we were separated. Desmond had gotten picked up on an indictment charge for an armed robbery that I told him not to do in the first place. Funny, the one time he chose to wear the pants and ignore me ended up costing him his marriage. He had made his choice and his loyalties lied in the streets with his gang so there was no room for me. His vice lord brothers ended up talking him into taking the rap for the robbery so that was it for me. I felt like if you went and got yourself locked up for something I begged your ass not to do in the first place then you got what you deserved. The thing that pissed me off most was this wasn't a robbery to benefit the family, this was simply a lick for the gang so he sacrificed his freedom for nothing. I told him them niggas would turn on him in the end and use him as a scapegoat because he was the youngest and the only one without a felony yet. Now he had one, and nothing to show for it. I feel like if you listen to your big homies before taking the advice of your wife then you're married to the streets, not me and you needed to be calling the gang on collect calls and putting them on visitation lists and wait on them to put money on your books because they were the reason you were in there. Of course they didn't do none of that shit. He said I abandoned him but I felt like he abandoned me when he landed his ass in jail for some bullshit in the first place. I had three mouths to feed and I wasn't doing time with nobody, not even my own husband. He was cool though, he had him a ride or die bitch, a lil red bone bitch he used to fuck with before we got married and continued to fuck her after we got married on the side. He thought I didn't know about that though. The bitch was going to see him every Sunday and his messy ass momma was the one taking her because the broke bitch didn't have a pot to piss in, let alone a car. Of course my mother-n-law was happy to do it because she never liked me in the first place. She was another country ass momma on that weird shit, always acting like she was his bitch and not his mother. When Desmond said that she said I was trying to steal him away from her my response to him was, "so what nigga, you should've been jumped off the nipple anyway!" I knew if I married Des, she would be outraged and I would bask in the glory of seeing her defeated. I guess that's how I broke my vowels so easily, because my intentions weren't in the right place from the start. His mother couldn't stand me and I was trying to hurt her by taking him because she wouldn't accept me. She thought I was too old for her son and maybe she thought I was trying to be his momma because I damn sure thought she was trying to be his wife. When we first met, Des still lived with her. She would walk around in her boyshorts, calling him bae and touching him all the time. She even went so far as to ask him to adjust the ring in her nipple piercing while she was in the bathtub. He claimed to have told her ass no but I wasn't there and I wouldn't be shocked if he did that shit. He was a sucker for her and way too much of a momma's boy for me. The way that woman was about her sons, I prayed my relationship with my kids never got that creepy. It was like she didn't want him to be happy or something. I'll never forget how Des's phone got stolen at a house party and he had to use his mother's phone to call me that night. She answered the phone politely but as she passed it, she snapped at him, "Tell your bitches not to call my mothafuckin phone!" Then, during our entire conversation she was in the background saying bullshit like, "Well you know that one girl said you done got her pregnant," on some hater ass shit like that was supposed to make me feel some type of way or run me off or something. The next day, I still went to see him but all of a sudden she had something for him to do that was so important and couldn't wait. She did shit like that all the time, have these out-the-blue plans, that of course didn't include me, so we'd end up having to cancel our plans because hers made it impossible for ours to happen. I could really go on and on but I think I'm going to just leave that where it's at, just like I left him- and his momma.

Chapter 3: Mercedez

Still killing time making sure Justin had left, I listen to Solo talk, not really paying much attention to what he is saying. I started to daydream, thinking about how long we've been together and how long ago it had been since we first met.

I met Solo from around the way; he used to hustle in the projects I lived in. We knew of each other and had seen each other before but we'd never actually hung out. That was until we met through a mutual friend. What started out as the three of us hanging out eventually ended up as just the two of us as Solo started to grow jealous of the third wheel. One day, he showed up by himself, it was raining outside and he knocked on my door, and asked me for a ride.

"So you mean to tell me you gone give me twenty dollars to run you right around the corner?" I asked him through my screen door. A bitch was broke back then, with babies, so I needed that lil twenty.

"If you go head and open the door, I can show you by putting it in the pocket of those lil ass shorts you got on," he smirked, pulling out a pocket full of money. I couldn't help but smile, the knot was so thick and all I could think about was what I could do with that kind of money. Des was in prison, left me on stuck, and I still hadn't found a job. That's why my mother-n-law suggested my three boys go to live with her for a little while, until I got my shit together. At first I protested but she insisted and eventually, I caved in. With the type of cash Solo had, I could send for my boys in no time because the ultimate goal was to get my kids back but I knew in order to do that, I would have to be financially stable. I eyed the money enviously and all I could think at that moment was I need to get this nigga on my team. So I did what any bitch in my position would do, I opened the door and let his fine ass in. I pretended to look for my keys, making sure to bend over and give him a sneak peek of my ass that was hanging out of my hot pink daisy dukes. I wore a black, spaghetti-strapped tank top with hot pink words on it that read, "Hot Girl" with a built in push-up bra that made my c-cup sized breast look like double D's. I felt his eyes on me as I bent over to "search" the couch and I smirked, knowing I looked good.

We walked out and when I closed the door and started walking away, he stood there and asked, "You ain't gone lock your door?"

I shook my head. "No. People around here know me, they not gone break into my shit."

He just looked at me like I was crazy. "I don't trust nobody," he said seriously.

"It's not about trust, it's about respect. I got too much respect out here," I countered. "I've been staying in these same projects for years and I've never been robbed or even disrespected for that matter. I'm a different type of female and they know it." They also knew who my brothers were and that them niggas was ruthless so people that knew them knew not to play with their only sister. What they didn't know was that I hated getting family in my business so my brothers would be the last people I called for help in the event that something went down. My pride wouldn't let me. If I needed something I got it out the streets, but, I was not the average hood rat that had to do something strange for a piece of change. Whatever I asked was given to me and I never had to fuck for a thing. "Whoever said "nothing in life is free" was a damn lie because I got stuff for free all the time or at least it was fronted to me. Niggas had trusted me with large quantities of dope to sell plenty of times and I can only name one out of a dozen times that I didn't deliver. Even then, that one time was because my kids needed a place to stay so I put them first, did what I had to do, ran off on the plug and worried about the consequences later. To my surprise, the plug had actually respected the motive behind me fuckin up the pack and ended up not only waiving my debt, but also fronting me another pack to get back on track. I had genuine love in these streets so me worry about a break-in? Not likely. As a matter of fact, I was the one you needed to be worried about breaking in your shit because Des had taught me a thing or two about his line of business. Solo had better been glad I was trying to change during that time or else I would've had to pull a fast one on his paper'd out ass. I was still thinking about that bank roll he'd pulled out of the pockets of his sagging shorts on the quick drive to his crib. I knew he was a dope boy and he must've been getting money if he had a twenty to blow to get one block over. He could've easily walked around the corner and been there in no time. Nevertheless, I was grateful for his generosity so I thanked him for the money and he thanked me for the ride. Before he got out of the car he asked me if I smoked weed and I told him no, but I sold it. For some reason he thought that was so funny. "What," I asked him, slightly offended. "You never met a female dopegirl before? Everybody not out here fuckin niggaz for money,"

"Don't knock it 'til you try it," he said with a sly smile. Then he looked as if he had an epiphany. "Yo, you like to turn up?"

I stared at him blankly, knowing what that was code for. I had never done cocaine a day in my life, although I was curious about it. "Every now and then," I said casually, lying my ass off. *Why are you lying to this boy?* I screamed in my head.

He then reached in his pocket and pulled out a little white baggie, holding it up as if he was offering it to me.

"I don't have any money to be spending on that," I said honestly. Cocaine was a rich man's high and at that time, I was far from rich.

"I don't want no money; didn't I just give you some money?" he asked pointedly. I felt dumb, feeling like I said something stupid. His tone was almost chastising, as if he were talking to a child. Then he said, "Let me come chill with you later and we can do some together." He then placed the little baggie in my hand and I could tell he was the type of nigga that didn't take no for an answer. That shit was sexy as fuck, so I agreed. He got out of the car and closed the door without even looking back. That was the beginning of our on and off relationship. It wouldn't be till after he'd practically moved in with me that I'd find out about his live-in babymomma, Ashley. Apparently she had just had one baby and was pregnant with another, As far as I was concerned, she was a non motherfuckin factor. According to him, the first baby wasn't his anyway but the one she was pregnant with was. Apparently she had lied to him about the paternity of the first child so he and his mother would take her in, off the streets and by the time the truth came out, he had already gotten her pregnant with her second child. I remember trolling her social media accounts one weekend when I didn't see Solo for two days trying to see if they were together. After that desperate attempt to keep tabs on him, I allowed him to move in, thinking I'd be able to keep up with his ass. Besides, he was already paying all my bills anyway. Not only that, but he was doing extra shit, like giving me money to send my boys the newest name brand clothes and sneakers, and furnishing my house with the latest home decor, knowing I wanted my house suitable for when my kids came back. Plus he kept my refrigerator, deep freezer, cabinets, and pantry full. It didn't take long for me to feel like I was ready to get my boys back.

What I didn't know was that Des's mom had set me up by taking my sons. I had a whole DHS/CPS case out here and didn't even know it. Apparently, she had told them I was on drugs and unfit and that she had to take them in her custody because I was incapable of taking care of them. She painted the perfect image of me as an unfit mother and her as the god-fearing granny and she had no intentions of giving me my boys back. Solo had to drive me way to New Orleans for me to attempt to get my boys back because Des's mom moved and changed her number and we had no idea where they were. We didn't even know where to start looking. We called the police but since Des and I had no custody agreement, in Louisiana the kids belonged to him just as much as they did me and he was living with his mom at the time. My mother-n-law wasn't giving them up willingly and I wasn't willing to wait on the judicial system to bring them back to me so Solo and I conjured up a plan to basically kidnap my own kids. Legally, I was the guardian as far as the state of Mississippi was concerned, I just had to get them over that Louisiana state line. So we ended up finding out what school they were attending and I wasn't surprised I was on the "NO CHECK OUT" list. That's why I was glad I never threw anything concerning my exes away. Birth certificates, socials, expired licenses, I had them all. I never knew when I might need that information and the day I needed it had come. I had Solo take Des's old identification card in there wearing a baseball cap pulled down low and pretend to be my kid's father and check them out of school for the day. Little did they know, they weren't coming back. The girl in the attendance office was so busy flirting with "Des" that she didn't even notice me waiting for the kids in the hallway. I knew that, not knowing Solo, they would not have walked out with him without knowing what was going on. They were so happy to be back with me, I vowed from that day forward, I would never send them alone with Des's mom again.

During that time, even though my life was starting to piece itself back together again, I was still battling a nasty pill and cocaine addiction. Shit was starting to slowly spiral with solo and I as well. I mean, he was a good provider and my kids absolutely adored him (because he spoiled them), but it was the side of him they didn't see when we were behind closed doors that perturbed me. Solo definitely had a dark side to him. On days he wasn't doing drugs he was moody and easily irritated. His mood swings got out of control when he started yelling at me and getting physically assertive. I can't say he ever flew off the handle and hit me in the beginning but the screaming in my face and punching holes through walls was just as intimidating. I grew tired of buying new paintings to cover up the end result of one of his tantrums. It's like the man I fell in love with had completely changed before my eyes. So many times I wanted to say fuck it and leave but everytime a situation would turn into a physical altercation he would apologize, crying and begging me to stay. I want to totally place blame on him but in reality, I was toxic as fuck too. One day, I got fed up and had him locked up, and like always I forgave him but things had changed. While we were apart and Psycho and I had started our operation, I was making so much money on my own that his money no longer controlled me and he was blind to the fact that I was hustling. He thought all my extra income was from the nursing home I had started working at to cover up the fact that I was out here getting money. What he didn't know was that during my "work" hours, I was road-running with Psycho. We could have hired people to do the trafficking for us but we trusted no one and so far it worked for us. I didn't want Solo to find out what I was doing because he was so jealous and crazy, he'd swear i was fucking Psycho when I wasn't. He'd swear I was giving up the pussy for the product. He just didn't know that I was the brains behind the tri-state operation and Psycho was the muscle. He wouldn't understand that I was a boss bitch because all he'd ever known were trifling hoes. From his momma to his babymomma, his sisters and all of his homegirls, all of those hoes left a bad taste in my mouth and looking at them I understood why he would think I was on some bullshit. So I had no choice but to keep my operation low key. After I accidentally left my laptop in his car that day, the shit hit the fan. Besides the photos, there were several calls and text messages between Psycho and I so I could understand how it looked bad. Their dumb asses really thought we were having an affair and nomatter what we told them, neither Solo nor Jessica believed us. He really believed that Psycho and I had something going on, they ended up fighting over that shit and everything. They eventually got back cool but Solo and I had stayed broken up for a long time after that. It wasn't until I found out I was pregnant with the twins and I had moved into my new condo that we ended up getting back together. Him coming home and the fact that I was pregnant was reason enough for me to quit hustling. Solo had spoiled me the entire 9 months, it was as if all was forgiven and we were back in love again. The material things were nice but I found myself missing him at night. He was staying out in the streets a lot. He said it was to make enough for the babies but something in my heart kept telling me it was more to it than that. When he was home, he was so much of a nurturer, washing my hair and rubbing my feet that I let my suspicions go and against my better judgment, ignored my intuitions and kept quiet, not wanting to come off as insecure. It wasn't until six months after I'd had the twins that he got picked up for violation of probation and had to do that last bid that I found out exactly what he had been up to all those late nights he was out while I was pregnant. He had definitely been cheating on me because his little brother, John, confirmed it. Although he wouldn't tell me who the bitch was, I knew John was a stand up guy, God fearing, good kid, and he wouldn't lie to me about the bigger picture. I guess Karma's a bitch. But I wasn't the one to sit around sulking. The best revenge I knew was to get money so once Solo got popped this last time, Psycho and I had jumped back in the game, full force. **Just recently, however, an out of state deal went wrong and I ended up owing Psycho one hundred thousand dollars. I started hanging with Justin to get my money up because I knew he had clientele and I had to hustle harder than ever to get Psycho his money. In the midst of all of this I started to have feelings for Justin, going against my own rule of not mixing business with pleasure. When it came to Justin, it was hard not to though. On top of the boy being so damn fine, he really wasn't a bad dude and he had been dumping so much cash on me lately that I really couldn't see me paying Psycho without him. Justin had a plug in Baton Rouge on pure cocaine which was selling out on college campuses from Oxford, Mississippi to Hattiesburg. Justin had put me on game; we were doubling up on student prices and charging white people twice as much just because they had it and we could. We were selling grams for $180 a pop and I could see why Justin stayed hanging around college campuses so much. Especially during mid terms and finals, I saw kids spend their last on coke then call their mommy or daddy like they had a flat tire or something just to cop enough dough for another bag. What could I say? Cocaine is a hell of a drug. This shit was so expensive you could easily go broke behind it and the stimulating high was so potent, it would still have you chasing that brief moment of ecstasy you experienced when you first used the drug everytime. Only that was a feeling that would never come again. You just kept chasing and chasing like a gambeling addict at a casino spending their last, hoping to hit big. Then ultimately you would have to face the "come down". All cocaine did was get you so high that when you came back to normal you'd feel so down and anxious you'd want to die. So to avoid that crashing feeling you just kept using and chasing and using and chasing until eventually the inevitable feelings of hopelessness and doom completely consumed you. And the fucked up part was you just couldn't sleep it off like weed and alcohol because the stimulant in it kept you awake to experience every unwelcoming moment of angst. Then, when you finally did sleep you woke up only remembering the highs and not the lows and the chase began all over again. It was the epitome of insanity. A person had to really be smart and have the willpower to JUST SAY NO to avoid all that shit.

     Solo is still talking while I stand here appearing to be listening but really, I've gotten so lost in my thoughts that I really have no idea what the hell he is talking about. I'm sure Justin is long gone by now so I need to wrap this shit up. I need time to think. I have to come up with a new way to get Psycho his money back other than juicing Justin now that Solo is home before Solo finds out what's going on. If he does, all hell is going to break loose and I'm not trying to be the one to set it off. That's why instead of answering the phone for Justin and simply explaining why I couldn't do lunch, or responding to Psycho's text and explaining I need a little more time to get the money, I blocked both of them niggas. I know I have to properly break things off with Justin and have a conversion with him now that Solo is back in the picture, i know, but now is not the time. It has to be soon though because Justin's careless ass is reckless. He'd been done called my phone at three o clock in the morning talking about "what you doing?" or "can I come over?" And how can I say it's the wrong number when I'm probably the only girl in Hattiesburg with a 313 Detroit area code? Solo was far from dumb, that's why when I saw the text from Solo saying he was outside a little while ago I quickly deleted my google chrome history and did a quick factory reset on my phone because I didn't have time to delete texts and log out of facebook messenger or erase call logs, ect. After I blocked them I reset the entire phone, thus eliminating and erasing any incriminating paper trail I may have left behind. I'm not no dummy. I don't have time for that nigga to be like, "give me your phone" just to take it and throw it to the bottom of the Mississippi river once he discovers what's in it. I believe that nigga would do it too, Solo's ass is crazy. The longer I know him, the more complex he becomes. Even after all these years, I'm still peeling off layers to him; he's so guarded. Our relationship is complicated. I do what I do because I feel justified based on what he did. Sometimes I wonder does he even want to be with me or does he just not want anyone else to have me. He told me once, "If I can't have you, nobody can," and I took it as he would murder my ass if I ever tried to seriously leave him. He definitely ain't the type to just let go; he says he invested too much time in us over all these years and he refused to "let another nigga benifit" from his work. I'm like, nigga what work? That's not the problem, the real problem is he just don't know how to let go of the past. He'd rather hold on to his past pain and dwell on that shit than simply let it go. He don't want to let shit go because he uses the bullshit excuses to justify his bad behavior. And although I do my thing too, nobody can't tell him shit when it comes to me. I remember he fell out with a few of his thot ass cousins because they tried to tell him I was seeing someone else. He cussed out all them bitches and just stopped coming around. It wasn't until he saw the evidence in my phone that he even believed them. He broke down and cried like a baby. He never thought I would actually do to him the things he had done to me. When that happened, I wasn't sure what to feel because he used to be so good at manipulating me through his anger, I wasn't sure what to do with the tears. I had been so prepared to confront him about his anger and where it came from. It took me to see him vulnerable like that to realize the anger derived from fear; the fear of losing control; the fear of losing me. I had taken a few psychology classes when I was in college so in my mind I had already diagnosed his ass and the prognosis was extensive. My problem was I needed to stop trying to be captain save-a-hoe and stop trying to "fix" him. Every boyfriend in my past had been like a little project, something I had to build up or fix. This time is no different. Here he is, with his toxic ass, fresh out of jail and already in my presence when we are supposed to be broken up and here I am, acting like I'm still his woman, feeling guilty for moving on with my life. I can't keep doing this dance with him. This shit is getting old. Like I know that when he leaves my job, he's going straight to the hood to pull up on and flex for these hoes but he's not going to tell me that of course, so he says he's going to his mother's house instead. I'm no dummy. He might stop by there but that's not ultimately where he is headed. But white lies are to protect my feelings. So he kisses me on my forehead and tells me what I want to hear instead. At what point does innocent "white lies" turn to straight up lies? Where there should be black and white we both bask in the shady gray.

It's later on in the evening and I'm just getting in from work. I'm not surprised that Solo is not home, I didn't expect him to be even though he said he would. As soon as I slip my shoes off my phone rings.

"Hello?" I ask, ready to hear what excuse is going to roll off Solo's tongue tonight. "Where are you?" I ask, after he greeted me. I put the phone on speaker and toss it on the bed so I can multitask.

"I'm on the block," he admits, pausing to hear my reaction.

"Already Solo, what the fuck?" I ask, rolling my eyes. I pull my pink scrubs off and toss them in the dirty clothes basket next to the bathroom in my bedroom.

"I wasn't planning on jumping back into the game this soon, I know you want me to look for a job but I need paper now. I can't be out here depending on you till I get my first paycheck."

I twist my face up in a frown. "That was kinda the plan," I remind him, annoyed. He hasn't been home five minutes and already he ready to get on the corner. Shit's ridiculous. "Why the sudden change of heart?"

"I went to go see my momma and the first thing she do is look at my shoes, talkin' bout I need to hurry up and make some money and get me a fresh pair of J's," he said solemnly. "She know how i get money so i don't even know why she fixed her mouth to say that shit, but she right though."

I'm shaking my head in disgust. What kind of fucking mother sees her son home from *prison* for the first time and the first thing she says is he needs a new wardrobe *knowing* good and damn well he ain't got no job. So she's basically insinuating he should go sell drugs, pushing him to do the very thing that got him locked up in the first place. I can see why he has issues; clearly, his mother does. That money-hungry heifer just wants him to start hustling so she can start poor-mouthing and begging for shit. It's always been all about the money with Janice. She thinks as long as he got it, she can get it and if that's the case, she needs to think again. That scheming shit been got old to me and after witnessing her straight play him out of cash like a hoe would with my own eyes, I quickly grew tired of her little antics. I told his ass if he wanted to take care of his momma then he needed to be living with his momma. Unlike her, who still lives off section 8 housing, I have *real* bills, not just a tab with the weed man and poor spending habits. I told Solo this and he turned the faucet off on her ass for a while too and that lady has been hating me ever since. He must've told her that I was the one who planted the seed in his brain because now her and her ugly ass daughter both act like they got a problem with me and I don'r give two fucks.

    I take a long shower and lotion up with my *Bath & Body Works*, anticipating the sound of keys jingling in the front door, letting me know my man is home. Fresh out the shower, robe still on, I open up a bottle of *Chardonnay* and grab a wine glass from the cabinet. Pouring me a glass, I can't help but ponder over how many times

I've told Solo it was over and how many times I've taken him back. Or the other way around. This time I'd been the one to call it quits, yet here I am, half naked in a candle lit room with a bottle of wine, waiting for him to come home. I already know tonight the sex will be nothing short of amazing and just like that i'd be "Dick"notized back into my feelings again. I had come so far. One step forward, two steps back.

What I need is time to get my shit together. I got too much going on and I don't need him in my way. I've been operating just fine without him these past six months and now that he's home I know it's going to be hard to move around him. I sigh a sigh of frustration knowing that Solo being in the picture is just going to make things messier than they already are. If I don't pay Psycho his money and Solo finds out i owe him; I don't know who'd kill me first. If I pay Psycho his money but Solo finds out I've been working with him behind his back; I may as well go sign my own death certificate. I let my mind wander to Justin for a minute. Justin is like a breath of fresh air from all this bull shit. When I'm with him I'm stress free not to mention the nigga's pockets are endless. He has just the type of cash flow I need to get me out of this mess because I don't have time for Solo to get his post-prison pockets up. Psycho is not going to wait around forever for his money and the clock is steadily ticking. Isn't it funny how time stops for no one?

As much as I like Justin, the more time passes it's looking like he is going to become my victim instead of my hero. With Solo in the picture he's not going to willingly hand over his cash so unfortunately for him, I'm going to have to take it. Switching up the narrative and becoming the villain is the fastest way to get this cash and right now the only thing important to me is securing the bag. I know how Justin moves around. I know when and where he makes his drops because I was always with him when he made the major plays. He said I look good on his arm. Justin is consistent to the point of being predictable so I know just about when he will be ready to re-up, which is when he'll have the most money in his pockets. I'll have to find a way to stick him for his paper in order to get Psycho squared away as soon as possible. I'll also have to find a way to cop several bricks from him without him knowing it too. That'll be enough money in profit to start building my own little empire. I don't have a clue as to how I'm going to do this yet but I know it can be done. I just hope things don't take a turn for the worst case scenario which is me having to kill his ass because I actually like the poor guy. I'm not a killer but if it comes down to it being him or me, I know who it's not going to be. I just pray it doesn't come down to that.

Chapter 4: Chassidy

It had been two weeks since Mercedez's boyfriend, Solo, had slipped his number to me at the nursing home that day. He had caught me so off guard with it, I didn't know what to do but quickly shove it in my pocket right before Mercedez approached us. I was unsure if I even wanted it or not. Don't get me wrong, Mercedez was my girl and everything but I'd had a crush on Solo's fine ass since the first day I laid eyes on him. If Mercedez was a loyal girl I might've felt some loyalty to her but she wasn't. She was a two-timing bitch who played with people's hearts like that shit was cool or something. She didn't deserve a man like Solo but she had him and I envied her for that. He'd send her flowers and shit to the job, doing all the things for her that my husband never did for me. And the way she described their sex life OMG, let's just say I ran through plenty of AA batteries fantasizing about that man. I had never been the type to have an affair with another woman's man but after the way Mercedez dogged these men out, they deserved some good nurturing from a real woman. I found myself entertaining the thought of having a secret rendezvous with Solo and that is what ultimately gave me the nerve to call him. I knew Mercedez was at work covering another girl's shift so I had the perfect opportunity to place the call. *It's not like she's faithful to him,* I reasoned, trying to justify my calling someone else's man. Fantasizing was one thing, actually doing it was another. After the second ring, I thought about hanging up and changing my mind all together but then he answered on the third.

"It took you long enough," he answered in a sexy, masculine tone.

"How did you know it was me?" I asked curiously. Had he gotten my number out of Mercedez's phone? And if so, why hadn't he just called me? So many questions swarmed my mind but I didn't want to sound like a total geek, asking twenty-one questions and shit.

"I know a lot of shit people think I don't know," Solo said, sounding like he was blowing a thick cloud of smoke into the air. Even the way he exhaled was sexy. "But what's up, what made you finally call?"

I sat there trying to think of something clever to say but came up with nothing. I didn't really know how to answer that question because I didn't know why I had called him. "I'm not sure," I answered honestly. "I guess I wanted to know if you were really interested in me or not." I mean, out of all the hoes in Hattiesburg or even the girls at Brooksdale, what made him come at me? I wasn't half as pretty as Mercedez was and I didn't have any of her vibrant characteristics that kept men pawning after her. I was just a simple, heavyset, 5'5" dark skinned girl with natural hair and eyeglasses. What could he possibly want with me?

'I don't know," he said as if he had been reading my mind. " I just see something in you and I want to get to know you better ."

"What does Mercedez think about that?" I asked cynically. I was officially a thot, this girl was my friend. I didn't even know why I was entertaining this conversation. "She'd kill me if she found out I even have your number," I said pointedly.

"What she don't know won't hurt her or you," he said.

Her or me? What the hell did that mean? Was that a subliminal threat? What the hell was I getting myself into?

"What you doing right now," he asked, interrupting my thoughts. Before I could even come up with a lie he said, "Meet me downtown at the train station. You can jump in with me. We'll kick it for a few minutes."

I hung up the phone and rampaged through my closet trying to find something cute to wear. I wanted to look pretty without seeming like I tried too hard. After trying on a few pieces I finally settled for my cut off shorts and a tee shirt. The T-shirt read, "I Can't Breathe" in reference to a slain Minneapolis black man that was gunned down while unarmed and non-resistant by a racist, white police officer. I ruffled my natural curls to give it that on-the-go look. I then added some oil sheen to my hair and lip balm to my lips. I looked in the mirror at my face after applying a little foundation, blush, and mascara, and was pleased at the vibrant look I had quickly pulled off. So when I hopped in Solo's blue *Infiniti* with the dark tinted windows and chrome wheels, I was feeling myself.

"So where are we headed?" I asked, trying to contain my excitement. On the outside I was calm, cool, and collective. On the inside I was nervous as hell but I was happy just to be in his presence. His car smelled like weed and I hoped the smell wouldn't stick in my hair. We wouldn't be in there for long though. He told me he had got us a room so we could "Netflix and chill." I knew what that meant. My mind was telling me no, my body was saying yes, and my heart was experiencing the vulnerability you felt when you still haven't gotten over a broken heart. So, against my better judgment, I went with him to the room.

"Make yourself comfortable," he said once we were inside. I just stood there for a moment, basking in the beauty of the room. It was a king suite, simple, but plush. There was a flat screen television, a coffee table and a pull-out couch. There was a desk and a view of the city behind it. There were kitchen accommodations and a table with two chairs and an ironing board in the closet. In the bedroom area, an all white, king-sized bed that was soft as hell sat in the middle. It was, by far, the softest mattress I'd ever sat on in my life. I looked at the balcony, overlooking the city and the skyline view and I knew Mercedez had been right, this nigga had plenty of money, even though he just got out. He explained how he kept his money in a savings account and he had a couple places where he stashed his money without Mercedez knowing sometimes.

After I got comfortable, he went into the nightstand and pulled out a glass mirror with a small bag of what looked like cocaine in it. At first, I declined because I had never experimented with a hardcore drug before in my life. But after watching him do a line and he seemed fine afterwards, I gave in and did a line too. I put my nose down and snorted the powder and it took about one minute for me to feel the effects. It was like a wave of excitement and energy came over me and all I wanted to do was talk. The next thing I know, I was telling all of Mercedez's business. Once he had heard enough, he walked over to me, dick in hand, stroking it as he approached me. His exact words were, "Let me see what that mouth do," then he shoved his large, erect penis in my mouth and down my throat. I don't know if it was the effects of the drugs or because I hadn't had any in a while but my juices were flowing in overdrive and I wanted him in the worst way. I continued to suck ferociously with the intention of giving him the best oral he ever had in his life. When he ejaculated all over my face I simply wiped it away with my hands and licked my fingers clean, laying down on the bed, eyes closed, expecting to get dicked down. I was ready to have the best sex in my life, my body tingled and my clitoris throbbed at the thought of him inside of me. When I didn't feel him climb on top of me I peeped open my eyes and there he was, zipping up his designer jeans and putting his shoe's back on. It wasn't until he threw a few twenty dollar bills on top of the dresser and told me to "call an uber," that I realized what was going on. Clearly, I had gotten played.

"You're leaving?" I asked, confused.
He didn't even give me the courtesy of looking me in the eye, as he never

stopped getting dressed. "Yeah, I gotta go pick my girl up," he said casually. "The room is paid for the night so you can stay till morning."

I was speechless. I jumped up and ran to the bathroom and washed my mouth out with tap water. I heard the door open and close and knew Solo had left without so much as a goodbye. I stormed out of there moments later, slamming the door hard. I needed a drink like no other so I decided to head down to the hotel bar and wash away my sorrows. I felt like a fool. I clenched my jaws tightly as I felt the onset of my high coming down. I was an emotional wreck and frustrated as hell. The alcohol took the edge off a bit but not much. I ended up having a triple shot of tequila and I was asking the bartender for another round when this fine ass white man that resembled a young Tom Cruise approached me and said, "I take it you have a room here and you're not planning to drive home drunk?" My first instinct was to ignore his ass, hoping he'd get the hint and just keep it moving. But after looking him over out of my peripheral vision, I decided he didn't look half bad and a little flirting wouldn't hurt anything. It wasn't as if my night could get any worse anyway.

I really didn't know what to say so I said, "Does your wife know you're down here trying to find a black girl to fuck?" I noticed the ring on his left hand the moment he sat down. He ignored my rude ass remark and decided to introduce himself anyway.

"My name is Trevor," he said, extending his right hand for me to shake. "And you are?"

"Drunk," I slurred, and we both started laughing.

Trevor placed a one hundred dollar bill on the counter and told the bartender, "This ought to cover the tab. I believe she's had enough for tonight." He then turned to focus his attention on me. "You look tired," he said. "If you don't have a room let me atleast give you a ride home."

"I have a room, " I said, looking him in the eyes. "Care to join me?" I asked, seductively.

"Don't mind if I do," he quickly said, grabbing his suit jacket which was draped over his chair. He took one last swig of his drink, picked up his briefcase and followed me out of the bar without another word. There was no reason to talk. What was understood didn't need to be explained.

We entered the room I had been in with Solo just moments before, and I closed the door, being sure to put the *Do Not Disturb* sign on the knob. Trevor ended up being a big freak who liked to role play. I was high as fuck, but not too high to remember the man had sex toys in his briefcase, including a strap-on. We didn't use that though. I had plenty of tricks of my own I used to turn his ass out. We fucked all night and when it was all said and done, I woke up the next morning alone. There was a note on the dresser written on the hotel stationary that read, *Keisha, I had a great time. Give me a call at 555-621-3652.* "It's Chassidy dumb ass!" I said out loud, crumbling the paper in frustration. I was disgusted to find two crisp twenty dollar bills on the nightstand. I crumpled the money with the note and tossed it in the trash can. I was feeling the onset of a headache.

    My phone vibrated and I read eight missed calls on the call log. Two from mom, three from Mercedez, and three from work. I instantly wondered why Mercedez had called and I prayed she didn't find out about last night. How could she? Solo made sure we were in a discreet location and I knew he wouldn't say anything. Suddenly realizing I was late for work, I jumped out of bed and into the shower. There was a meeting this morning and it was important that I be on time. The staff was meeting the new administrator and I was supposed to bring donuts. I quickly finished my shower and lathered my body in the hotel brand body lotion, glad that I had decided to bring a duffle bag with my work clothes in it. I slipped into my gray scrubs and slid into my Nike Reacts, then rushed down the stairs. Too impatient to wait for an elevator, I made it to my car in record time. I frowned, looking at the pollen on the hood of the red Dodge Charger, and made a mental note to drive through the carwash on my way home from work. I hit highway 98 towards Hardy st. and was at Krispy Kreme in less than twenty minutes. After purchasing a French Vanilla Cappuccino and a few dozen donuts, all original glazed, I was finally on my way to work. I laughed at the radio host, Charlamagne the god, as he gave his "donkey of the day" scenario on his radio show, The Breakfast Club and before I knew it I was pulling up at work. I got out of the car hastily, donuts in hand, and as I was entering the building, someone was exiting at the same time and we collided. "I'm sorry," I stammered nervously. I was such a klutz, I had gotten the cappuccino all over the poor guy's shirt. "Cappuccino on the go," he said. "Just how I like it." I looked up at the familiar voice and was shocked to see it was the same white man I had slept with the night before. What did he say his name was? Trent? No, Tre? No, It was definitely Trevor. What was he doing here at my job? Was he lost? Maybe he was visiting a family member. "At least the donuts aren't ruined," he smiled. I smiled politely and was relieved to see Mercedez approaching us.

"So, you've met the new administrator already?" she asked without so much as a "hello". She usually said hi first. Was she being shady or was I just being paranoid?

"No, I haven't seen him," I said and both Mercedez and Trevor burst out laughing.

"What?" I asked, not getting the joke. Mercedez just shook her head while Trevor scratched his. "This," Mercedez said, elbowing Trevor, "is the new administrator. Say hi to your new boss!"

You gotta be fuckin' kidding me, I thought, but all I said was, "Hey," with a weak smile. All I could think about was that rendezvous I had with him the night before.

My smile quickly vanished when Mercedez said, "And this is his significant other," pointing at the person making their way across the room as Mercedez motioned for them to come over. As they stood before me, my mouth dropped and I thought I would have to pick my lip up off the floor. "Chassidy," Mercedez gushed, "Meet Paul." I almost dropped the donuts. Paul was about 5 foot and two inches, an orientle man with long black hair that he wore pulled into a slick ponytail. He wore slacks that may as well have been leggings with a colorful top that made him look animated like a flamboyant cartoon character with pointed toe shoes.

"Pleased to meet you," Paul said with a fake ass grin. He extended one hand and placed the other around Trevor. I had a feeling that Paul wasn't pleased to meet me at all. It was as if he was a hound dog and I had left my scent all over his owner the night before. Suddenly I felt hot and nauseous like I wanted to throw up.

"Excuse me," I said, holding my index finger up and placing the donuts I had been holding in Mercedez's hands. I managed to escape to the bathroom and began searching for my phone. I planned to text Trevor,"WTF" and I realized I threw away his number after I had fucked him all night. How promiscuous was that? I sighed. I wasn't about to sulk and have the pity party I felt like having. Instead, I would put on my big girl panties (as my momma used to say) and face the rest of the day chin up. If that meant hiding out in an empty stall all day, so be it. My cell phone vibrated the short vibrational patterns of a text message and I saw I had one new message from Solo. What could he possibly want from me now after humiliating me like he did the night before? I heard voices approaching the bathroom and I instinctively closed the message. I recognized Mercedez's voice on the other side of the door, so I jammed my phone in my pocket, making a mental note to see what the hell her man wanted with me later. I listened carefully, waiting for her to leave before I emerged from the bathroom. It sounded like she was on the phone with him when she walked in. Niggas aint shit.

"That doesn't mean shit, I still don't know where you were last night because you left the kids at your cousin's house until eleven o'clock when it was time for me to get off," she was saying. "Your cousin already told me yet you had them at the house when you picked me up like yall had been there all night. Where were you?" I don't know why but I felt flushed and hot as sweat beads started to trickle down the side of my face. "Boy, bye," she said before ending the call. I wiped the sweat from my forehead. A few seconds went by and then she said, "Hey Justin, what you doing?" She paused. "Oh you are? I didn't even realize what day it is." She was lying, I could tell because I'd seen her lie to these niggas so many times before. "I should go with you, you know it never hurts to have a second set of eyes." There was a long pause before she said, "Okay, I'll see you tonight baby." Then, she ended that call before calling another. I peered at her through the cracks of the stalls, wondering who she was talking to. "I said I'll have your money tonight after eleven. All of it." Whoever she was talking to had her distressed, I could see it all over her face and hear it in her voice. What the hell was this girl up to now?

Chapter 5: Solo

After I dropped the kids off at my cousin's house for the day, I hop in my Infiniti and shoot Chassidy lil' thick fine ass a text to see what's up. I haven't spoken to her since last night and I know she probably thinking a nigga just wanted to smash but really, I got other tricks up my sleeve. I have an agenda. All the other shit is just what came with it. What I'm really trying to do is get this money. Did I really have to fuck her to get her to rock with me? No, but, a lil' head ain't never hurt nobody. I know I could've gone about doing things another way in order to put this money scheme in motion but I've got my reasons. Up until last night, Chssidy was loyal as a mothafucka to Mercedez, more than Mercedez was to her. These are straight facts I've observed over the past couple of years. Having grown up around women, a gang of sisters, cousins, aunts, and homegirls too, I know even the tightest bonds can dissipate over money, clout, and dick. As for me, I got all three, so I know it'll be easy to get shorty to rock with me. The shit I'm tryna scheme up on, I wouldn't dare risk my lady being involved. I can't have the mother of my kids jeopardize her freedom for me. That's why I need Chassidy as a pawn. I need her to make a few moves and I don't need my Queen to get mixed up in no bull shit if shit goes wrong. My plan is air tight though but you can never be too careful.

    One of the reasons I know I gotta keep this shit between me and ole girl is because Mercedez is jealous as a muthafucka. She don't like me doing business with no female period. To be honest, I wouldn't be so bold in my endeavors if I hadn't heard about Mercedez fuckin' around with that ole clown ass nigga, Justin while I was locked up. She think I don't know but I been known about the shit because Justin has a kid by my first baby momma, Ashley, and just like he tell her everything, she tells me everything. I know about Mercedez and Justin's "secret" lil trip to Vegas and the weekend in the carribeans too but, I can't let Mercedez find out I know because that'll be a dead giveaway that I still be talking to Ashley and she'd automatically assume we still fuckin. The truth is, I still fuck her everytime I get a chance. Why not? She know that's gone always be my pussy for life. She even got my name tattooed on the small of her back so a nigga know who it belong to everytime he hittin' it. I know I'm wrong and that two wrongs won't make it right but Mercedez really pissed me off, having that nigga around my kids and shit. I know I can't believe everything my ex says about the woman I left her for but a lot of that shit be true. At the same time, it's my own fuckups that cause me to be insecure. One thing I do know, while a nigga was in these streets, my girl was loyal, no doubt about it and until I see it with my own eyes, I won't treat her otherwise while i'm in her presence.

    I'm not surprised at all to hear the rumors about Mercedez with another nigga; I knew how she rocked when I met her. She wasn't doing time with nobody, she made that shit clear when she left her own husband while he was doing time. But that nigga went to jail on some fuck nigga shit so that nigga deserved to get left. I don't know dude like that but I do know that Ashley tried to fuck dude to get back at Mercedez but the nigga wasn't gettin no money so that shit didn't last long. Ashley is a gold digger. True enough, I left Ash while she was pregnant and even though the first kid didn't turn out to be mine I still let her stay at my momma's crib and continued to take care of her because by the time we found out I wasn't the father, she had gotten pregnant with my son for real. I just hate that I'm the reason she got strung out on drugs. I wasn't the one that gave it to her, I would've never done that to my son's mother. What happened was, I left her at home while I was out sneakin' and geekin' with Mercedez and she was so hurt, she just wanted to ease her pain. I know once I heard she was fuckin with different niggas and trying to get at my homeboys I told her something to hurt her soul. I told her the rumors were true about me and the cocaine but that everybody around me did it, including her coke-head ass mother who I let snort a line off my dick because the bitch was a trick. I can't make this shit up. So the whole time I'm basically living with Mercedez, Ashley was stealing out the stash I kept hidden in my momma's attic. She was selling the dope *and* gettin' high with my own gang affiliates. Mercedez tried to tell me them niggas ain't shit but I didn't want to believe it until Ashley made a fool out of me. I remember she hit my pack hard by the ounces one time, it was around christmas. I beat that girl so badly I cried for her, not just because of what I'd done but because of what I'd done to her life and how it will affect my son. Now she was a dike with four kids and four baby daddies and all but one of her kids are in dhs custody. The girl couldn't even stay sober long enough to pass a piss test to get her kids back. Luckily, my mother got my son under the strict circumstances that Ashley doesn't come around. I accept my accountability in the fact that Ashley was a dopefiend but at the same time you have to want to do better badder than I want you to do better. She was supposed to be a better mother than her mom was to her and she wasn't. She allowed the cycle to continue; funny how history has a way of repeating itself. For instance, consider the new drug, ice, code for crystal meth. That shit hit the streets like crack hit the 80's; the game don't change, just the players. Meth isn't a drug I choose to slang though, that shit come with fed time and I ain't got that shit to do. Besides, my homeboy SciFi put me on this pill shit. America is in the middle of an opiate crisis and everyone is connected to it in some way. Even the old folks got in on that hustle but the doctors are the biggest dope dealers of us all. Prescription pills is booming, that's why I need to get at Chassidy, a licensed practical nurse, in school to become a registered nurse. Chassidy has access to narcotic prescription pads and I got a guy at this pharmacy in the hood, that's gone run that shit through the old people at the nursing home's medicare and medicaid like it ain't shit. Then, I'll pay a crackhead to go pick it up. This is about to be the beginning of an extremely profitable business, all I need is a solid team. I got Paul at the pharmacy, Chassidy and Sci-fi at the commulesant home, a couple smokers, and I'm in there. Me getting my dick sucked was just to see if shorty really fuck with me. When she let me bust a nut all over her face last night she passed that test with flying colors. If she plays her cards right I might fly her lil' thick ass out to Miami for a tummy tuck or some shit, everybody wants to get done up these days. I let Mercedez get that brazilian buttlift she kept worrying me about and I must say it turned out quite nice. Shit, rich people did it all the time and my ole' lady can have whatever they have and then some.

My phone starts vibrating on my lap while I'm rolling a blunt. It does the start and stop pattern indicating it's a message. I assume it's Chassidy's hittin' me back so I lick my swisher and pick up the phone. The message says, "In the bathroom stall, I think I'm still high and possibly hungover. HELP." I burst out laughing and I'm not even high yet. I mean it wasn't funny that shorty was tweekin', and she would most likely become a dopefiend, it was just funny the way it came across my screen. I'm not surprised at all, in fact, I was expecting that message. The dog food (heroin) I put in her coke will keep her coming back. She'll think it's just good coke but I'm really lacing it with the heroin because it's the most addictive drug of them all. Her body will start craving that shit so bad that she'll be sick without it and I'll be there to supply her every time. That's how I'm going to control her. It was my plan from the jump, I knew she never got high before so that first time would blow her mind. She was going to feel out of this world and consequently her world would come crashing to an end once she came down off the high. The only place left to go will be back up. I got her where I want her, you see, a fiend will do anything to feel that first high again, the orgasmic, euphoric feeling they felt the first time they did it. The catch is, that day will never come and inevitably, they'll spend the rest of their lives chasing it. So Chassidy needed me now because she knows I got what she's looking for. And since nobody knows her little secret but me, she gone have to keep spending money with me too. Shit, the way Mercedez been trippin' on bread lately I got to come up with new ways to eat and Chassidy plate seems big enough for the three of us. I pull on my blunt and decide to text Chassidy back, "Meet me at the same spot we met last night. I got something for you."

Chapter 6: Mercedez

I hang up on Solo's lying ass, deciding to deal with him later. Right now, I need to talk to Justin. It's time for me to put my plan in motion.

"Hey baby," Justin answers in such a sweet voice I almost feel bad for what I'm about to do to him. Almost.

"Hey baby, what are you doing?" I ask, as if I don't already know.

"Bout to go pick up my bread so I can meet my guy in Columbia. I gotta re-up tonight, you know that."

"Oh, I completely forgot what day it was," I say, lying my ass off. I didn't forget shit. I know exactly what time it is, in fact, I know more about the re-up than he thinks I know. I know what he's picking up, how much he has to spend and how much it's worth. It's the same thing every time but, little does he know, tonight is going to go a bit different than usual. I suggested I take the trip with him because I'm about to take this nigga for all he got. I told Solo that I was working a double so he isn't expecting me till seven in the morning. As long as Sci-fi can deliver the counterfeit cash after the welcome brunch, my plan is going to go smoothly. Sci-fi, whom you know as *Trevor* and I go way back since we were kickin dust in the sandbox; his mom and mine are best friends. I'm the reason he got the job as the new administrator even though he had a degree in science and had zero experience running a nursing home. I made his resume' on *Career Builder.com* using the counterfeit BSN that he printed. Sci-fi is a computer genius so it was nothing for him to hack into *Pearson View*'s registry to make it appear as if Trevor was an actual RN with a degree in Healthcare Administration, which qualified him for the position. It was all part of a prescription pill operation that I had nothing to do with. All money ain't good money and if you ask me, Trevor is in way over his head with this one. They're giving pill-pushers more time than crack dealers these days and I want no parts of it. I got over my addiction and that kind of access to something that would ultimately be the death of me isn't exactly appealing to me. I won't even let Solo sell pills and he knows I'm not playing when it comes to that.

I hang up with Justin and call Psycho. "I'll have the money tonight," I promised him and just as the door is closing behind me the strangest thing happens. It sounds like something hit the floor in one of the stalls. I stand there, frozen with my heart racing, Now who the fuck was that? The last thing I need is for these white people to be all in my shit. I swing the door back over, preparing to face whoever it was so I can know who's all up in my business when Trevor comes charging behind me, barging us both into the bathroom.

"What are you doing? This is a ladie's room," I say, slightly annoyed that he was distracting me from finding out who was hiding out in the bathroom stall. Trevor blurts out, "I cheated on Paul last night," his white face turning beet red. I tried not to laugh at the way Trevor could go from masculine to extremely feminine in two seconds.

This wasn't Trevor, this was SciFi.

"With who?" I ask, not believing what I'm hearing. I swear, my attention span is so short because just like that, I forget that we may not be alone in the bathroom.

"With the chubby chick that had the donuts. I think Paul knows it because he's glaring at me and rolling his eyes every chance he gets. I swear he's got senses greater than a hound dog," says Trevor.

I twist my face up in confusion. "How is that even possible? I just introduced her to you less than an hour ago." This doesn't make sense to me.

"No bitch, we already met," Trevor says, pushing my shoulder playfully. "At a hotel on the south side."

"What the hell SciFi?" I ask, wondering what the hell he was doing at a hotel in the first place. The interesting thing is that was the same location I tracked Solo's phone to last night. The cheap app didn't give off an exact location and there were six hotels on that side of town. That's the only reason I didn't run down on his ass. I was really tracking him so I wouldn't get caught slipping my damn self. "So how did you end up sleeping with the girl with your bi-polar ass; you don't know what side of the tracks you want to stay on," I say, joking him about his sexual prefrence. Trevor and SCiFi were two totally different personalities.

"Let me run it down to you real quick," he says and proceeds to tell me exactly what happened, play by play. I'm standing there laughing my ass off as I listen to the bizarre events that took place the night before. We finish our conversation and Trevor asks me to come out and join him for a smoke break, anything that will distract him from facing Paul. It's not until Trevor is practically dragging me out of the restroom that it finally dawns on me that someone had been eavesdropping. I try to double back and check the back door but by the time Trevor loosens his grip, it's too late; whoever it was is already gone. I shake my head, not knowing what else to do because now I have a whole new problem; someone knows way too much. Oh well, there's nothing I can do about that now so instead of dwelling on it I decide to think about what I have to do tonight.

I really don't want to do it and if there was any other way i would choose that but there's not so it is what it is. I remember the day I met Justin. I was leaving my apartment, walking to my car when I heard this voice from way across the street.

"Damn, there she go! Hey beautiful!" Justin was saying. "Ain't she beautiful everybody?" He was standing on a balcony that overlooked the street with a few other guys who all chimed in and agreed with Justin. I just blushed and continued to fumble with my keys, slightly embarrassed from all the attention I was getting. By the time I unlocked the door, sat my purse in the passenger seat and climbed in the RangeRover I was driving at the time Justin had made his way down stairs and was walking towards my car. I glanced at myself in the mirror to make sure my lipgloss was poppin' and my hair was in tact and just as i was cranking up my car, I heard him say, "I just want to know your name love." I looked up to see Justin's fine ass hovering over my window. He was caramel colored with dark brown eyes and pretty white teeth. He wore a yellow Polo shirt and the smell of Christion Dior lingered on his smooth skin. His jewelry was a little bit too flashy for me but he made it look good, rocking a gold watch, two gold and diamond chains and a gold band on his pinky finger. "I don't know what it is about you, I see you everyday and you're so pretty to me," he said, looking into my eyes.

"Thanks," I said with a smile. "Mercedez," I extended my hand through the window.

"Mercedez? Like the Benz?" he asked, shaking my hand.

"Yeah, like the benz," I said with a laugh. We were silent for a moment, gazing at each other..

"Man, come on while you harassing that girl, let her go on!" a female voice said from behind him.

I raised my eyebrows.

"That's my sister," he explained. "I guess I'll see you around beautiful," he said, licking his lips.

"Yeah, I guess so," I said, with a smile plastered across my face. He backed up, walking backwards, still looking at me while rubbing his hands together. I pulled off with butterflies in my stomach and Mr.Handsome (I didn't know his name at the time) on my mind.

A few days later when we ran into each other at the beach we exchanged numbers. I remember him calling me that night, asking me to go to a party with him. I was hesitant at first, because I didn't want to run into any of Solo's people. Then I remembered how it wasn't that long ago that he flaunted another bitch around those same people behind my back right after we had our daughter. My ego bruised with scars of betrayal, I decided to take Justin up on his offer. I was glad that I did because I ended up having the best night of my life. Justin showed me off like a trophy and catered to me the entire time. We ended up in VIP with his people and his friends actually turned out to be cool as fuck. His sister, Aneika and I hit it off big and we all partied till the break of dawn. Aneika and I were click tight ever since that night. After the party we all went to Waffle House and ate an early breakfast. I wasn't worried about getting home because my kids were in Detroit with my mother for the summer so I was as free as can be so instead of taking me home Justin took me to his place where we made love, having passionate sex for hours. His dick was long and his stamina even longer. I could see why he had a big ego. Afterwards, we slept in his King sized bed and didn't wake up till six o'clock that evening. We probably would have slept longer if it wasn't for the loud banging on the door that woke us up. Some girl, who I would later learn was his babymomma, was screaming to the top of her lungs about why he wasn't answering her calls and who he had in there. He put his finger to his lips and threw on his boxers and was out the door. But not before locking me in the room, which he did with good reason because as soon as he opened that front door this bitch comes barging in. She pushed right past him and headed straight for the bedroom and started banging on the door with one hand and twisting the knob with the other. I know Justin probably thought he was protecting me from her but what he didn't realize was that he was protecting *her* from *me* because if that bitch came through that bedroom door, she was going to get a beat down and slashed with a box cutter just for good measure. I heard him rough her up a little bit and it sounded like he was dragging her out of there.

"Now calm the fuck down before I throw yo ass out instead of walking you to yo car cause either way you gettin the fuck out of here with that bullshit!" I heard the front door slam and I peeped through the blinds nosely. I don't know what he was saying to her I just saw a lot of hand motions and I couldn't do nothing but laugh at how animated he looked and how goofy this bitch was. I couldn't see her face at first because she was facing away from the building but when she turned around to walk around her car I got a good ass look at her and my stomach dropped to the floor. I had no idea his babymomma was Ashley! I kicked myself for not asking him about his relationship status from the beginning. This town was too small, what were the odds of me running into her like this. I blew out a breath in exasperation, suddenly glad that she didn't come through that bedroom door. She would've loved to tell Solo I was fucking her babydaddy and that would've been the worst possible way he could've found out. I continued to peep out the window and noticed she had calmed all the way down. I don't know what the fuck he told her but this silly bitch actually kissed him (after all that) and got back in her car like a civilized human being instead of some crazed, mad woman and waited for him while he ran back up the steps and into the condo. He came in the room and reached in his night stand and grabbed a scale and what must've been an ounce of coke. Hold this bag open for me, he instructed me, tossing me a miniature ziplock bag. I held open the bag for him and smirked thinking I must've been as silly as this bitch because I asked no questions, I just did as I was told. He sealed it up, tossed it on the scale and it weighed 1.0 exactly. "I'll be right back, let me go give this to her so she can get the fuck on. Fuckin powder head ass, that's all she really want." Before I could comment he was out the front door again, this time leaving the bedroom door open. I peeked to make sure he was outside before I grabbed a few bags and filled them all up with that fish scale, which is what we called uncut coke. I hopped out the bed and slid them into my jeans pocket and was back in the bed in the nick of time. He walked in and dropped his boxers. "Round ten?" he asked climbing on top of me. I wrapped my long legs around his strong back and pushed his shoulders down.

"I seen where yo mouth been so you know where yo mouth goin," I said with an arched eyebrow and a slick smile. He chuckled and dropped his head, shaking it from side to side.

"You cold, bruh, that's some shit I'd say. You up in here talkin' like you a nigga, you must think you me or somethin?" he laughed. "What am I gone do with you?"

That's when I looked him in his eyes and said, "I can show you better than I can tell you." I placed my hand on my clitoris and he stuck his tongue in my pussy, up and down and around with long, deep thrusts while his fingers played in it, causing my juices to flow all over his chin. I palmed his head as he buried his face in my love box, his fingers doing magic in my walls while he sucked on my cit, bobbing his head like he was bobbing for apples. "Oh shiiit," I moaned, feeling myself about to cum. "Ohhh shiit," I whined as I grasped the sheets, pulling them from the corners of the bed. And just when I was about to come he stopped. I opened my eyes but before I could ask why he stopped I felt him push inside of me, his thick, long dick filling me up to the max. This wasn't love making. We were straight up fucking. He flipped my little ass over so quick and slid in me from the back, shit felt so good I thought heaven had opened its gates and let me in because nothing could feel better than this. He was pounding this pussy so hard, all you could hear was the loud slapping sound of my ass hitting his pelvis over and over again.The dope made his nut stall so we fucked like animals for hours, raw dog and all.

"I'm bout to nut," he said, jumping out of my love box and into my mouth. I didn't care, I was cuming again anyway, he could've nutted all over my face and I wouldn't have gave a damn. I swallowed that shit like a fish swallowing water, and then I drained him dry. I Sucked it so good I made his toes curl. He was fisting my hair, biting his lip, and looking intensely into my eyes, I think that was the moment I made that nigga fall in love.

Chapter 7: Chassidy

I can't believe I dropped my phone and almost got caught eavesdropping like that. For some reason, I didn't want to face Mercedez, not when her boyfriend's name kept coming across my screen. I was saved by the bell when Trevor came barging in. I was grateful for Trevor's dramatics because I'm sure Mercedez forgot someone else was in the room. Otherwise, the conversation wouldn't have gotten so juicy with information I know Mercedez didn't intend for me to hear. Her absent-mindedness made "dumb blonde" so non-cliche' at times. Not wanting to make my presence known, I put my phone on silent and tried to be as still as possible as I leaned in on the tea.

"So let me get this straight," I heard Mercedez say. "You book a room as a surprise anniversary gesture for Paul, and instead of giving him the threesome he always wanted as a gift, he gets too wasted and passes out, then you end up at the hotel bar where the two of you were supposed to pick the girl, only, you went alone?"

"Right," Trevor confirmed, "And that's where I met your friend-"

"Co-worker," Mercedez cut in and corrected him and I felt a bit slighted?

"Whatever, co-worker," Trevor says. "And the rest is history honey; ya homegirl is a hoe."

The two of them shared a laugh and I could see them give each other a high-five as I peered through the slit between the door and the wall of the bathroom stall. I was sitting on the commode with my feet up so they wouldn't discover me hiding out like a creep.

What if one of them actually has to use the bathroom? I thought, and as if on cue, Trevor said, "Let me pee real quick before we go back out there to face the crowd. When he turned in the direction of my stall, sweat beads formed on my forehead as panic set in and I could feel the saltiness trickle down my face. Trevor placed his hand on the door and I thought, *Oh shit, this is it*, then Mercedez blurted out, "Bitch!" I squinted my eyes shut and braced myself for the blows I was sure I was about to receive, but instead, I heard her say, "This is a girl's bathroom." I opened my eyes, relieved to see the door to the stall was still closed. "You're going to blow your cover," she hissed at Trevor. "We can't risk that. There's a side door that leads to the parking lot out back, you go that way before we get caught. I'll go back out through the front."

"Oh no bitch," Trevor said as he released the door handle to the stall, "you're coming with me. It's time for a smoke break and I ain't talkin bout no cigarettes either," he says and pulls her towards the back door. Before they exited I could've sworn Mercedez looked directly at my stall and I let out a tiny gasp as if she could see through it. Luckily, Trevor was adamant about their smoke break and he dragged Mercedez's curious ass out the bathroom. I made a quick dash for the front door before her curiosity got the best of her and she decided to double back. As I made my way through the crowd of fellow co-workers and their family members, my phone vibrated and lit up in my hand. "WYA?" flashed across the screen. I scanned the room, in search of the Director of Nursing to let her know I would be leaving for the day. I would tell her I had an allergic reaction to something I ate or that I felt like I had food poisoning. I didn't know, anything that would get me out of that damn building. The DON was not happy and I could tell she was not satisfied with my lame ass excuse but oh well, I was out of there.

"Damn baby, what took you so long?" Solo asked when I jumped inside his car at what seemed to be becoming our usual meeting spot. I looked around the train station, a bit paranoid about my close encounter earlier.

"I have something to tell you," I said, turning to face him. He just looked at me with a blank stare. "Okay, this is the part where you say, 'Well, what is it?'" I said with a laugh.

"Spit it out shorty, I don't got time for games," he said, so I decided to just go ahead and give him the information.

But not before I said, "It's going to cost you."

Again, the blank stare.

I pushed my glasses up further on my nose with my index finger, suddenly feeling nervous about the whole situation. After a few more moments of awkward silence he said, "Don't ever try to play me again with no lame ass shit like that shorty. If you need something from me, all you have to do is ask. If you have something I need to know, all you have to do is tell me." The authority in his voice made me feel like a child being chastised by their disappointed father. The logic made sense though and I made a mental note to never come at him that way again.

"I want a gram of the coke you gave me last night and a few hundred dollars." I explained, "My rent is due and we don't get paid till next week and I'm a little short on cash."

He held up his hand as if telling me there was no need to explain and reached into his pocket. He pulled out a small white bag and placed it in my hand. "That's a eight ball shorty. That's ya gram plus two and a half more to make ya few hundred."

"But, I don't know how to sell coke, hell, I don't even know who I would sell it to," I protested.

He smirked and shook his head. "I'ma have to teach you the game shorty and as for sellin' it, it's safe to say you can start with a few of ya co-workers; I be servin' all them hoes."

I looked at him, shocked. "But how will they know to get it from me?" I asked, genuinely wanting to know how I was supposed to sell illegal drugs at my place of business. I wasn't a dealer, I didn't know what the hell I was doing.

"They'll know because I'll tell them."

"And what about Mercedez?" I asked.

"Shit, what about her?" he asked rhetorically.

"Aren't you worried about the girls running their mouth to her?" I knew if Mercedez was cool with him dealing to her friends then she would be the one doing it, not me.

"Fuck no, them hoes know not to cross me," he said, sounding something like a pimp. Hell, maybe he was. This guy had more than a few tricks up his sleeve and I found him quite intriguing. "But fuck all that, tell me what's up, what you gotta tell me?" That's when I told him everything I overheard in the bathroom that morning. I intentionally left out my encounter with Trevor, however. He didn't need to know all that. What he needed to know was that his girl was running circles around him and that he couldn't trust her.

"But, you can trust me," I assured him, speaking softly and seductively. I placed the eight ball in my bra and let my hands find their way to his lap.

"That's a bet," he smiled, that million dollar smile of his, unzipping his pants and allowing me access to his manhood. The way it was growing hard in my hands let me know that we weren't going to make it to the hotel. He reached over my lap into the glove compartment and pulled out a Magnum. I instantly got wet, excited at just the thought of feeling him inside of me. He slid his seat back and reclined it all in one motion. Then he lifted the steering wheel, giving me room to climb on top of him. I exhaled loudly as I slid on top of his huge pole and began riding him like a cowgirl right there in the parking lot of the downtown Hattiesburg train station. Thank God for tinted windows. The rain beat rhythmically against the window and I didn't know what was wetter, me or the weather, as Muni Long's "Hours and hours" played on the radio.

"Ooh, when you do what you do, I'm empowered

You give me a super power

Together the world can be ours…"

This was, hands down, the best sex of my life and any girl, including Mercedez, that let this good dick get away was a damn fool. I knew exactly what I was doing by snitching on Mercedez then fucking her man; I was getting her the fuck out the way. I'm tired of being in the shadows, living vicariously through her. I would no longer be mediocre. I was bossing up.

When we were done with our escapade I reclined in the passenger seat and actually hit the blunt Solo had rolled up. That shit had me feeling good. I sat back and relaxed as he drove through the city and let the weed carry my mind to another day and time. It was last spring and I was still married to my ex-husband, Franklin. It was a beautiful day and when I got to work there were too many people scheduled so the boss let me go. I knew Franklin was probably buried in his work and probably wouldn't take a lunch break so I decided I'd bring lunch to him. I went home and slid out of my work clothes and put on a cute, yellow sundress that I bought out of Dillards and put on my yellow sandals. I tamed my hair with some JAM and oil sheen and used edge control to slick down my baby hairs. I sprayed Franklin's favorite fragrance that turned him on when I wore it (Japanese Cherry Blossom from Bath & Body Works) and I even put on some light makeup. Once I was completely satisfied with my look, I went down to the kitchen and prepared Franklin's favorite meal (lasagna) and packed it into a lunch box with his favorite lemon seltzer. I was going to call him and let him know I was on my way but I thought it'd be more romantic to surprise him instead. Franklin had been acting a little distant and I was afraid our relationship had become a stalemate so I was going to spice things up a little with a quickie in his office. I pulled up to his job at about a quarter till twelve and parked in the garage. I took the elevator to the fifth floor where Franklin's office was, picnic in one hand, smoothing my dress out with the other. When the elevator doors opened I got off on Franklin's floor and immediately noticed his assistant wasn't there. Assuming she went to go grab Franklin lunch I walked past her desk and headed straight for his office. I waved to a few familiar faces and proceeded to open Franklin's door only to find it was locked. I frowned, thinking that was strange because his door had never been locked before. I called his phone and was surprised to hear it ring right next to me on his assistant's desk. I noticed his keys were lying next to the phone as well. I was going to knock but then I heard something crashing to the floor on the other side of the door. Thinking something was wrong but not knowing what was going on, I picked up the keys and hurriedly found the key to the office. *Boom!* another crashing sound, so I stuck the key in the door while still carrying the picnic on my arm. I turned the key and pushed until the door flew open and just like I thought, books and shit were all over the floor like they had been knocked off the desk and it was obvious how they got there. I dropped the picnic on the floor, tears welling up in my eyes as I made eye contact with Franklin. There was nothing wrong except what he was in there doing. He had his assistant butt naked on all fours on top of the desk and his pants were down to his ankle, his shirt and tie loosened. There my husband was, committing adultery right before my eyes and to make matters worse, he seemed to be unapologetic about it. Do you know he kept fucking her like no one else was in the room, his shaft going in and out of her pussy like he owned that shit. He looked me in my eyes the entire time, only breaking contact when he busted a nut and his eyes closed in deep pleasure. He smacked her on the ass and pulled out of her and pulled his pants up. His assistant walked right past me with a little smirk and walked into the bathroom and closed the door. I looked to Franklin for an explanation, an apology, or something but all he said before he walked right by me and spoke in a low tone, his lips near my ear, was, "Go home." I just stood there, tears streaming down my face. It's like I was stuck there, frozen in time. I didn't want to attack him because if I did I wouldn't be able to stop myself from killing him so instead I turned around and flew out of that office like a bat out of hell and not knowing what else to do, I did as I was told, and went home.

Chapter 8: Mercedez

Solo's not answering his damn phone and I need to know why and what the fuck he got going on. My phone tracker tells me he's at his mother's house but when I call over there, Janice is happy to tell me he's not there.

"Solo left here hours ago, matter fact, right after he dropped you off he took them kids to my niece's house then he came and dropped the phone off over here. He said in case some money calls but chile' you know how these men lie honey ain't no tellin' where that boy at, what he doin, or who he with.. Now, my niece done brought the kids over here so unless you coming to pick up yo' children, don't call here lookin for Solo nomo', that's a grown ass man, if he want to be found, he will resurface." Then she has the nerve to abruptly end the call in my face. I can just picture the smug look on her face as she seemed to be happy to have that bullshit to tell me. That bitch will throw her own son under the bus just to get off. She know he on some bullshit with all her subliminal hints but three can play that game. I know how to pull a disappearing act too and when I get lost I won't be found. I need to ride off with Justin tonight to put my plan in motion anyway.

The rest of the work day went by fast, probably because there were only 3 nurse's in the building and there are four halls so shit was kind of hectic. Them old people act like the worst kind of dope fiend when they don't get their pain medicine on time. Chassidy stupid ass left early for some bogus ass reason so nobody got their pill on time. My work load seemed to double, which is a lot, considering we're already short staffed around here. She claimed to have gotten sick or food poisoned or some shit but I think the bitch is just pregnant. I've been pregnant six times so I know what it looks like. The real question is by who though? This had to be a new nigga she was fucking because her and her husband just finalized their divorce. And you know if they're divorced they've been separated for a while so they definitely wasn't getting it poppin' in the bedroom. Her ex had definitely been screwing somebody while they were going through the motions because Chassidy says he has a "new family". It sounds like to me that he was cheating on her long enough to make a baby by the side bitch and that they probably had the baby already and everything. But the whole time, he "wasn't ready" for kids. Niggas is triflin' for real, but, If she would've been paying more attention to her man instead of playing wifey to a nigga in prison that couldn't do a damn thing for her then none of this shit would've ever happened to her. Knowing Chassidy, she was probably pregnant from a one night stand and she don't even know who the baby's daddy is cause she be all on them hookup sights and shit. Chassidy is dumb as fuck, her husband had that paper, I'm talking walstreet money and the bitch signed a prenup. Fuck her problems though, where the fuck is my babydaddy at? He still ain't called and I ain't mad either, I'm actually more concerned at this point. No, not what you're thinking, fuck his well-being, I need to know his whereabouts so I don't have to worry about him popping up on me while I'm with Justin. That's what I'm concerned about. I look at my pink Rolex, growing more annoyed by the minute because I'm impatient as a mothafucka. I text Justin, *I'm ready,* then I sit down at my desk in the main office to finish my charting. As quickly as my computer screen flashes on it flashes back off and my irritability is on ten right now. I press the power key over and over knowing that the battery is probably dead but I left my charger in Solo's car and he's not answering the phone. Since it's against the rules to chart on someone else's laptops, I decide to use Chassidy's charger instead. I almost get frustrated when I realize her drawer is locked until I remember I still have her spare key. She gave me one last summer when she kept locking her keys in her drawer once we got the new office space. I turn the key and open the door and am shocked when I discover a chrome 9mm glock with a case of bullets sitting next to it. What the fuck is Chassidy's lame ass doing toting iron? I jump at the disturbance of my cell phone vibrating obnoxiously on the desktop. "I'm on my way out," I tell Justin and I slam the drawer closed, forgetting to lock it behind me. I'm too busy wondering what the fuck Chassidy has going on as I clock out and make my way out to the parking lot. I try Solo again and again it goes straight to voicemail. I'm annoyed by my own voice as I hear myself say, "You've reached Solo. Unfortunately his mouth is full right now so he can't take your call. Leave a message-" I hang up, pissed off, knowing Janice must've blocked my calls. *Miserable bitch,* I think bitterly. Just the thought of that evil old lady put a bad taste in my mouth like poison and her son was starting to have the same effect on me.

"Damn, baby, what took you so long?" Justin asks, kissing me on my cheek. He is looking good of course in Dior jeans and a crisp white tee, smelling like new money and I'm thinking I should at least fuck him good before I fuck him out his paper.

"I had to pee," I lie, scanning the parking lot for Solo's car.

"That nigga ain't gone touch you long as I'm around baby so stop actin' all paranoid and shit," Justin says casually. "I need you thinkin' clear so you can count this money and cut these bricks with me later."

Boy, Solo will beat the fuck out you, I think cynically. Justin is a gangsta but he is no match for Solo. I smirk, thinking I'm about to take this nigga for everything he's got and he has not the slightest idea. Being this close to him in the small space of the car has me feeling uneasy as if the betrayal is radiating off my skin or something. I hope I'm not giving off opp vibes tonight and my Chanel number nine is strong enough to smother my deceit. The fact that he actually trusts me enough to hold his money and his weight is also contributing to my guilty conscience. No one has ever put that much trust in me in my entire life and here I am about to jeopardize a great friendship with this awesome guy, all because I don't want Psycho telling my nothing ass baby's daddy about a few power plays I made in order to survive out here while he was locked up. It's starting to not make sense and I'm wondering if it's even worth it. I'm having major second thoughts until I get an incoming text from Psycho that says, "I need my money tonight no BS I gotta leave the country and I'm not crossing that border without my bread. And if I don't leave yo BD won't live. I just upped the ante lil momma." My heart drops to my stomach, which is in knots from the anxiety. Psycho just upped the stakes. Now not only is he going to rat me out if I don't pay up but now he's threatening to murk my babydaddy too? I lick my lips in anticipation as I go over my plan again in my head. There's no time to feel bad about it now; shit just got real. I'm just going to have to do what I have to do. I think about just asking Justin for the money but quickly decide against it, thinking, *what if he says no and I expose my hand for nothing?* He'll know that I'm desperate and won't trust me anymore. I can't take that chance. I have to make a safe bet, it's all or nothing at this point, do or die. Tonight I will kiss my friendship with Justin goodbye.

"Pull over so I can pee," I say anxiously.

Justin frowns. "Damn bruh, I thought you already peed? He asks, his annoyance evident in his tone.

"Well I gotta pee again so pull up at that Fast Mart over there so I can go or i can just piss all over your leather seats," I say, bouncing my knee as if I really have to go, but really that's what I do when I'm nervous.

"Hurry up," he snaps, pulling up at the store. "I'm not on yo' time tonight you on my watch and I got shit to do."

'Yeah," I say, rolling my eyes and getting out of the car. You can tell when a nigga not on no drugs, Justin is grumpy as fuck right now. " I don't know what type of time you on but I'm not feeling the attitude, I'd rather get out and walk than ride with you when you're like this." I know I'm acting childish as if starting a petty argument will make this easier. I hate myself for what I'm about to do to him. "I'll be right back," I tell him, slamming the door because I knew he hated that shit.

"Really?" he asked, looking up at me. I avoid eye contact with him, genuinely pained by what I have to do next. I feel a few raindrops so I quickly dash in the store, trying not to get my lace front wig or my false lashes wet. It's been raining all day, making it a dark and stormy night. It feels like the beginning of a horror story. The stage has been set, now it's lights, camera, action. In my script, Justin's the star and I'm the muthafuckin villain. Once I'm in the bathroom I reach into my scrubs and pull out two bottles. One was *Seroquel* and the other was *xanax.* My hands are shaking as I open them both and pour two of each on the counter. I tuck the bottles back into my shirt pockets and take a credit card out of my wallet. After placing the card over the pills, I pull out my phone and began to flatten the card over the pills, crushing them into mere dust with the weight of the cell phone. I then pull out a twenty dollar bill and hold it out to catch the dust I'm scraping off the table with the card. I fold the bill with the crushed pills inside and use it to carefully pour the dust into a half empty two ounce shot bottle of VivaZen Max, a form of liquid kratom. Justin drinks them faithfully, claiming the miracle shot is what got him off percocets, he consumes at least three or four a day. It sounded to me like he just went from one addiction to another but hey, who am I to judge? I'm battling my own demons. I shake the bottle ferociously for about sixty seconds then I jam it in my jacket pocket. Before I walk out I scan the stalls, which I should've done first, to make sure no one had been watching me. When I didn't see anyone's feet on the floor I pushed the two stalls open, which is what I should've done this morning. I don't know who had been in there and why they were hiding but for some reason my thoughts travel to Chassidy's gun and I try to remember what time she'd left the party this morning. I wonder why she hasn't mentioned the whole Trevor thing yet, then I realize I haven't heard from Chass all day. Maybe she was too embarrassed. Trying to connect the dots, I wonder if it could've been her eavesdropping but that's reaching. A part of me prays it was her and not some random person because I'm not sure what incriminating statements Trevor and I may have made with our juicy conversation. I can mind fuck Chassidy's gullible ass into believing what I want her to believe but anyone else would possibly pose a threat. I shake my head in an attempt to shake off the paranoia that was creeping. I wish I could just shake off Psycho's crazy ass. I'm still in disbelief that he actually threatened to hurt my man over this shit. If it weren't for the incriminating messages that may still be in his phone I would just murk his ass myself but my loose lips would give the police enough evidence to fry my ass. So murdering him was out the question. I exit the bathroom after checking myself out in the mirror. Time to get this show on the road.

    I can see the agitation on Justin's face as soon as I get back in the car but I have something that's about to calm all that. "I was in line getting you this," I say holding up the sealed bottle of VivaZen. "That's what took me so long," I lied. I already know what he was going to do and I'm right; he passes it right back to me and tells me to open it up for him. *This nigga making this shit too easy,* I think to myself before grabbing the bottle and swapping it out with the drugged one. This nigga is so damn prefictable, i'm amazed no female has tried to rob his ass yet. As much weed as he smokes and coke that he does kind of makes him an easy target for bitches that liked to hit licks. I bet his charm alone kept a bitch from getting out on him though. I give him the shot and look at the clock. We have thirty minutes to make it to our destination and fifteen minutes before this nigga passes out.

Once I see he's getting groggy I suggest that I drive. "You know this car is hot as fuck with these rims and these tinted windows already so we can't afford for you to be swirving," I tell him truthfully.

"Good thinking," he slurs and he pulls over to the median since we're on the freeway. He shakes his head back and forth like he was trying to shake the sleepiness off.

"I don't know why I'm so tired all of a sudden," Justin says, scratching his head. He gets out and I slide over into the driver's seat and readjust my mirrors. He pulls on the door handle, telling me to unlock the passenger side door and I hit the unlock button so he can get in. I'm grateful that his phone is on GPS, that way the phone will still be unlocked after he passes out. As long as the Google Maps app is running, I have full access to Justin's phone. I have to be able to communicate with the nigga that's doing the drop. This nigga is about sleep when a text message comes through.

I suck my teeth when I realize that even when the phone is unlocked, you still have to unlock the messages. This nigga think he a real player. Once he's knocked out, I place his thumb on the fingerprint sensor on the phone and the messages instantly unlock. I mount the phone to the dashboard with a grin. Access *granted.*

Chapter 9: Chassidy

I looked at Solo in disbelief. Did he really just ask me that, like was he serious? Maybe it was the drugs talking because we had did a few lines but what he was proposing was ludacris. How the hell was I supposed to basically rob the pharmacy, the old people, and the insurance companies, simultaneously without getting caught? I could end up in prison for the rest of my life with all those felonies.

"I'm just an LPN," I reasoned. "I don't even have access to prescription pads."

"That's where my boy SciFi comes in," Solo said. "He's going to make sure shit goes smooth. He's the one over this whole prescription pill operation."

Sometimes it was best to use the vocabulary of silence. The less I talked, the more I could hear and I heard Solo loud and clear. This nigga didn't give a fuck about me, he was just using me as a pawn, a way to make some money. I was merely a means to an end. He wanted me to push coke at the job and probably eventually in the streets too. I guess his girl was too good for all that. Besides that, I just found out that his guy "SciFi" he's always talking about and Trevor are the same person. So Travor was working with Solo behind Mercedez's back. None of them were to be trusted. They were the last people I'd consider going into business with. On the other hand, I could use the money. And working closely with Solo wouldn't be all that bad. As a matter of fact that's what made me cave in and agree to go along with this grand scheme of his.

Solo looked at me with a sly smile. "I knew that brain had to work up there as good as that head work down here," he said with a laugh.

"What the fuck ever Solo," I said pushing him playfully. "You're using me for your own personal gain. That's fucked up."

He stopped laughing and placed his hand on my thigh. "I'm not gone lie, those were my intentions at first, but when we connected and I found out you were cool as shit, I started to really like you. That was then, this is now."

"That was last night!" I snapped and he just shook his head.

"I'm not talking about last night per se," he said seriously. "I Found out you were cool when you were talking to Tragic. This was supposed to be strictly business between us but you make it hard for a nigga shorty. I could've done this with or without you but I'd much rather be in your presence than without you. Us vibing like we do is just a plus."

As I listened to him spit game, a part of me knew I should've been mad because it was just that- game. But the more I heard him talk my heart warmed anyway. I couldn't stop thinking about how good it felt to be wanted or in this case, needed for a change. I was getting from him what I had longed for in my marriage, the right to feel needed. The satisfaction of being wanted. I wished that I could have that feeling for life. But, this *wasn't* real life, at least not my life because he wasn't my man, this wasn't my feeling to keep. I was his on borrowed time, which was never too long.

"So is you wit' it shorty or na?" was the question he'd asked me. My head was saying, "Hell no!" but, against my better judgment I said, "I'm with you."

"Do you believe in love at first sight, Chassidy?" was the next question he hit me with. He was either putting his mac down strong or he was really feeling me, like for real.

"Yes," I said in almost a whisper.

He leaned over to kiss me then he said, "You ready to get this money?"

I nodded my head. "Let's get it!" I said, giddily, then I sat back and listened intently as he laid out the plan. I had to give it to Solo, he had all his bases covered, from the desk clerk at the medicare office to the cashier at the pharmacy. Everybody had a role. Solo was really smart to be a hood nigga. His plan was nothing short of perfection. In fact, it was genius.I listened eagerly as he explained to me how I played a key role in the operation and he stressed to me how important it was that I didn't fuck this up.

"I need you to be sure you're ready," he said, looking me in my eyes and the beauty of his naturally green eyes didn't go unnoticed. I gazed at them as he continued to talk business and I couldn't help but wonder what his life would've been like he hadn't dropped out of high school. The nigga was clearly a mathmetician. He was a beast with the numbers, he probably would've excelled in business school or been a celebrity accountant or something by now. He would've been with someone like me, not someone like Mercedez's superficial ass. I didn't feel bad for fucking her man because karma's a bitch and Mercedez put a lot of bullshit in the atmosphere, it's no wonder she'd been hit with a dose of her own medicine.

I looked at the clock in Solo's car and wished that he'd hurry up and pay for the room already. He had been in there for ten long minutes and I was anxious to spend the rest of my night with him.

"Finally, I've been sitting out here forever," I complained moments later.

"Oh, my bad shorty, I got a business call when I was in there."

"Must've been some important business" I said with a hint of an attitude.

"Don't do that," he said, giving me a quick peck on the cheek. Just my brother-in-law wants to meet up to handle some business. But really it is important enough for me to have to leave you here for a couple hours after we go up here and handle our business if that's cool with you?"

"Yeah sure," I said, punching my glasses up the bridge of my nose, attempting to sound unbothered. I was really disappointed but I was so desperate for him that I'd take whatever time he would give me. Pathetic right?

He pulled around to the back of Red Roof Inn and we went in from the side door by the dumpster. A far cry from the first room was all I could say. As soon as we got upstairs he tugged off our clothes and tossed them on the floor. He handled me aggressively, animalistically even and while this was not the love making session I had planned, his consistent pounding and deep thrusts quickly brought me to my peak and then I felt him reach his. When we were done Solo immediately snatched up his clothes and began to get dressed.

"Are you coming right back?" I asked. I know i was coming off as needy but fuck it, I needed to know I wasn't gone get played like a forty dollar prostitute again.

"Why wouldn't I?" he asked and kissed me on my lips. "I told you I need you and you know he," he said, pulling at his manhood, "can't stay away from you too long."

The way I was grinning you would've thought that nigga said he loved me. My head was swimming in the clouds and I hadn't even touched my pack yet. I was in lust and I wanted Solo in the worst way. And it seemed like whenever I wanted him, i wanted the coke or whenever I wanted the coke I wanted him. So I sprinkled a gram on my little glass tray and kicked my feet up, deciding I'd catch up on some H.B.O. while he was gone. My favorite show *Love Craft Country* was on tonight so I'd be entertained without Solo for a little while. The cocaine had me so on edge though, i couldn't even enjoy the show and I couldn't seem to sit still for shit. Not wanting to appear too high when Solo got back I decided to take a xanax so I could relax. Despite the fact that I'd done a generous amount of cocaine, thanks to the pill, I felt myself growing tired and drifting off to sleep. I dreamed of my ex for some strange reason. We were out on our yacht, fishing at sunset and he reeled in a humongous catfish but when he saw that it was already dead, he threw it back into the sea and I woke up. The room was dark except for the glow from the t.v. light and there was still no sign of Solo. I decided to be proactive and work on some things. I had a little money scheme of my own and I wanted to put some things in motion so I pulled out my work laptop and got started. I was going to show Solo he wasn't the only one that could come up with a bomb ass plan to make some money. Once I let him in on my new ideas I was sure he'd want to leave his girl and be the power couple we were destined to be. So I hit a line of cocaine and got to work. It seemed like I came up with the best ideas when I was high, or so I thought.

Chapter 10: Mercedez

After not hitting me up all day, all of a sudden, Solo is blowing my shit up. Luckily Justin is out like a light so he doesn't see my phone constantly lighting up and vibrating. I keep on letting that shit go right to voicemail, twelve times and counting just so he can see how that shit feels. I could easily answer and lie like I'm out with Chassidy just to ease his mind but fuck that, I'ma let that nigga sweat like he did me. Obviously he's done entertaining bitches and now he wants to make time for me when it's convenient for him. So i'll be damned if I pick up, his actions or lack thereof got me feeling like I don't owe a nigga shit, not even an explaination. If he continues to blow my shit up I'ma turn my shit off because i don't have time to be distracted. I'm almost to my destination, some address in Jackson google maps is leading me to. Justin has the plug name under P which I assume is for plug. So, pretending to be Justin, I text P from Justin's phone informing him that Justin wouldn't be picking up the dope but he was sending his sister instead. I was glad Justin only seemed to communicate with "P" through texts. He seems to think that the police can't hack your phone and check your messages like they can tap your phone and hear your calls so it's not out of the ordinary for them to communicate via text only. My hands start to itch in anticipation of stealing the money and the product too. I already swapped out the cash for counterfeit , leaving the real bills on the top and bottom of the stacks. Thanks to Sci-fi, P won't know the bills are fake unless he takes them to a bank and tries to deposit them and I'll be long gone by then. At first I was only going to rob Justin. Hitting P wasn't even in my original plan, he was supposed to have been Justin's problem once Justin presented him with the counterfeit cash. but greed got the best of me as I thought about the possibility of walking away with the money and the drugs. That roofie has Justin so gone I have to stick my finger under his nose a few times to make sure the nigga is still breathing. I know after a while the effects of the medications will start to wear off so I have to move quickly. I have to drop the duffle bag full of "money", get the drugs, and get ghost by the time Justin wakes up. When he comes to and calls me, I'll act like I was never there and I didn't know what happened or what the hell he was talking about. Luckily, a side effect of the xanax is short-term memory loss and I gave him at least four milligrams, enough for the whole night to be a black out. He wouldn't remember a thing and P wouldn't be able to identify me with my black wig, dark powder-pressed make-up and huge oversized shades I pulled over and put on. P would probably off his ass before he could even figure out it was me who set him up anyway. Damn, that's fucked up but better him than me.

    When the GPS alerts me that we have arrived at our destination I find myself outside of a huge warehouse that sits in a big empty lot surrounded by nothing but woods. The security guard pats me down and I instantly recognize him as the bouncer that was at the Youngboy show that night. I'm glad that it's dark and I'm wearing a pound of makeup. Tim has a duffle bag in his hand, which I assume has the five-hundred thousand dollars worth of bricks in there. I hold up my bag which is supposed to have two-hundred thousand dollars in it. "You wanna count the keys?" he asks me as he unzips his bag.

I hold up my hand and say, "No need, Justin says P is good people," and I unzip my bag as well. "It's all accounted for," I tell him, then he holds up his hand to silence me so I nodded as we mutually agreed to trust each other.

"Justin has never done bad business before so we good sis," he said assuringly. We exchange bags and shake hands, then finally, I turn to leave. I can't walk the quarter mile back to the car fast enough. When the car is in view again, I pop the trunk remotely and when I reach it I throw the bricks in next to the real money bag. I jump in and turn around to head back out but this time the gates don't automatically open like they did the first time.

"What the fuck," I mutter with a frown. I'm ready to get the fuck out of here. I didn't plan on getting locked in this motherfucker. Suddenly there is a tap at my window and I shriek, startled by the unexpected noise. I'm in panic mode like a motherfucker, my anxiety on ten, but I got my poker face on. I crack my window and look at the guard with a raised eyebrow, motioning my hands towards the gate. "You gone let me out this motherfucker or what?"

"The boss needs to see you," he said, ice grilling me.

My heart drops to my stomach as it begins to turn knots but I maintain my cool. "That's cute, but I don't work for your boss," I say, trying my best to sound confident, cocky even. "Now could you please open the gate and let me the fuck out of here?"

"No," he growled at me. "Psycho ain't opening that gate until you see him."

Did he just say what the fuck i think he just said? So P stands for fucking Psycho??? Ain't that a bitch. I should've known! Now I know I have to get on down. I just gave $200,000 counterfeit cash to the same nigga I already owe a hundred thousand to? I have to get the fuck out of here! Suddenly I look at the passenger seat I had reclined Justin back in and realize the motherfucker is empty! The panic is setting in for real now. Where the fuck did he go? Had Psycho or should I say, motherfucking "P" snatched him up while I was doing the exchange? Knots are forming in my stomach now. My phone rings and Psycho's number flashes across my screen. The gig is up. I'm fucked. I want to run but there's no use, he'll just find me. I need to face him so I can lie my way out of this somehow. I take a deep breath to calm down before answering the phone because an innocent person wouldn't be panicking.

"What's up Psycho?" I ask, glaring at the guard.

"I saw you coming in on camera. If you this nigga sister, yall some incestuous mothafuckas cause this the same nigga you was fuckin' when my brother-in-law went to the penitintury."

I try to come up with the words to say but a large lump forms in my throat and I can't seem to speak. The guard is giving me a menacing glare and I see pure malice in his eyes. I also notice the two goons that are approaching us and all I know is I definitely gotta get out of here now so I hang up and throw the car in drive, pushing the pedal to the metal. I pray the gates open and I don't just crash into them as I brace myself for impact. Luckily, I come crashing right through them. I high tail it out of there and let out a laugh as my adrenaline starts to rush. Right now I have the upper hand. I have the money, the drugs and a fast ass car. I'm sure the grill is fucked up from the wreck and I think I ran over the guard too but fuck it at least I'm free. It ain't my damn car anyway and fuck that guard. There is a few miles back to the highway and I'm going at least 100 miles per hour. My mind travels to Justin and I feel bad for leaving him but there's no use in both of us getting killed, I had to save myself! I look in my rearview mirror and notice large, bright headlights approaching me, and fast. Fuck! I finally reach the highway and the vehicle behind me is in high pursuit while I'm weaving in and out of traffic trying to shake them. I slow down to 90 mph, not wanting to cause an accident. I'm acting as if I'm going straight then I turn at the last minute to get on the exit. I check my mirrors, the high beams are gone and I know I've lost who I'm assuming to be Psycho and his goons. I pull up at a semi-crowded hotel parking lot, ditch the car, and call Solo. If anybody knows how to get me out of this situation it's him. He won't be too happy about it but I'm confident that all that anger will subside when I show him the duffle bags I have full of dope and money.

"Where the fuck you at?" he hollers through the phone. He sounds pissed and I haven't even told him what was happening yet.

"Look, I need you to come get me, now," I say panting, walking quickly along the shadows of trees. I keep looking over my shoulder because I'm paranoid like a muthafucka.

"From where?" he asked, sounding frustrated.

"I looked around and noticed the golden arches not far from me. "There's a

McDonald's about a half mile from the hotel I'm walking from," I tell him, knowing he is about to make assumptions about me being at the hotel with a nigga . Before he starts yelling and cursing me out, I let him know that I just went there to ditch my ride. I run down the location as best as I can by telling him what exit I took and what is surrounding me. I tell him to meet me at the McDonald's because I want to be somewhere well lit with a lot of people in the event some shit pops off, at least there'll be witnesses. I'm not trying to get snatched up like Justin. A wave of guilt overcomes me and I start to feel remorseful over my friend. I quickly shake off the notion, knowing if there were any other way to handle what went down tonight, I would've done things differently. I briefly peek inside the bags and a sly smile creeps on my face, knowing I've landed a small fortune. I plan on doing whatever to keep this money, even if it means relocating to get away from Psycho's crazy ass. The city isn't big enough for the both of us and me, not being from here, will gladly take my ass back to Detroit, Michigan and take over the streets with this cocaine I'm sitting on. I have enough bricks to last until I find a new connect and enough money to live good when I get there. What happened to Justin tonight is fucked up because I'm alost sure his life has come to an end but as for me, I'm not going out like that. Thoughts of what I will do with the money consumes me as I hustle through the trees on the side of the road. I can't let all this bullshit go in vain. No, this is the beginning of the come up.

Chapter 11: Solo

I purposely hit every pot hole on the freeway, going a hundred miles per hour. I'm not trying to fuck up my truck but I want this nigga in the trunk to feel every bump and I hope it bruise his shit up too. How the fuck this lil' weak ass nigga gone try to play me like I'm a lame ass nigga or something? I come home from jail and this nigga out here playin bonnie and clyde with my bitch. That's right, that lil' app she put on my phone, *ilocate mobil*e, the one she think I don't know about, work both ways. She probably didn't know that because she never read the fine print just like she never thinks a plan all the way through. And from what she told me on the phone, she clearly didn't think this one through. Her plan had more holes in it than swiss cheese, like really, how the fuck she think she gone rob the same nigga twice? Even if she claims the first time wasn't her fault, it might as well have been because she was rockin' with the nigga that did it, so she might as well have done it. If she would've just been honest with me and told me what the fuck was going on I could've helped her before the situation got this bad. But, I had to hear it from another bitch too little too late, and now, shit was out of control. I knew exactly what she was up to thanks to Chassidy's coke head ass. I been telling Mercedez that bitch ain't her friend. With the information Chassidy gave me, it didn't take long to put two and two together because I had already heard about the Psycho beef from my little sister. I believed the rumors just because I already know how Mercedez is; she'll rob a nigga without blinking or thinking twice. I slam my fist on the steering wheel in fustration because Mercedez is in way over her head this time and i'm probably gone have to body a nigga before this shit is over with.

I push the pedal to the metal knowing I only have so much time before Psycho catches up to my girl. I'm reeling wondering what the hell she was thinking going into business with this nigga? And then she crosses the nigga at that. A chill went up my spine as I thought about what happened to the last person that crossed Psycho. He had cut the nigga into pieces while he was still alive, part by part until he eventually bled out. Then he put the nigga in a box and sent him to his momma. Luckily, Sci-fi's bills are so authentic that even if the weight was off it wouldn't be by much, and they can pass the pen test. If anything Psycho's thinking she shorted him and she's just being paranoid because she knows the whole bag is counterfeit. The bills could easily fool anybody and they even work in a money counting machine. Mercedez should've just kept her cool when the nigga told her the count was off instead of panicking and acting guilty. By losing her head instead of keeping her poker face, she was showing her hand, exposing herself. The number one rule in a situation like this is to never let them see you sweat. *I'ma tell that nigga he better count that shit by hand because his scale must be off,* I think, trying to come up with a way to keep him off Mercedez's ass. He probably used a marker by now and thinks the bills are real and she just took some off the top. When he counts it and sees that it's all there he won't be a problem 'til Monday morning when the banks open and by then I'll have everything under control. Those bills definitely won't make it past the bank though. If he deposits it himself, he won't make it past the bank either. His ass will be aressted on the spot and a nigga ain't a threat behind bars. I'm just saying. I just hope my little sister don't get caught up in all this shit. I want to protect her but there's no way I can warn her without throwing Mercedez under the bus so I'm not gone say shit. If it was me or her nigga she'd save her nigga first. So, fuck her. I told her about fuckin' with hood niggas and that one day she would face the consequences like every other bitch. She wasn't exempt. The players gone change, but the game remains the same.

My eyes travel to the back of my truck through my rearview mirror to make sure the nigga is still tied up and ain't broke loose somehow. I scoff, wondering what my girl ever saw in that clown ass nigga anyway. I know the nigga was gettin' money though and that's what probably gravitated her to him. She wasn't a gold digger but she wasn't messing with no broke niggas for real. It hurt me to know that my girl was out here in trouble and she had to turn to another man for help. I keep thinking if she would've just been honest with me instead of having me solve a fuckin' mystery to get to the truth I could've helped her out of it like I've helped her so many times before. I'm supposed to be her hero but she playing games with me like I'm the villain. How the fuck she ain't gone tell me that a nigga was threatening to take my life until now? That nigga called me earlier and told me to come over and now I see why. I was about to walk right into a motherfuckin' trap. I move to the right lane, headed for the exit. Mercedez said she got off. She's still on the line on my car phone, not wanting to hang up in case some shit pop off before I get there. I continue to listen to her ramble in a hurried attempt to explain the details of the situation to me but I can tell she's still lying and leaving some parts out. I just shake my head, one hand on the steering wheel, the other holding my blunt. To be honest, I don't give a fuck about what she did, I'm not bout to let a nigga play with me or mine in no type of way. She did her dirt, I did mine, I can't even be mad at her. In my heart I knew that every action Mercedez ever took was just a reaction to the way I was moving. I know I'm wrong for fuckin' with her slut ass coworker but it's a part of the game. Shit happens but it'll all be worth it in the end when this pill operation takes off and her ass is swimming in new money.

"I'm pullin' up in the SUV," I tell her so she won't be alarmed and take off, thinking it's Psycho or his goons.

"Open the trunk so I can throw these bags in there," she said walking towards the back of the truck.

I take both duffle bags off her shoulders and say, "I'ma just toss it in the back. I got some trash in the trunk I need to throw out," opening the back door and tossing both bags onto the back seat. "You know this my sister's truck. I borrowed it to come get you."

"I thought you was Psycho in this mothafucka," she said, eyeing the big black suburban. "Where is your car?"

"I lost my keys," I lied, opening the passenger side door for her to get in. The truth was I was following them the whole time, since they left her job. I knew my car would've been a dead give away so I opted for my sister's new truck instead. She looked at me skeptically but didn't say anything as we got in the truck. My phone rang and broke the silence. "Talk to me bruh-in-law, what's good?" I say, trying to sound casual. Mercedez looked at me with large eyes. She looked like a deer caught in headlights.

"I was expecting you to come through. I need to holla at you about a few things," Psycho said evenly.

Tired of the charades, I decide I need to holla at him about a few things first. "We got yo' money, she told me everything, including the threat you made about me."

"That's why I don't like to mix business and family. The same rules apply to everyone in the game whether we kin or not. It wasn't personal homie, just business," Psycho said.

"You can come by and pick up the dough once we make it home," I tell him, assuringly.

"Bet," Psycho said before we ended the call.

"We about to pay that nigga back with his own money," I say to Mercedez. "If there's as much as you say it is in there, we can give him half and still come out on top with a lot of cash and a whole lot of dope."

"But I thought he was after me for the counterfeit?" she says, looking confused.

"He talkin' about his cut out the New orleans deal. He won't know about that counterfeit until Monday morning when that nigga try to go to the bank. They gone lock him up on the spot and that's fed time dealing with counterfeit shit, especially the amount he has. He won't be getting out no time soon," I explained, passing her the blunt I had been smoking on. "I just gotta see to it that Jessica don't make the drop or it's gone be her ass in jail and then we'll still have to deal with this nigga." My phone starts ringing again. I look at the number and realize it's Psycho calling me back. I said, "What's up bruh?"

"Ya boy Sci-Fi, that computer geek yall be fuckin' with," Psycho started.

"Yeah, what about him?" I asked, confused as to why he would be asking about Sci-fi. My stomach drops. I assume Psycho knows about the money.

"What's his number?"

Needing an excuse as to why I can't give him the number, I stall for time. "For what?" I ask pointlessly. It didn't matter what Psycho said he needed the number for, he wasn't getting it from me.

"Shit, I'm trying to get out the country and I heard he be makin' them passports. Tell him I got him ten racks right now if he can make that happen for me."

The pit that was forming in my stomach stopped, realizing he wasn't calling about the cash. I still wasn't giving him the number though. Hell. Nawl. What if he tried to pay that man with that fake ass money? Sci-fi might think I tried to cross him and I would never set him up like that. So I wasn't coming up off that number.

"Shit, to be honest bruh, Ion even think Sci-fi into shit like that nomore," I lied. "Ever since he got engaged and got that good ass job down at the nursing home he ain't really been fuckin' with the streets like that. He say he goin legit."

"Damn, for real?" Psycho asked, sounding disappointed

"Yeah for real," I continued with my lie. "The nigga don't even go by sci-fi nomore, he use his government name, Trevor."

"Damn, I guess I gotta find someone else then," he said solemnly.

"If I come across somebody I'll let you know," I lied again before ending the call. I look over at my girl.

"This nigga talkin' bout leavin' my sister and they kids to flee the country? Who the fuck he owe, the mafia?"

At first she laughed, then she turned serious. "You said the only reason you wouldn't kill the nigga is because of your nieces and nephews. But now the circumstances have changed. For one, he'll be trying to kill us if he doesn't go to jail and two, he talkin' bout leaving the country anyway and leaving them behind so what good is he to them then? He might as well be dead, it'll be one less problem on our hands."

I look at my girl, shocked she would be down for a 187. "So you wanna dead this nigga? I ask, trying to make sure I heard her correctly

"Shit if we don't he gone be tryna' dead both our asses come Monday morning.

What if things don't go the way you plan? Shit, your nieces and nephews will still have a momma if we off his ass but if he get to us first our kids ain't gone have nothing but each other." She took a long pull on the blunt and passed it to me.

I didn't have to say anything but, "Say less." She knew I heard her and what was understood didn't need to be explained.

Loud groaning sounds and movement started to come from the back of the trunk. Mercedez almost jumped out of her seat as she exclaimed, "What the fuck!" She turned around with her back to the dashboard. Noticing I was still cool, calm, and collective she said, "You must know who or what is in the trunk."

"Oh yeah," I said, rubbing my hand over my goatee. "I forgot to drop off the trash."

"What the fuck is in the trash?" she asked, looking terrified.

"Relax," I grin. "We had another loose end so I tied him up."

Mercedez glared at me as if to say this was not the time to be telling jokes. "So you tied someone up and stuffed them in the muthafuckin' trunk!" exclaimed. She was furious and I hadn't even told her who it was yet. "Who is that Solo?"

I ignored her and said, "Thanks to you the nigga was passed out already. What you slip him, one of your xan bars?" I laugh. "That nigga was like dead weight in my hands! His body was so limp when I snatched him out of that car that for a minute I thought the nigga was dead already," I admit.

"Already?" Mercedez starts shaking her head, looking bewildered. "What have you done?" she says in almost a whisper. A moment of silence goes by and then she asks, "What were you doing at the warehouse?"

"Trying to see what the fuck you was doing," I snap at her.

"How you find it? Even I had to use GPS to find it," she asked, folding her arms to her chest.

"I followed you from your job but I lost you trying to keep a few cars back so I had to use ya lil' app you snuck and put on my phone. You must didn't read the fine print because thanks to you, I can always locate yo' ass too! Right back atcha! Muthafucka," I tell her with a chuckle.

She turns back around in her seat, facing forward, face beet red, probably with guilt. She said nothing.

"Yeah mu'fucka," I keep going cause I'm with the shit now. "You thought I ain't know you had a tracker on my phone? That's why I used to leave it at my momma house all day just to piss you off cause you knew I wasn't there."

"And where were you," she asks, rolling her neck like a snake.

"Hustling," I bark. "Unlike you, out here ridin' wit' niggas and shit," I say, trying to flip the script so we were no longer talking about where I was but what she'd been doing instead. Luckily, my phone starts ringing. *Saved by the bell,* I thought, until I looked at the number and saw that it was Chassidy. I quickly sent it to voicemail and shoved the phone into my pockets.

"Who was that?" Mercedez asked me incredulously.

"Business," I tell her, then the phone starts ringing again. Again I send it to voicemail and decide to shoot her a text message instead, telling her I had some important business to handle and I would catch up with her shortly.

"You can text but you can't talk?" Mercedez asks with an arched eyebrow. She tries to snatch the phone out of my hands and I accidentally swerve into the left lane, barely missing a collision with another truck. *BEEEEEP!* The horn blared loudly, scaring her into keeping her hands to herself.

"What the fuck is wrong with you?" I exclaim, heated that she almost caused us to wreck. I decided then that it was time to drop her off.

A text from Chassidy came in, *Good news, I placed an order for the pills you asked for, they'll be delivered to the office tonight so I'll need to be at the job.* I smirk, thinking about the money that's about to come my way. Fuck a bitch, money make my dick hard. My smile is short lived though when I realize Mindy is ice grilling me. Besides that, i still have to do something with this nigga in the trunk. "Show me you don't love nobody but me," I say to Mercedez as I'm pulling up to our garage.

"How the fuck I'm supposed to do that?" she asked, irritably.

"Dead ya lil' boyfriend in the back," I say seriously.

She looks at me with wide eyes shaking her hea., "Are you fucking serious?"

"Dead ass," I say, reaching for my gun.

"You want me to *murder* someone to prove that I love you? That's not love, that's insanity." I can see her visibly shaking, something she does when she gets really nervous, as I attach the silencer to the pistol, I don't care about her being nervous, I want this nigga dead and she's going to be the one to do it since she's the one that brought him into our lives in the first place.

"Call it what you want but either way it's gonna happen. And if I do it, it's not gone be quick and easy. I'ma make that bitch ass nigga suffer and die slow."

"I can't do it, Solo," she says as I peer at her while twisting the silencer in place. Her eyes got the nerve to be watering and shit. "I've never done this before," she says in a hushed tone, I ignore her and place the gun in her hands anyway. I can see her hands trembling and I almost feel sorry for her. My sympathy fades quick when I think about her fuckin' this nigga and my heart hardens. I want her to prove she ain't got love for this nigga so I reach over and take it off safety. If she can't do it then that can only mean one thing- she in love with that nigga. And if that's the case, I'ma shoot her and bury her right next to that nigga because the only way they gone be together while I'm alive is in death.

"Get out the truck," I say as I open my door to get out as well. I feel her eyes on me while I'm moving and I know she don't want to be a killer. But at the same time I want to know she don't love this nigga more than she love me. We make our way to the rear of the truck and I push the button to make the garage door close. I pop the trunk and I see the nigga squirming, bound and gagged. I spit on him and start to walk away. She glares at me so hard that for a second, I wonder if she's going to shoot me with my own gun. I throw my hands up as if to say, "I surrender" and take a couple steps backwards, giving her her space. As a matter of fact, she can handle that business on her own. I don't want to see her all teary eyed over this nigga so to protect my own feelings, I choose not to watch. As soon as I turn my back I hear the gun cock and I pause. Before I can take another step she shoots and everything goes black.

Chapter 12: Mercedez

What the fuck does he mean, 'he need to know I'm only in love with him'? All I know is I'm way too emotional to have a gun in my hand. Because, fucking with me anything can happen. He wants me to commit murder to mask his own insecurities? I feel like crying but I know that ain't gone solve shit either so I suck it up and hold my head up. I dread what's next. One thing about me, you're not going to lil' girl me and tell me what to do. *But if you don't do it he's going to kill you.* Unless I kill him. I pause for a moment to picture what life would be like without Solo. *Freedom.* Free from him and all his toxicity. It's true what they say, there's a thin line between love and hate and Solo is crossing the line this time. As soon as he turns his back to walk away I cock the glock and he stops mid-step.

"I'm sorry," I say, a single tear rolling down my cheek. I never thought it would come to this. I wipe away the tear and before I can think twice I pull the trigger. *Psssst*, I shoot and in a state of shock I stumble backwards against the wall causing myself to accidentally turn the lights off. I take the opportunity to wipe my face, not wanting him to see me cry. Once the lights are on I look directly in his eyes. He looks shocked as if he didn't see it coming, his eyes, even though lifeless, burning a hole through mine. That was the last time I'd ever see his pretty eyes. It was the last time I'd see Justin. "I'm so sorry," I say again, closing his eyelids. "But you knew too much."

The silence between us is thick, making it seem as if I'm going to suffocate, so I'm glad when Solo finally backs out of the driveway and disappears into the night. As soon as I'm in the house I lock the door and break down. I put my hands over my mouth to muffle my sobs, remembering the kids are home. Luckily it's late and they are sound asleep. I try to stop the tears from falling but they flow freely like a river. Justin was my friend. In another lifetime he could've been my lover. I shake my head, disgusted at myself for what I did to him. This was a different feeling from when I thought I left him at the warehouse. I murdered him at point blank range. But I did what I had to do. He knew too much of Solo's and my business. Solo was right, he was a loose end. Why the fuck did Solo have to kidnap him if he felt some type of way? Why not just kick his ass and keep it moving? No, he wanna tie mufuckas up like we in a street novel and leave me to do the dirty work. Had I known the nigga was in the truck I would've watched my fucking mouth. Solo did that shit on purpose, he knew it would play out like that all along. Suddenly my anguish turns into anger. I hate feeling played. I look down at the gun that's still in my hand. Solo thinks the clip is empty but little does he know I lifted the box of bullets I found in Chassidy's drawer when I was at work earlier tonight. That bitch been moving real suspect lately anyway and I don't trust her. Something is definitely up with her. After all, who hides a gun in the office at their job? For all I know, this bitch could be planning a mass shooting like the others that's been happening in the world lately. The bitch might be a terrorist. Besides that, my gut keeps telling me that that was her fat ass in the bathroom eavesdropping this morning and if that's the case that bitch can get it too. I make sure the gun is on safety and I stick it in my back pocket. Is this what killing does? Make you think about killing every fucking body? I pace the floor back and forth, feeling like I'm losing my mind. I need to relax. I've got some xanax but I'm not trying to be sleep. My thoughts travel to the Dilaudid I have in my locker at work. I stopped taking pills a long time ago but they were too expensive to throw away. I could've sold them but I wanted to keep them in case I really needed them one day and today is one of those days. I decide to go down to the office, glad that the office is in a separate building than the actual nursing home. But not before I pack some clothes. Something keep telling me some more shit about to go down and that only makes me more anxious to get the fuck out of town. I go through the house throwing shit in a couple of suitcases I had originally bought for our trip to Cancun this summer. I get my mother on the phone to let her know I'm sending the kids to her till shit dies down. I'm sending them with a bag full of money so she won't ask any questions. After purchasing their tickets on southwest airlines website I wake my kids up and get them ready for their 2:00 am flight from Jackson to Michigan. They wake up groggily but are excited when I tell them where they're going. They love my mom to death, I hate that she lives so far away. In less than thirty minutes we loaded up the benz and headed to the airport. During the hour and a half drive I reflect on the events of last night and how everything spiraled out of control so quickly. Thoughts of the counterfeit cash invade my mind and how Jessica is going to be going away for a minute if she's the one to take that shit to the bank. Even if she's with him, she's still going to jail. *Oh well, not my problem.* I pull up at the Southwest terminal and immediately notice the young white girl holding a sign that said "Sitter". The kids were under 18 so they had to be accompanied by an adult. Luckily the airlines provided sitters for minors. The kids are so excited to be flying they barely said goodbye as they hurried through the airport doors. I tip the sitter two hundred dollars and with that I'm on my way back to Hattiesburg.

No sooner than I reach city limits, I get a call from Trevor. He sounds distraught and the only thing I could make out was that he was at Forrest General Hospital. "I'm on my way, just stay on the phone," I say in an attempt to calm him down. My words fall on death ears as I can hear Trevor sobbing hysterically. I haven't heard him crying this much since the eighth grade. We were walking home from school one day when a group of bullies pulled up on us with dirt bikes. I instantly recognized them as the white boys that gave Travor a hard time at school. They formed a circle around us and started taunting Trevor. "Hey Trevor, or is it Trisha?" one of them said. "Hey Tevor, my sister called, she's going to need her panties back!" They all laughed hysterically.

"Leave him alone!" I shouted, not afraid of them like Trevor was. He was literally shaking in his boots. He and I stood back to back, as they seemed to make circles around us. Trevor was clutching his books for dear life, I was clenching my jaws.

"Let the faggot tell me to stop!" One shouted at me. I balled my fist so tight, my knuckles had to have turned white.

"I said leave him alone," I said through gritted teeth.

"Make me!" the boy shot back. "I dare you nigger!" When he said that my blood began to boil. I was from Detroit and wasn't used to the ignorant ass white people in Mississippi throwing around racial slurs. Trevor could let them clown him all he wanted but I wasn't on that type of time. Before I knew it, I had hauled off and punched the boy dead in his mouth. *BLOOP!* The boy stumbled backwards, holding his hands to his now bloodied lip.

"I'm gonna kill you little nigger bitch," he spat, looking at me with an evil eye. "You and that faggot friend of yours. Tie her up!" All of a sudden one of the sons of a bitches came out of their backpack with a brown rope and gray duct tape. Another one snatched me up and held my hands behind my back while one of them grabbed me by the legs. I kicked, squirmed and screamed to no avail. They were much stronger than me when they worked together. They knew if they didn't make it a group effort to bring me down that I would've gotten free and beat their asses one by one. They tied Trevor and I to two trees parallel to each other. We were both sitting on the ground. First they took turns punching me and kicking me. A few of them even spit on me. When they got through with me they started attacking Trevor. First they beat him until he was a bloody mess then they did the unthinkable. Those little motherfuckers unzipped their pants and whipped their little dicks out and started laughing, evilly. But instead of attacking me like I expected they went for Trevor. The leader of the gang said, "Since you wanna be a dicksucker, you're about to get some practice!" They all hooped and hollered and proceeded to approach Trevor with their penis' in their hands. "Suck it punk!" one of them said to Trevor and one by one they defiled him, violently. Trevor screamed and cried as they laughed. I continued to wiggle out of the weak ass knot they had me tied up in and when my hands were finally free I was able to reach into my back pocket and pull out the box cutter I kept on me at all times. They were so busy violating and pissing on Trevor that they didn't even notice me cut the rope from around my ankles and break free. I ran up on the biggest one and slashed his ass across his back and down his spine. He fell to the ground screaming like the little bitch he was, as the others looked on in horror. One by one they hopped on their bikes and fled the scene, except for the one I had cut. Once I cut Trevor loose, I handed him the knife so he could finish the job. He must've stabbed that boy at least twenty times. We weren't worrying about anyone finding out because we knew if they told on us then they would have to tell what they did to Trevor. I did tell my parents and needless to say, they went out that night. The next morning when I turned on the television, "Breaking News!" flashed across the screen. The caption read, "Four teen scuicides following a teen homicide in Hattiesburg" A reporter said, "That's right Bill, it was a group of friends, police are thinking they must've murdered the victim and then killed themselves with drugs later that night. All four died of an overdose on the same lethal drug, Feytenol. The authorities are trying to find out where they could've gotten a hold of the drugs…" I saw the spelling of the drug in the caption and instantly recognized it as one of the pills Trevor's mom kept in her medicine cabinet. I knew then exactly where my parents were all night. We never spoke on it but I knew. I still don't know exactly how they did it, I just knew they did that shit. In my house what was understood didn't need to be explained. My parents were ruthless. Anybody could get it, women and children included, no one was exempt. I hadn't thought about that day in so long, but hearing Trevor cry was a trigger.

I get out of my head when I reach the emergency room and I ask for Trevor Watson at the front desk. The receptionist escorts me to a little room that looks like a small waiting area. I immediately notice Trevor sitting in the corner with his head down and I rush over to him. "What happened, are you okay?" I say looking him up and down trying to find out where he's hurt. When I don't see any sign of him being physically harmed a look of confusion comes on my face.

"It's Paul," he says quietly. "He's dead."

Chapter 13: Chassidy

"Damn, where have you been?" I asked Solo as soon as he entered the hotel room.

"Handling business with my family," he answered, looking a bit annoyed. He seemed different than before he left. He set a brown paper bag on the dresser. I ignore his emphasis on "family" and decide to share some news that will brighten him up.

"There's a 2 hour delivery shipment of narcotics going to the office. I need to be there to sign off on the meds."

Solo looked confused. "How the fuck you gone do that without getting caught? And who told you to make a play, I'm the one calling the shots here." He sat on the edge of the bed and pulled out a big wad of cash and started to straighten up the bills and put them in order.

"I thought this shit was a partnership?" I say, getting offended.

"This is," he reassured me. "But that shit is sloppy and I don't move sloppy."

"How is it sloppy?" I say, placing my hand on my hips.

"Because you can lose your job by signing off on those meds. Then what about the cameras?'

"I have an R.N's badge that used to work there and I'm having them delivered to the office not the workplace. Oddly enough, they're in separate buildings and there's no cameras at the office.

A smile crept on to his face and he stopped counting his cash. "Come here," he said, patting the spot next to him on the bed. I walked over to him and sat down beside him. He gave me a slow, sensual kiss and then stood up. He walked over to the dresser with his back turned to me and I can hear the cork pop on the bottle of wine he pulled out the brown paper bag. "Lets celebrate before we go with a toast. To our partnership." He turned around to look at me. "Go ahead and be puttin' ya clothes on, so we can ride out after we have this drink," he instructed me.

I jumped up smiling ear to ear and ran into the bathroom so I could fix myself up. When I came out of the bathroom he was holding up our glasses and he motioned for me to take one. "This must be really good champagne, it's still bubbling and fizzing,"

"It sure is," he said, wrapping one arm around my waist. "To new beginnings," he toasted then downed his glass. He then tilted mine, ensuring that I swallowed every bit. "Now, let's ride." He grabbed the keys to his truck and we were out.

He had to make a few stops so the fedex truck was already at the office when we arrived. The older man was looking at me kind of funny like he was suspicious of something but he didn't say anything. Once the fedex guy was gone I walked back to the truck to tell Solo he can load up the boxes. I could've done it myself but I was feeling dizzy all of a sudden, like I may have had too much to drink. I tried to shake it off and decided to do a quick walk-through around the office to make sure no one was there to witness us stealing the drugs. I was almost sure no one was there because the lights were all out. I flicked the switch to turn the lights on in my office but nothing happened. That was strange. I wanted to get the charger to my laptop so i held my hands out in front of me so I wouldn't bump into anything while walking to my desk. Suddenly I tripped over something big in the middle of the floor. I stumbled a bit before gaining my balance. I frowned, wondering who left something in my office area because I wouldn't leave anything out of place, especially in the middle of the floor. I used the flashlight on my phone to see what the hell I tripped over. I gasped when I realized what it was. Or who it was rather. There lay sprawled in the middle of the floor was Justin's lifeless body. There was a hole in his forehead and blood was all over his face. He was almost unrecognizable but I noticed his custom transformer chain and the gold grill because his lips were partially opened, gagged with a rope. I started to scream and a leather gloved hand clasped over my mouth. I couldn't see who the person was because they were standing behind me. I spotted the 9mm handgun in the center of the floor. I knew if I even so much as attempted to move in that direction, every hair on my naturally curly head would be ripped from my scalp. His grip was just that strong on my bush. *Fuck it*, I thought. *There's some wigs in my closet I've been dying to wear.* I had to make a move or I was going to die in there. I kicked my foot backwards, my stiletto pump landing directly between his legs, causing him to wince in pain. I scurried from beneath his grasp as he loosened his grip and dropped to the floor in pain while I scrambled towards the middle of the room. For the first time in a long time I was glad I took my ex-husband's advice to have a handgun in my office. "We're living in an evil world with lots of weirdos out there; It's better to be safe than sorry," he said one night before he kissed me on my forehead and left me to go be with his new family. I was left, feeling sick 2 months into my pregnancy with nowhere to go. I opted out of mentioning it to him, not wanting to be one of those women that used a baby as a desperate attempt to keep a man from leaving. Now what stupid son of a bitch that went and broke into the office tonight, clasping their OJ

Simpson glove all over my mouth, preventing me from screaming was beyond me. Suddenly, I felt heavy and tired, as if I'd been drugged. My adrenaline seemed to be the only thing keeping me alive at that point. I thought about the baby. Was it even alive? My first time being pregnant, I couldn't decipher between fetal movement or nervous butterflies fluttering in my stomach. If in fact I had been drugged, I wondered if the drug I'd been given was too strong for the fetus. Or was it the champagne? All I knew was if something happened to my unborn child, whoever was behind this had better kill me or they were a dead man walking. I'd do anything to protect me and mine. I finally got a hold of the glock and picked it up with both hands in an attempt to control my shaking. I had never held a gun, let alone, used one so I was trembling, nervous as hell. I aimed it at the perpetrator's head and their eyes grew wide as they slowly stood up. I, on the other hand, felt like I was going to pass out. Not only was my vision blurring, but I was getting dizzy. "Don't make another fucking move," I instructed them. Something wasn't right with this though; the masked man seemed to be looking past me. He was being distracted by something behind me. That's when I noticed the shifting shadows on the dimly lit hallway walls and I realized we were not alone. I had seen enough scary movies to know that if whoever it was were there to help me, they would've said so by now. But this was real life and I had to do whatever to save my child's life and mine. I spoke with my eyes never leaving the attacker. "I don't know who either of you are but if you make another move I will blow your brains out with no remorse. I'm the one with the gun."

That's when I heard the shifting shadow say, "Your clip is empty and I have the bullets bitch." Then *WHAMM!* All I could think about as I dropped to the floor was my unborn child. As I laid there it was like pictures of my life flashing before my eyes and I thought about the events that lead to this point. I was almost certain I knew who my attackers were so this was no robbery. This was personal. Lately everything had been happening so fast. As I felt the blood trickle from my head, past my nose, and to my lips I pondered, *"Where did it all go wrong?"*

Chapter 14: Solo

Feeling guilty about condemning Mercedez for the same shit I'm doing, I decide to cut Chassidy off. I can't reprimand my girl for keeping secrets and gettin' money with another nigga when I'm out here telling lies and hustling with bitches too. Plus, shit is out of hand on my side, now is definitely not the time to put my plan into motion. I can't let a quick lick pass though so I use the key card to open the hotel door ready to tell Chassidy she gone have to handle that lil' business she was tellin' me about pronto.

I'm pleasantly surprised when she tells me the pills will be here any minute. Apparently she emergency expressed that shit or something like that. I really don't give a fuck how she did it as long as she gets it done. The sooner I get the work, the sooner I can be done with this bitch. I copped a few xans from Mercedez so as soon as Chassidy sign for this shit she gone be out like a light. I need her sleep for my new plan to work without no problems. I figured out a way to get rid of Justin's body once I saw Chassidy left her keys in my truck. I knew one of them had to be to the office so I drove straight over there. Just as I suspected, the key worked and after double checking to make sure there wasn't no cameras, I dragged the dead body in the office and planted it there as if that's where the murder happened. I wiped my prints off the gun and left it there too. My plan was to plant a sleeping Chassidy at the "crime scene" and make an anonymous call to 911 to report what sounded like a shooting in the office building. Chassidy would be the main suspect and the police won't even have me and Mercedez on their radar with all the obvious evidence at the scene of the crime pointing to Chassidy. I thought about just killing the bitch because I don't like loose ends but she didn't deserve that. With Justin, it was personal. I hate the girl have to go to jail for some shit she didn't do but I had to shoot a cross so somebody had to take a loss for my girl to be straight. The xanax will have Chassidy's memory so fucked up she probably won't even remember being with me tonight. While Chassidy is in the bathroom I slip the pills in her drink. It's still bubbling and fizzing when she comes out but she chalks it up to good champaign.

When we get to the office and Chassidy gives me the ok, I back up with the truck and we load up the trunk with the pills. I can tell she getting sleepy from her delayed reactions but she is still determined to check the premises to make sure there were no witnesses. I already know the place is empty and she won't be able to see anything because I turned the breaker off. She isn't in there five minutes when I hear a piercing shrill from inside. I'm sure she discovered the body, which wasn't supposed to happen. I thought she'd be passed out by now but I guess her body mass and extra fat is stronger than the xanax I gave her. The only thing I can do now is knock her ass out because I need her to shut the fuck up before she runs out causing a scene. I dart inside and notice the hallway is lit so apparently I missed a switch. Luckily her back is facing the door so she doesn't see me creep up behind her. I instantly place my hand over her mouth to muffle her screams. I put her in a headlock and get a good grip of her hair. When she bites my hand and kicks me in the balls simultaneously I kneel over, wincing in pain. All of a sudden I see the shifting shadows in the hallway as if someone is approaching. *Fuck!* The last thing I need is a witness. In the few seconds I was looking at the hallway I took my eyes off Chassidy long enough for her to pick the gun up off the floor.

"Who's there?" she called out, crooning her neck towards the door but never taking her eyes off me. "Say something," she demands. "I don't know who either of you are but I will shoot you both with no remorse! I have the gun."

That's when I realize who it is creeping up from behind her. Motherfuckin Mercedez. "But I've got the bullets, bitch!" *WHAMM!* Mercedez pistol whips Chassidy right over the head, causing Chassidy to hit the floor with a loud thud. Then she does something unexpected. She points the gun at me. "You wanna tell me what the fuck is going on or am I gone have to lay your ass out too?"

"Baby," I say with my hands up while moving towards her slowly. I want to say, "What the fuck is you doin' here," but instead I go cliche' and say, "I can explain. It's not what you think."

"You better get to explaining because what I think is the worst case scenario," she says, still pointing the gun at me.

All of a sudden Chassidy groans, holding her head and her stomach. "Please don't hurt me," she begs. "I'm pregnant."

"I'm not going to hurt you," Mercedez said, turning towards her, then *POW!* She turns and shoots her right in the forehead. "See? Quick and painless," she says, mockingly. Then she swiftly points the gun back at me. "How long have you been fucking her?"

I look at her like she's crazy. "Not as long as you been fuckin Justin," I snap. "And definitely not long enough to get her pregnant. Now get that fuckin gun out my face!" She puts the gun down. "I'll tell you everything you want to know. And I just started fuckin wit that bitch since I got home so that definitely ain't my baby."

Mercedez scoffed. "The fact that it's even a possibility is fucked up Solo!"

"Fuck that, it's not possible on God! But how could you just kill her knowing she's pregnant like that Mercedez?" I ask. "God damn baby, I've created a monster," I say, getting her hair out of her face and tucking it behind her ear.

She swipes my hand back and snaps at me, "Don't fuckin touch me!"

I put my hands up as if I surrender.

"Why do you give a fuck about this bitch or her baby? What are you a fucking republican now? All 'Pro life'" and shit," she says, tucking her gun into her back pocket.

"I don't give a fuck, I'm just saying," I tell her. "Let's just get the fuck out of here."

Once we're outside she tells me to meet her at the house and take the highway instead of the main roads. I do exactly as I'm told. After all, I'm dealing with a real killer here. Shorty ain't playin'.

Chapter 15: Mercedez

When Solo tells me all about his little plan, I'm shocked. Of course I'm hurt because he cheated on me but I can't do nothing but chalk that up to karma for my relationship with Justin. When he told me why he didn't want me involved I had to forgive him because in his own twisted mind, he was protecting me. I could kick Trevor's ass though, that bitch is supposed to be my best friend, he could've told me about Solo's involvement in the operation. I want to call him and get on his ass but i remember his fiance' was just murdered so I decide not to even mention it to him. He has enough to deal with.

"Have you heard from Psycho since I delivered the rest of the money?" Solo asks. We're standing in the kitchen plotting on our next move when gunshots ring out and the windows shatter as bullet holes fly over our heads. Instinctively, we get on the floor and stay there until we hear screeching tires.

"I think we just heard from him," I say, panting. "You think we should call him?"

"Hell naw," Solo says, getting up and dusting the debris off of his shirt. "Then he'll know we in this bitch and come back and finish the job."

"Right," I agree, thankful that I sent my children away. That's why they call him Psycho- that nigga don't give a fuck about human life; men, women, and children, they all can get it in his eyes. Suddenly I regret the day I went into business with him. "He probably knows about the counterfeit. Let's just give him the product you dropped off at the storage and the real money."

"Fuck no!" Solo declines. "That would mean everything we did this far is for nothing," he reasoned. "What we need to do is get to him before he gets to us. Put his ass in defense mode." He walks to the closet and pulls a black duffle bag off the top shelf. Inside the bag are all types of guns and arsenals. I know when he pulls that bag out he's serious and some shit is about to go down.

My phone vibrates and I see that it's Trevor. He sent a message asking where I am and if we can meet.

"For fuckin' what?" Solo wants to know. "What we need to be doing is handelin' this business wit' Psycho." He grabs the keys and I follow him out the door only for us to find both cars shot up like swiss cheese with flat tires.

"Fuck this, we going to the airport, we need to lay low until we have a real solution," I say. "How we gone ride on niggas and we aint even got no whip? I'll tell Trevor to come on and we can get him to take us to the airport." Solo nods his head in agreement and I give Trevor our location so he can come take us to our destination. Seconds later I get a text back from Trevor letting me know he's on his way. Before I can shove my phone in my pocket, I get another incoming text message. This time, it's from Psycho. "*I just want you to know it was all business, nothing personal. U fam n I fwu da long way. Preciate u payin me back. We can do business anytime. Once I get back. I'm on a international flight right now. I'll get at u wen i touch down*". I look at the phone and frown. If it wasn't Psycho who shot at us then who the hell was it?

Solo notices my frown and askes, "What's wrong?" He leans over my shoulder as I hold the phone up so he can get a better look. "It wasn't him," I muttered in utter confusion.

"What he mean he *fuck wit' you the long way*?" Solo asks.

I swing around so that I'm standing directly in his face. "Are you fuckin' serious right now? We just found out the shooter ain't the shooter and you got time to be insecure?" I snap, furious that he's insinuating that there was more to the message than what it was. Typical Solo.

"For real bruh, why he couldn't just text *me* then? If it's all *business*," he asked, making air quotations with his fingers.

"Because he wasn't in business with you, he was in business with me, and did you just use air quotations?" Just then I hear a car door slam so I run to the window to see Trevor hustling up the driveway, looking at our cars as he crutches his chest. I can't help but be embarrassed by the bullet holes and shattered glass decorating the ground. Solo dismisses himself to make a call and I rush out to meet Trevor. "Oh my God, Trevor how are you, I know you've been busy with Paul's situation. Again, I give you my condolences," I say when he walks through the door.

"It's okay, I'm coping," he says nonchalantly. He takes a look around and tightens his jacket as if he's cold. "What happened here?"

"A fuckin' driveby,' I admit. "Remember when I mentioned to you earlier at the hospital about going out of town until things cool off? Well I'm kinda gonna need you to take Solo and I to the airport."

"I actually came to talk to you about you leaving town. Who's going to watch over the storage and continue the business while you two are on your little break? I know that was Paul's position."

I frown. "I don't know, I guess I haven't thought about it." That was a weird ass question. Your fiance is dead and instead of running around trying to handle his affairs you're running around town trying to fill his shoes? Who does that? He doesn't act like a person that just lost a loved one, that's for damn sure. But, I guess everyone deals with grief differently.

"Let's cut the bullshit shall we?" Trevor says clasping his hands together. "I need the storage key. Paul had a few things put away in there and since he's gone, it's only right that I get it."

I just look at this fool like he's crazy. There's no way I'm giving him that storage key. Paul never said anything to me about handing over shit to Trevor. Call it intuition or a gut feeling, but something's telling me Trevor might have had something to do with Paul's death. But what would be his motive? Envy? Greed? Both? "Did you do something to Paul?" I ask bluntly. It's been a long night and I'm not beat for the bullshit.

"We're being a little bit presumptuous aren't we?" he asks rhetorically.

"I thought you wanted to cut the bullshit?" I retorted.

"Fine," Trevor says, reaching in his coat pocket.

When he pulls out a small silver revolver, it looks like a .22, and points it at me. I'm shocked. "What are you doing?" I ask, backing up slowly. There's a knife holster behind me on the counter. If I can just back up a few more steps I can get to it. "Why are you doing this?" I ask with watery eyes.

Trevor answers me all the while keeping the pistol aimed at me. "All my life all I ever did was be in your shadow. My mother loved you, her best friend's daughter, more than me, her only son. Women are so privileged, it's sickening. You don't know what it's like to wake up every damn day in a body you despise."

"' I was there for you when you didn't have no fucking body, not even Paul-"

"Shut up," he snaps. "You see, once I have all the money in that storage I'll have more than enough to have a sex change and start a new life somewhere where no one will know me as Trevor. Paul was so fucking stingy with his money so I made a plan to marry him but that was before I realized you don't have to be married in order to get a life insurance policy on someone."

"Murderer," I say in utter disgust.

Trever scoffs. "How easily we forget our own transgressions? How is she by the way? Chassidy right?"

My eyes grow large and my chest tightens. "She's alive?"

"No honey, you killed her," he said reassuringly. "I stopped by the office and to my surprise both you and your man's boo thangs are stretched out on the floor. Now, I can go make a statement and you can cooperate with the police or you can cooperate with me and hand me the damn key." Then his voices changes to a low baritone voice of a man. "What's it gonna be bitch?" The last time Trevor had an episode like this was in college when he stopped taking his bipolar medication and was on the verge of schizophrenia. He's definitely armed and dangerous right now so in an attempt to save my own life, I act like I'm reaching for the key behind me. "Fine, okay!" I shout then I grab the butcher knife and attempt to stab his ass with it but his little skinny ass is too fast.

"Oh, you just made the wrong move you little bitch," he spat and he holds the revolver directly at my forehead. I hear the loud shot and it causes my ears to ring. My life flashes before my eyes as I hit the floor and I can't help but wonder, was it all worth it? The addiction to the fast life, the money and the street fame or the obsession of lust painted pretty like love can place a spell on anybody who craves it and they'll do anything for it like a junkie for a fix, but at what cost? In the end, what is the ultimate sacrifice, your soul? Who would've thought I would go out like this? I guess it's true, if you live by it, you die by it. That shit came back quick. I never would've expected it from my best friend though.

Growing up, Trevor was like the sister I never had. My twin sister died at birth and all I had were my brothers. That's how I became so tough, I would knock a bitch out in a minute. There were plenty of times I had to do just that, trying to stand up for my best friend. I remember when he was the new kid on the block and susceptible to bullies like the ones that tied us up that time or mean girls such as my cousin, Sierra. One day I walked in the cafeteria and Trevor and Sierra were in a heated argument. It took me a minute to see it was them because of the small crowd that had circled around them. I don't remember the intricate details of the small feud but I do remember having my cousin's back even though she was wrong. When I saw Trevor sitting alone at recess I went over and apologized about my cousin's actions and we became cool. Then when his mom found out who's kid I was she adopted me as her god-daughter. We were inseparable ever since. I even pretended to be his girlfriend when the other kids started teasing him about being gay. And even though Trevor battled with schizophrenia, bi-polarism, acute depression, and anxiety I always had his back. So him being the one to end my life is fucked up. Was Sierra right when she said that I betrayed her by befriending Trevor and that one day, Trevor would betray me? Damn right she was right because here we are and this is the ultimate betrayal. Never try to battle greed with loyalty these days because greed will win everytime.

Chapter 16: Solo

I hear the back and forth between Sci-fi and Mercedez and I go into my duffle bag and pull out a gun that will lay that nigga down. With the red dot on the back of his head it's almost too easy. I shoot him where the red dot beamed and both of their bodies drop. *Oh shit!* I start to panic, rushing to Mercedez. *Did the bullet go through him and hit her?* Blood is splattered all over her face and I push Sci-fi, who had fallen on top of her, onto the floor. I sob loudly as I search for the bullet wound. *What have I done?* I think solemnly as I hold her limp body in my arms. I can't seem to find where the blood is coming from though. When I hear her mumble my name I almost think I'm imagining it but then I hear it again, "Solo."

"Are you okay? Damn, I thought you was hit," I stammer, thanking God that she is okay.

"What happened?" she asks, holding her head.
"I don't know, I shot him and I guess you passed out. You probably thought you were hit because I a gun to your face when I shot him. And I guess his nasty ass blood splattered all over you when y

dropped," I explained. I helped her to her feet.

She stood there and looked at Trevor as the blood continued to gush out of his head and a slow s[mile] crept on her face. "I just came up with a whole new game plan boo."What's up, spit it out," I say, n[ot in] the mood for guessing games.

"We gone blame all this shit on Trevor! Everything that happened since last night is on hi[m]
I look at her with skepticism.
"It'll be our word against his and he can't say shit," she reasoned.
I nod my head, agreeing to the brilliant idea. "That's why I love you," I tell her, using a rag t[o wipe] the blood off her face as she picks up her phone to dial 911. I listen to her speak to the co[ps] when they arrive. She told them that trevor

confessed to at least three murders and that we don't know why, how, or if it's even true.

When he tried to kill her that's when I came in and shot him and that's all we know.

The less we say without a lawyer present, the better. I marvel at how great of a liar

Mercedez is and her acting skills are on point. She could've won an oscar for that

performance. But, I can't help but wonder how many times she played me like that.

We also came up with a way to get around the counterfeit with Psycho. We gone put that shit on Justin because like Mercedez said it'll be his words against ours and that nigga dead. Mercedez will say she jumped in the car with me and he didn't tell her where he was taking the drugs. That keeps us in the clear, we get to keep the money and the product without starting a domestic war. However, avoiding a street beef is a simple task compared to evading questions in the interrogation room. They separated Mercedez and me but it didn't matter because we had our story down packed. They kept me in that cold ass room for six hours, most of the time just sitting as I looked at the window they thought I was dumb enough to think was a mirror. Once I felt like I had more than cooperated I asked to speak with a lawyer if they were going to arrest me and keep me there. "Finally a beautiful brown skinned woman entered the room and sat across from me at the cold, steel table. She looked at me with slanted, hazelnut colored eyes and introduced herself as Detective Baldwin. She was trying to get me to flip on Mercedez but I wasn't with all that so that's when I decided I'm done cooperating. I know they can't legally hold me here so I'm ready to go. Mercedez is waiting for me when I walk out and I'm relieved to see that she got out of there too. Now we could carry our asses home. She smirked when she saw detective Baldwin. Apparently the same detective was trying to get my girl to flip on me. Mercedez mocked her on our way out as she told me word for word what the detective said. "*I'm just gone keep it real with you. I think you're a nice girl, brilliant would be an understatement because I see me in you. Let me tell you something, love will have you in some fucked up situations, like the one you're in now. In fact, you might be ride or die but you're too smart to let a man make life decisions for you. You give him up, you can walk out of here free so you can go home and get to your babies. If you decline to cooperate Ms.Jackson, there's a possibility that you won't walk out of here free and you'll be gone for so long your youngest will forget he has a mother. Now I want the truth. Who robbed the pharmacy at your job and why do I have three bodies tied up in this mess. All you have to do is tell the truth and we'll give you immunity."*

"Damn, immunity?" I ask in disbelief. They didn't even offer me that shit. We decide to ride Uber home since we know we can't get dropped off by the police. I ain't got time for somebody to act like I'm snitching on nobody for a get out of jail free card. When people don't know what's going on, they tend to assume things and for some reason the assumptions are always the worst case scenario.

The next day, after the windows in the house were repaired and the vehicles towed to the body shop, Mercedez and I sat across the kitchen table from each other, eating the meal she had prepared for us. Neither one of us spoke at first. I was the first to break the silence. "This food is delicious. Thank you for cooking."

"You're welcome," was all she said in a barely audible voice, not bothering to even look up at me. She continued to stir the fork around on her plate.

I sat my fork down and sat back in my chair. "What do you want from me Mercedez?"

She sighed. It was a heavy sigh, as if she had the world on her shoulders and I empathized with her. Suddenly I lost my appetite. Was I the reason she was feeling this way? I was supposed to take that weight off of her shoulders and here I was adding to it. In that moment, nothing I did that was supposed to be all for her made any sense. I was way out of line with the Chassidy thing but I had done worse and she had forgiven me so this time would be no different, right?

"Baby, I can't help you if you won't talk to me," I tell her.

"I just want…" her voice trails off and I lean in, ready to oblige anything she asks of me to make it right. "Normalcy. I want a normal life. I want you to get out the game."

And there you have it, the one thing I can't give her is what she asks of me. I couldn't give up the game. I wasn't even where I needed to be yet. Just like every other nigga, I had hood dreams, plans to make it to the top. But, what did that make me? Average? I got up from the table and walked to her side, kneeling before her with her hands in mine. I wanted to tell her what she wanted to hear from me, tell her what would make her smile again. But I couldn't. I vowed that I would never lie to her again and that was a promise I intended to keep. "Mercedez you know i'm not where I want to be yet, baby, I'm not in the position to retire. I'm nowhere near that."

She withdrew her hands and rolled her eyes. "And whose fault is that Solo? If you listened to me at least half the time you would be so much further in the game right now. Fuck the game, you'd be so much furthter in life." I knew what she was saying was true because Mercedez was wise beyond her years and by age, she had me beat by a few years, almost four to be exact. "I don't want to keep doing things the hard way just because you have a hard head and you don't mind bumping it a few times to get it right," she continued. "It's like we're on this journey and I have the map to get to our destination but you insist on finding your own way and we just keep falling in a ditch. I'm tired of falling with you. Do you know how frustrating that is?"

My forehead wrinkled in concern. "So is that how you feel? Like I'm bringing you down?"

She nodded her head and my stomach felt hollow. Never was it my intention to make the woman I love feel like I'm her downfall. "You stayed down with me Mercedez, so I want you to be there, right beside me, when I come up. I just need you to hold it down for a little while longer." The last thing I wanted was for my girl to leave me before I had a chance to give her all the things she deserved. And Mercedez deserved the world. It was then and there I decided to get my shit together. For her. For my kids. For my family. I wasn't the nigga to go work a nine to five but I would become the biggest damn drug dealer in the city if it meant I could give her whatever she desired. I just wanted to be enough.

For the next few months I went hard in the streets. I didn't spend a lot of time at home but when I did come it was always with a bag so there were few complaints from my lady. She was so used to being right up under a nigga that the only way I could go hard in the streets was if I left her with a stack to get her nails and hair done, female shit that would occupy the time she was away from me. I stopped serving the hoes at her job and I let her handle that shit. She felt some type of way about me dealing with females on a regular basis so most of the females had to go through her to get to me. I wasn't even tripping because I didn't want them hoes in a nigga face anyway. Females were trouble so I tried to steer clear of them when I could. I didn't ever again want to disrespect my girl the way I had in the past by letting these hoes think they had one up on her because of some sneaky shit I was doing behind her back. Everything was going good, life was good, and although all good things come to an end, I prayed that I'd be happy in love forever with my lady.

Chapter 17: Mercedez

Call me a big kid, but the holidays have always lifted my spirit. No matter how down in the dumps I am, there's something about the colorful lights, the snow flurries and the silver bells around the city that cheer me up and make me feel like an innocent child again. The snow, which is rare in southern Mississippi, reminds me of being back home in Detroit, Michigan again. Especially tonight. There were Christmas carolers outside and kids in every house sneaking into their parents' bedrooms while they were out or at work to see what "Santa" would leave them this year. I put a lock on my bedroom door especially for my girls because they were nosey as fuck, just like their father. I glanced at him and my mood dampered just a bit. I couldn't believe Solo took advantage of our Christmas shopping spree to meet with his gang affiliates to make a play. We had a trunk full of toys but in every stuffed teddy bear was a kilo of raw, unstepped on cocaine.

I tried to enjoy the cool, brisk air as we strolled the streets of downtown Hattiesburg arm and arm like we were just a young couple in love. Solo was waiting on the call with the location and I was constantly looking over our shoulders and growing more anxious by the minute, suspicious of every white guy that passed us by.

"Will you relax?" Solo finally said, placing his hand at the small of my back as we maneuvered through the crowd.   "Everything is going to work out just fine, just chill."

"Chill?" I scoffed. "We picking up a dollar amount bigger than our tax bracket and I'm supposed to relax?"

"About that…" his voice trailed off into the night.

"About what?" I stopped walking. I knew he wasn't about to tell me I'm out here risking my freedom for some bullshit.

"The exchange gone be in two different locations because of the amount of weight."

I walked off, shaking my head. I was heated. I couldn't believe he was putting so much trust in them grimy ass niggas he called homeboys. How the fuck they want the product now but can't pay the price on sight? Drop now, pay later? Solo ain't never rocked like that but tonight he was on some new shit. I turned my nose up and snorted, deciding I was better than this conversation. Hell, at that moment I felt like I was better than him. I was raised by a mothafuckin' gangsta so I wasn't green to the game. Solo was moving wrong but of course he wouldn't accept that coming from me so I kept my mouth shut and my comments to myself.

"How about I take you to the spa tonight," he said, pulling me back to him. "You seem a little tense," he said smoothly, kissing me behind my ear.

I giggled because that was my spot. "This must be an all female spa because I know you ain't lettin' no man rub on all this," I said seductively, touching my breast and my thigh for emphasis.

"You lookin' like a whole two piece dinner out here girl come here," he said, playfulling biting me on my neck. "Lil' fine ass."

"I take it you like the extra pounds I put on?" I asked him, flattered enough to forget I was pissed. He knew me too well.

"Like it?" he said, still holding me from behind. "I love it," he confirmed. "I love this version of you. Clean and not on no kind of drugs. It's been what, six months now?"

"No pills, no coke, no liquor," I said proudly.

"Nothing but dick," he said loudly, just as we were passing an elderly white lady. She looked at us disdainfully, pulling her coat tighter and we burst out laughing,

"Man you play too much," I tell him and then the phone rings.

"Headed to you now," Solo said, ending the call. He looked at me. "Let's rock and roll baby." We picked up the pace walking towards our Porsche truck. Life had been good to us lately, we had been having our way out here for almost a year now. Solo was grinding harder than ever and it paid off nicely. Our relationship had gotten better as well. We weren't fighting, nobody was cheating, it was like we fell in love all over again.

Once we were inside the truck, I put on my seat warmer and seatbelt. I turned the radio dial from 106.3 to 102.5 and was instantly swooned by the Temptation's classic Christmas song, "Silent Night". I loved this song so the biggest smile spread across my face and I turned the radio up and started singing, "*In my mind…*".

"Nigga," Solo protested. "We goin' to make a drop not sell Christmas cookies while caroling."

I laughed but refused to change the station. I knew he probably wanted to listen to NBA

Youngboy or Money Bagg Yo, but the soothing sound of holiday tunes was keeping my anxiety at a minimum. We could get gangsta on the way back, once I knew we were good.

The location was a McDonald's on Broadway Drive. They liked to meet in public places, figuring they would look less suspicious. We pulled up and popped the trunk and appeared to be selling Christmas bears with SantaClause hats on. There were identical bears on each side of the trunk, one stuffed with drugs, the others stuffed with cotton. I fastened my coat and began shaking silver bells and saying loudly, "Come get your Santa bears! One for six dollars, two for ten!" I eyed the black Tahoe with black rims turning in the parking lot and getting in the drive through line. They were supposed to order food like any other customer and then stop at our car to purchase twenty bears without ever stepping foot out of their vehicle. Tragic, the driver, and Krystal, his babymomma on the passenger side, were supposed to drive to New Orleans and deliver the drugs. They were supposed to pick up four-hundred thousand dollars and bring it to us when they got back in a few days and then they would receive their cut for trafficking our product. We liked to call them road-runners.

"Aye, you got some stones?" Tragic hollered at Solo. "I got a lil' play to make before we hit the road."

"Hell nah," Solo lied, patting his pockets as if he was looking for something. "I got you when you get back, I'll put something together for you while you gone."

"No doubt," Tragic said, nodding his head. "I'll hit you as soon as I touch down."

"Say less," Solo said and we watched them drive away.

"You trust him?" I asked, watching the truck disappear into traffic.

Solo nodded slowly as he broke down a cigarillo. "Hell yeah, that nigga know not to play with my money. Not only is he the big homie but he looked out on me while I was locked up. I can't switch up on him now that he's out, that ain't me." He rolled down the window and dumped the tobacco before letting it back up.

"I get that but I'm talkin' bout the fact that this nigga fresh out the joint, out the blue, with no explanation. We still don't know how this nigga got out."

"Bruh says there was an error with his paperwork that his lawyer found. A technicality or some shit. The state fucked up so they had to let him go."

I looked at him skeptically because it all sounded like bullshit to me.

"Look, Tragic good people," Solo said as he filled the cigar with the finest weed I had ever seen. "Plus with that covid shit floodin' the prisons, they lookin' for reasons to let them niggas out."

"I guess," I said, deciding to keep my opinion to myself, knowing it would fall on deaf ears.

Just as we're pulling out of the McDonald's parking lot a cop car jumped behind us and threw their lights on.

"Fuck," Solo said banging his fist on the steering wheel. "I can't stop bae, I got a pocket full of stones. I should've just gave that shit to cuz."

I knew he was right. He could've made bail on the dope charges but he wouldn't be able to shake an MDOC (Mississippi Department of Corrections) hold. He hadn't been to see his parole officer in months. She would definitely place a hold on him and could potentially violate him, which meant he'd be going back to prison. I wasn't having that. It was too close to Christmas. So I put on my seatbelt and said, "Let's shake these muthafuckas bae." With that being said, he began weaving in and out of traffic so fast my head started to spin. The tires screeched and we literally spinned in the middle of the road. Solo switched gears on the porsche like a Nascar driver and it looked like a scene out of an action movie only this was real life and those cops behind us were not actors. We headed towards downtown going so fast I was terrified we might crash. "Maybe we should just stop," I say, fearful we might not make it out of this truck alive or even worse, cause innocent people to have an accident and die. Solo completely ignored me and my anxiety got the best of me. "Just stop the fuckin car!" I yelled, unable to control my fear that seemed to be taking over me.

"Shut the fuck up Mercedez!" He finally snapped. "What you think they gone do if I stop? Black lives don't matter to them blue muthafuckas and I'm not about to die at the hands of a pig with a badge on. Sit back, I got this." He hit the accelerator while switching gears, making so many sharp turns I just know we're about to flip over. All I could do was grip my seat in angst while silently praying that we made it out alive. When I reopened my eyes I noticed that the blue lights were gone although I could still hear the sirens, which meant that they were close. Solo pulled behind some old abandoned house and turned the car and the headlights off. We jump out and I run around the car into his arms and he pulls me to the stairs that sat on the back porch of the old house. We sat and watched the blue lights light up the night sky like the fourth of July until the sounds of the sirens faded and the flashing lights were no more.

I sigh a deep sigh of relief and I ask him, "Where the hell are we?"

Solo held up his index finger as if to tell me, "hold on" as he spoke on the phone. He was calling a ride to come pick us up because the car was definitely too hot to drive again tonight. "We can't come pick it up until after seven a.m. when the shift changes cause them muthafuckas gone be lookin' for our asses all night," he was saying. After he hung up the phone he answered my question. "This my aunt Tracy's old house. I basically grew up here. She died from breast cancer a few years ago but my family still owns the house."

"So your aunt Tracy and your mom lived here while you were a kid?" I asked, looking at the old, rundown house.

"My mom wasn't here," Solo explained. "She didn't raise me, my grandma and my aunt did. That's why I call aunt Tracy my momma and my momma Janice. She dropped me off over here after her and my dad broke up. She left me and kept my little sister and eventually made my little brother. Everyday I used to sit on these steps and wait for her to come back. She never did." I could hear the hurt in his voice. He stood up. "Finally I got old enough to jump off the porch. I stopped waiting for her and took to the streets instead. That's how I got in the gang. Shit them niggas was like my real family, they showed me more love than my own blood did. They used to look out for me so in return I looked out for them, watching for the police while they did their drug transactions and shit like that. Once I was old enough to start making my own money, I got my first kilo on consignment."

"How old were you?" I asked with sympathetic eyes because I couldn't even imagine if that happened to my sons.

"Thirteen," he said, looking out into the darkness. "I ain't even have to get jumped in the gang, the O.G.'s had raised me, they knew what I was about. They knew my hustle game was strong and although I was in the gang they knew if it came to it, I could hold my own so they named me Solo. I was always rockin' Solo and a few bitch niggas was hatin' but I ain't lost a fight yet. Come on, my lil' brother pullin' up."

I followed him to the blue nissan altima with a heavy heart because I felt sorry for him. His story was so sad but it didn't seem to phase him one bit, like he had built a wall up around his emotions but for the first time, he was letting me in.

"What's up John," I greeted Solo's little brother as I climbed in the back seat. John was the youngest boy out of Janice's six kids. He had just graduated highschool last Spring. He attended the local university, the University of Southern Mississippi, on a baseball scholarship and he was the only rookie who got any real playing time on the field. He had the potential to go pro and no matter how hard Solo tried to keep him out the streets, at the tender age of eight-teen, John was enticed by the street life. Because of that, he often found himself in compromising situations and Solo would have to handle whatever the situation was to get him out. That's why when Solo called tonight, John didn't hesitate to come because his brother had done and would do the same thing for him. I guess keeping him away from the street life was null and void when he needed a getaway driver. I shook my head.

Solo immediately started filling John in on the details of what happened and I looked back at the house until the darkness consumed it and was illuminated by the night. Solo had had such a hard life and I was beginning to understand the root to some of his issues. The anger, the attitude, the possessiveness, the fear of abandonment, it all started to make sense somehow and it made me wish that he would open up to me more so I could love him through his pain. I sighed and shook my head. That's what I get for being so damn spiritual, I'll always attract men that need healing.

Chapter 18: Solo

It's been twenty-four hours since I led HPD on that high speed chase and I can tell she's still pissed about it. I tried apologizing but it seems like the more I say I'm sorry, the more agitated she becomes. So I decided I'd give her some time to cool off and soon it would all blow over just like all the other bullshit. Like my granny always said, "This too shall pass," and "trouble don't last always". So I was kicked back in the living room with the kids watching the christmas classic, *Home Alone 2: Lost in New York* while Mercedez was in our bedroom with the door locked, wrapping gifts to put under the 10 foot, fully decorated Christmas tree. I had just smoked a blunt so the children's movie seemed extra funny to me. I laughed so hard my stomach hurt and that's when I realized I was starting to get the munchies. I called out to Mercedez to see if she wanted to go for ice cream.

"Aye baby, let's go to Sonic's and get hot fudge sundaes!" I knew she couldn't resist a good sundae with strawberries and bananas in it.

"Yaay!" The kids erupted with cheer and I laughed because she had no win against the kids. She walked into the living room with pieces of tape all over her face and colorful bowes stuck to her arms. "Mommy, you look like a Christmas present," our youngest daughter giggled and we all laughed.

"I move quicker when my ribbons and tape are already laid out," she explained and I pulled her down on my lap, missing my woman's touch. One day without touching her feels like an eternity.. "I love you so much," I said to her genuinely.

"Get off me, you're messing up my tape," she resisted, her forehead wrinkled in frustration. Even in her frustration she was still the most beautiful girl in the world, next to our daughters.

"You need to take that shit off anyway," I said whispering in her ear. "Matter fact, take all that shit off," I said nibbling on her ear.

"Gross, get a room," one of the boys said and the other kids laughed. Family moments. I'd been in the streets so much that I forgot to appreciate times like these. I love my kids, even the ones that aren't mine, you can't tell me they're not because I love them all the same.

Fifteen minutes later we were parked at the Sonic Drive-In and I was going off on whoever was on the speaker. "The fuck you mean the ice cream machine broke?"

"We can sell you the ice cream but it'll be more like a shake," the voice said over the loudspeaker.

That shit sounded nasty as fuck. "Nawl my nigga, we good," I crank up the Porsche and we pulled off into the night.

"Where we goin' now, McDonald's?" Mercedez asked because at this point she didn't care where it came from, somebody was going to give her an ice cream sundae. Knowing her, she already had her mouth set for it.

"Now you know McDonald's ice cream machine stay broke," I said with a laugh. "We goin' to Dairy Queen."

We went inside Dairy Queen and I let Mercedez drive back so I could use my hands to eat my food before it got cold. Once we pulled back into the driveway of our home I couldn't find my change and I began to wonder if the lady had in fact handed me any change. When Mercedez backed out the driveway to go back I remembered it was in my coat pocket and not my pants pocket where I usually kept my money. So we pulled right back in and as soon as she threw the car in park, she cursed, "Shit," looking out my window. I asked what she was looking at, then I turned to see a police car sitting at the stop sign on the side of our house. I stuffed my crack rocks in a makeshift hole in the waist of my jeans and waited for them to make their move. But they just sat there. "What the fuck do we do?" Mercedez asked in a panic.

"Nothing," I told her, still eyeing the cop car. "Just act normal, we ain't did shit wrong."

"But they're gonna think I pulled back in because I saw them sitting there," she said and I knew she was right. I kissed her on her forehead, told her to keep calm and take the ice cream in to the kids before it melted. "But, what about you?" she asked. "You just gone sit in here until they leave?"

"I don't know. I might have to," I said.

"You can't," she said back. "They're going to think you're hiding something if you don't get out. I'm sure if they're watching us they already know you're in here."

She had a good point but I really had no other choice. I wasn't about to get out and give them a reason to come fuck with me. "Just do what I said," I told her and she reluctantly got out of the car. The moment she closed the front door they threw the blue lights on and pulled up behind the Porsche. "Muthafuckas," I say, lowering in my seat and locking the car doors. They hopped out and began beaming their bright ass flash lights in the truck.

"Get the fuck out of the car with your hands up!" one of them yelled while his partner called for backup.

"What did I do?" I hollered back at them angrily. I had no intention of stepping out of the car. I saw Mercedez peering through the blinds and I was glad she was smart enough not to come back outside.

"What is she hiding for you in the house?" an officer asked and I instantly recognized his voice as the officer who had taken me to jail the last two times I went. This white boy has had a fuckin vendetta against me since I was a teen goin' to juvi cause I used to outrun his punk ass. "This car matches the description of a vehicle involved in a high speed chase last night. Get the fuck out of the car!" The other officer knocked on the door to the house and hollered, "We don't want you, it's your boyfriend who has a warrant for his arrest. So either you're going to unlock the doors to the truck or they're going to bust your windows out with a club and drag him out, so what's it gonna be Miss?"

  The sight of them on my doorstep fuckin' with my ole lady made my stomach hollow. I unlocked the doors and put my hands up. They snatched me out of the truck and slammed me down on the ground hard. "Man close my girl car door bruh she got a weak battery and she gotta take my kids to school tomorrow. Yall gone come give her a jump off?"

  "Shut the fuck up," officer asshole said, slamming me again. This had to be police brutality. "Tell us what you just sent your girlfriend to hide in the house for you."

  "Nothing," I said, spitting blood out from a busted lip that I got as a result of being slammed a third time. I'm telling the truth but of course they want to believe a nigga lyin' anyway. Next thing I know, three more cop cars pull up and they kick in the front door ready to raid the house. Now I know this shit is illegal, they ain't said shiit about no search warrant, no nothin'. "Man I got kids in there!" I shout to no avail. "And these handcuffs are too fuckin' tight!" I'm not an expert at the law but I know they were on some illigal bullshiit tonight.

"Why are they taking you to jail? Are you a drug dealer?" The question came from The Hattiesburg Patriot, an unofficial news anchor that showed up on every crime scene in the city.

"Fuck you," I spat at him and this muthafucka says, "Looks like you're the one getting fucked tonight, don't drop the soap!" I wanted to rip his fuckin head off his shoulders.

"Man Hattiesburg Patriot you a bitch boy," I said and the police officer snatched me up and threw me in the back of a cop car. My anxiety was on ten right now because I can't protect my family from these pigs. I felt helpless and it was all my fault. I started to question every decision I made that led to this moment and suddenly I understood where Mercedez's angst came from. By moving wrong in these streets, I was putting all of our lives in jeopardy.

"We found a gun sir," a young lieutenant said into his radio as he walked out with a clear ziploc evidence bag. The door swung open and it took everything in me to find balance and not fall out of the car. "Is this your gun?" My face twisted up in anguish because that wasn't my gun. And although I'm a convicted felon, I would have to take the rap for my girl. The gun actually belonged to Mercedez and to be honest, I don't even know where the fuck she got it from so I hoped it didn't come back hot or with a body count. "In addition to the gun, we found enough evidence to know he has been cooking crack cocaine in the residence most likely with the minor children in the home," the officer continued, holding up another ziploc bag.

"Man my kids ain't never seen me do no shit like that. I smoke crack," I lied. "So you can leave my family out of this."

"You brought your family into this the moment you decided to manufacture illegal drugs in your home and harbor illegal firearms while being a convicted felon," the officer argued.

"This ain't my home, my name ain't on no lease," I shot back, knowing wouldn't none of this shit stick in court. I was more worried about my parole officer if anything.

"What the fuck ever." It was officer asshole. "Take him to jail."

A young, black, rookie cop caught my eye and I yelled, "Aye, say bruh, let me holla at you."

"I got him," the black officer said to the asshole. He waited for the officer to back off before saying, "What's up young brother?"

"I got a couple racks in my pocket and I want you to get it out and give it to my girl." The officer looked unsure and I continued, "It's the holidays bruh and my girl got them kids. I'm all she got plus you know they just gone keep half that shit anyway. Can you do that for me man please?"

The young dude hesitated and I reminded him again, "it's Christmas."

"Anything over a thousand dollars we have to compensate," he said.

"Well it's nine hundred and ninety-nine then," I said with pleading eyes.

He looked from left to right then lowered his voice. "Which pocket is it in?"

I lock eyes with Mercedez and can see the hurt all over her face. She was scared I might be gone for a long time this time and honestly, I was too. I just hoped she was hurt enough to wanna hold a nigga down this time. Damn.

Chapter 19: Mercedez

I stood there, mortified, as the police ransacked my house looking for anything and everything that could put my man in jail. They really had the nerve to ask me if I'd testify against him like I would actually do that shit. Of course when I said no, they tried to scare me into it.

"You know we could call DHS and have them take your kids," a female officer said.

"For fuckin' what?" I snapped, craning my neck back with my hand on my hip.

"For manufacturing drugs while your children are here," she said matter-of-factly.

"I ain't manufacture shit," I said and that was the God's honest truth.

"Okay, well *allowing* the manufacture of drugs around your kids," she said mockingly.

"You don't know what you're talking about," I said, crossing my arms over my chest. What I wanted to say was, "You're barking up the wrong tree bitch," but somehow I didn't think getting disrespectful was a good idea. "He doesn't do that shit around my kids." I kicked myself for even saying that much. I was talking too much.

"But he does do it?" she asked, arching one brown eyebrow.

"No," I said flatly.

"Oh yeah?" the detective smirked, walking up behind her. "Because I got a whole lot of evidence that says otherwise." He placed a pyrex cup in front of me.

I laughed out loud. "The fuck? I like to measure my ingredients." He placed a jumbo size carton of arm-and-hammer in front of me. My dumb ass just had to buy the biggest box because it was on sale at the CornerMarket. "What? It's great for cleaning. Mixed with a little bit of vinegar." I winked at him. Next he placed a box of sandwich bags in front of me. I shook my head because now they were just reaching. "I got a lot of kids that eat a lot of snacks. Like what the fuck he manufacturing? School lunches?" I sneered. Then, he placed a scale in front of me with a bag of crack rocks sitting on it.

"Hardly a school lunch," he said with a smirk on his face.

"Yeah, well, he smokes that shit," I lied, knowing he would say the same thing. A simple possession charge would be less than an intent to distribute.

"You seem like a smart girl," the detective said. "Why are you letting him make a fool of you?"

I frowned. "Excuse me?"

"You and I both know where he gets his money from and it ain't no nine to five," the detective said, staring down at me.

"I provide for my family," I said, about tired of him coming at me with his circumstantial ass evidence. "I work full time as a med tech at the county nursing home, check for yourself.

"And he contributes nothing? Again, why do you let him make a fool of you?"

I recognized the reverse psychology bullshit he was trying to pull and although it felt foolish coming off my lips I said, "I work while he takes care of the kids." The female officer rolled her eyes and I focused my attention on her. "And as far as DHS, they're going to have to have a real warrant with some real evidence, not this circumstantial bullshit, before they take my kids. Now if you don't mind, I'd like to get back to them while you continue to fuck up my house." The detective stepped back and allowed me to walk towards the boys room where the kids were all crammed, waiting for the raid to be over. Before I could place my hand on the door knob another cop approached me from behind.

"Miss Jackson, a word with you please?"

"What now?" I asked without even turning around. I was over it. "I told you everything I know."

"This revolver, who does it belong to?"

I tensed and turned around slowly. "I don't know," I lied. "I keep a lot of company, that could be anybody's. Excuse me," I said, placing my hand on the door knob again. If I could just get on the other side of this door so they could stop asking me questions I could just wait this shit out with the kids.

"Nice try," the officer laughed. "You know he's going down for this right? I mean a convicted felon with an illegal firearm is a clear violation of his probation. He probably won't get a bond because of the high speed chase, he's a flight risk. Terell has been running from me since he was a juvenile as if he's above the law. Tell me, where were you two coming from last night?"

I gave him a tight lip smile and said, "You've been following us. You tell me. Because I'm not going to do your job for you." I was glad Tragic hadn't given us the two-hundred thousand because it would've been gone, states evidence and collateral damage. I made a mental note to pick up the money as soon as the cops cleared my house because I would need it to get Solo a decent lawyer and to post bail.

"You know," the officer started. "We're going to be watching you and if you do anything suspicious, you'll lose your kids for real. Have a good night." And with that, he rounded up the other guys and they went to leave. The brisk, cool air swept through the house, across the marble tile floors as the cops exited my house one by one. The cop car that they had placed Solo in was gone. I shut the door. With my back pressed up against it I slid down to the floor and began to sob in defeat. My house had been literally turned upside down. It would take days to clean it. I fired up a cigarette and pulled out my cell phone to call my mother. As I began to run down the events of the night it got harder for me to fight back tears. I wanted my man back. The cops had been right, he had no bond due to an MDOC hold. That meant he would have to face his parole officer and she would decide his fate. He had stopped reporting to her a couple of months ago though so she would probably want to violate him. If she did, he would have to back up five years in prison for violation of probation on a receiving stolen property charge. On top of that, the way they pieced together that evidence with the crack he was bound to do some time and with the gun charge, it was inevitable.

I went outside to crank my truck the next morning only to discover that the battery was dead. So I drove the Lexus instead. I would have to give myself a jump off later when I had time. I called Tragic on the car's bluetooth speaker while I sat in the car line to drop the twins off at school. There wasn't a bus for pre-k students so I dropped them off every morning.

"Damn, that's fucked up," Tragic said as I told him about the shit that went down last night. "That nigga took that gun charge, he really love yo' ass."

"Yeah," I said dismissively, because I hadn't really called to talk about that. "I'm coming to pick up his money when I leave the school."

"How long you think he got?" Tragic asked, seeming to be dismissing me his damn self.

When I told him about the possibility of Solo doing five years I instantly regretted the moment it rolled off my lips. Something was telling me I should've kept my mouth shut but i didn't and I could hear Solo in my head telling me I talk too much. "It's a hold up on that bread," Tragic told me.

"What the fuck is a hold up, where's our product?" I asked, somehow knowing I wasn't about to get a straight answer.

"I already dumped it. I'm just waitin' on the bank to release the funds. You know how long it take to clean money."

"No, I don't," I snapped, tears burning my eyes because I was growing more angry by the minute. "Nigga we sent you to do a transaction, not a lay-a-way! The plan was for you to post up in New Orleans until the check cleared ya babymomma's account. When did twenty-four hours turn to three days?" I was furious.

"That's the agreement I made with Solo so y'all on some miscommunication shit because the plan never changed," Tragic said, not caring that I was practically yelling at him through the phone. He kept a cool head like he was unfazed like a muthafucka. "I'm not with all the dramatics though shorty so don't hit my line until I hit you."

The call ended and I slammed my hands against the steering wheel. "Bitch!" I exclaimed, accidentally blowing the horn. "No not you," I apologized to the white lady walking in front of the car with her daughter. The lady grimaced as she pulled her daughter closer and they hurried to get out of my way. The bad ass little girl threw her middle finger up and put it back down before her mother saw it so fast, I questioned if the shit actually happened.

"Is everything alright Mrs.Jackson?" a teacher asked me with sympathetic eyes as she let the twins out of the car.

"It's fine," I said, pursing my lips, trying to control my anger. "Have a great day sweeties," I said to the girls and with that I was on my way. I had a nagging feeling that Tragic was playing games with the money, knowing he had that shit. Niggas was really thinking Solo gone have to do some hard time. I hoped my gut was wrong this time because I really needed that money to get a good lawyer because wasn't no public defender gone get him off those charges. I decided I would at least wait the three days, to see if Tragic was going to give me the money before I brought the situation up to Solo. I didn't want him to flip the fuck out and catch a body in there because when he got mad he liked to fight. He didn't need any more charges so I would have to handle this on my own. I flicked the ashes to my newport out the window. Tragic picked the right bitch on the wrong day to play with. I was going to get that money and get Solo out one way or another. A part of me wanted to leave his ass in there for lying to me. He made it seem like they were just roadrunners, he had failed to mention the part about Krystal cleaning the money through her hair shop in New Orleans. It's not like Krystal ever crossed me before but for some reason I just couldn't bring myself to trust her or Tragic. Two-hundred thousand dollars could cause a bitch to cross you, ain't nobody safe in this street shit. I dialed Krystal's number three times in a row and all three times it went straight to voicemail. I know this bitch ain't blocked me. I don't know where that little shop of hers is in New Orleans but I'm sure it's not hard to find. There can't be too many hair stores with a salon in it run by a red-head bitch from Mississippi. I'd burn that shit down if I was still set in my ways, but I've grown and I realize that won't get me my money either. But one way or another Krystal and Tragic were going to have to pay me the money. And I ain't have time to wait.

Chapter 20: Solo

Worst case scenario is I'ma have to do twenty-five percent of them five years. I could be out in eighteen months or less. I was devastated when the judge denied bail. What the fuck was I gone do now? The head narc came to see me this morning tryna get a name for a deal. Apparently I'm the small fish they want to use to bait the big fish, the problem with that is I ain't no snitch. Truth be told, I don't know how the fuck Tragic got an early release now that i can't trust him and I'm starting to wonder if he'd set me up. Mercedez told me it wasn't a good idea to fuck with that nigga on that level and I wish I'd listned. How did I go from meeting him to being on a high speed chase to my crib being raided all in twenty-four hours? Shit, my girl could've lost our kids to DHS behind that shit. Luckily the detective was sympathetic with her and decided not to call child protective services. Somebody had to have tipped them off though, otherwise the shit just don't add up. I tried to make it make sense in my mind all the while wondering if I was crazy. They say the definition of insanity is doing the same thing over and over again and expecting different results. I can't keep coming to jail over the same shit and leaving my girl out there for one of them bitch ass niggas to try to fuck her.

"Stokes!" I hear the female guard calling my last name so I sit up on my rack. "Visitation," she said and I gladly followed her out the steel door. I was more than happy to be away from all them niggas in there. All they do is talk shit about what they used to do. They sounded like a bunch of washed up ass has beens. I didn't talk to none of them niggas. The less I associate with them, the less chance of me gettin' in some bullshit and the last thing I want to do is add more time to my time.

The visitation room was cold. The floors were made of cement and the walls were concrete too. The ceiling was low and the lights were flickering between bright and dim. I struggled to sit down with the cuffs chained to my legs. The booths were made of metal, including the stool to sit on. I took a seat, the thick glass separating me from whoever was coming to sit on the other side. Moments later I saw Mercedez take a seat in front of me and pick up the phone so we could hear each other. She was beautiful. Her honey blonde hair hung loosely over her shoulders in jumbo curls. Her hazel eyes seemed to dance when she looked at me. Her lips were glossy, like always, with that beautiful smile plastered on her face. I picked up the phone receiver that was hanging on the side of the booth so I could hear that beautiful voice.

"Hi," was all she said but it was like music to my ears.

"Hi," I responded, taking her all in. Her beauty was timeless, priceless like the Mona Lisa or something. Words can't even explain the beauty that sat in front of me. We just sat there for a few moments, basking in each other's presence. Finally, I broke the silence. "I think that nigga

Tragic set me up," I said.

    Mercedez just nodded, probably trying her best not to say, "I told you so". Instead she said, "And that nigga still aint paid up either. We need that money to get you a lawyer. Even the retainer fee is high as fuck. I don't know what we're gonna to do."

    "We do whatever we gotta do to get me up out of here," I said in a hushed tone.

    Her eyes studied mine for a moment then she spoke softly, "Say less." She knew what time it was. I hadn't reached out to detective Ted Miller in a while because it's been a minute since I needed his help. I had no intentions of snitching on my homeboys or my connect but I knew a few bitch niggas that I had beef with who was probably safer in jail than on the streets with me because I didn't hesitate on that gun play. These niggas were opps so it was time to get them out the way. Once they were locked up and I was free, I would take over their blocks, clientele and take over the city.

    For the remainder of our time we talked about the kids and the storefront we had recently purchased downtown to start washing our money in. Krystal and Tragic owned a percentage as silent partners but the store belonged to Mercedez and me.

    "I love you bae," I told Mercedez before hanging up the phone. We both kissed two fingers and pressed them on the glass to each other. It pained me to see her walk away because all I wanted to do is be with her. She was my life, my future wife that I just wanted to love, protect, and never neglect. How the fuck was I going to make good on those promises from a jail cell? I prayed she'd catch up with Detective Miller fast. When I got back to my cell block I thought about calling Janice to let her know I was in jail because Mercedez don't fuck with her so I know she ain't told her shit. After waiting an hour in the phone line it was finally my turn to place a call. After saying my name to the operator there was a long pause before I finally heard Janice's voice on the other end.

"Boy what the hell you done got locked up for this time?" her voice blared through the phone. "What that bitch done called the police on you again? I keep telling you that bitch ain't for you!"

"Watch ya mouth!" I said a little bit louder than I intended to. "That girl ain't do shit, me and her not even into it right now."

"Well what the fuck you done did now? I swear, you and Jessica runnin' a damn race!"

"Mercedez house got raided. They found drugs and a gun. I think i'ma be in here for a minute this time Janice and I need you and Mercedez to get along for the girls' sake," I said somberly.

"Yeah, okay," she said dismissively. "What the public defender say?"

"Fuck a public defender, I'm gettin' a lawyer," I said, slightly offended. "A nigga done came a long way from using public defenders Janice. Anyway it's up to my P.O. whether she gone send me up the road or not and I think she just might do that shit this time cause I ain't been goin' to see her."

"Cause ya ass know you can't pass no piss test," Janice scoffed. "You might as well find you a lover while you in there because you keep carrying yo' ass back, it must be somethin' in there you like."

"Get the fuck outta here with that bullshit Janice," I snapped, in disbelief she would actually say some shit like that to me.

"And you might as well kiss that girl goodbye cause she gone be out here fuckin' everybody-" *CLICK!* I hung up on her hateful ass. I can't believe that woman just said that shit to me. How could a mother even think to utter those words to her son? I was disgusted. That's exactly why I call her Janice and not Momma because she aint never been no mother to me noway. I remember the day she took my siblings and then left them to go be with their daddy like I wasn't even a part of the family. It ain't my fault she fucked another nigga while her nigga was working off shore trying to provide for her ungrateful ass. It wasn't until I was seven years old that a man approached me while I was sitting on my grandmother's porch and introduced himself as my father that I'd even known I had a different daddy. It was like I was her mistake and she hated me for it and still a part of my heart yearned for her love. I would be lying if I said I didn't long for her attention and acceptance. Even her affection would be too much like right. The reality was, no matter how hard I tried she would never love me like she loved my siblings. She even loved that nigga more than me, as crazy and abusive as he was, she still loved his dirty drawers. I just wanted to protect her. She stayed with a black eye or a swollen lip and there was nothing I could do about it until I did something about it. It was a cold winter night, it must've been around christmas because the holidays and summer were the only times I stayed with them. I remember my momma was fussing at him for not allowing her to turn the heat up and it was literally freezing outside. He didn't care because he had a heater in his room. Out of nowhere he backhanded my momma so hard blood shot out of her nose or her mouth and she dropped to the floor. You would think he would've left her alone after that but the beating just continued. He proceeded to talk shit to her while kicking her several times in the stomach. She was pregnant with my baby brother John at the time. I couldn't take it, seeing my mother beat like that, I winced in pain with every kick as if I was receiving the ass kicking myself. Before I knew it I had grabbed a butcher knife from the holster and stabbed him in the leg. He fell down and I could hear my mother screaming, "Noooo!" but it was too late. I was on top of him stabbing him over and over again until my mother pulled me off of him. But, it was too late, he was already dying. She smacked me harder than she'd ever hit me in her life and kept screaming, "What have you done?!" I took off running up the stairs, afraid she might murder my ass next. I remember her calling my uncle Sug to get rid of the body and my aunt Tracy to help clean up the mess. Of course, she put me on the first train back to Hattiesburg with Aunt Tracy, where I would remain for the rest of my adolescent years. By the time I was sixteen I was a young nigga gettin' money. I had more hoes than i could count, even old hoes was tryna throw me the pussy. I used to sit in the trap and read this book, *The 48 Laws of Power*, tryna learn something because I already had the money and the respect.

    I met Mercedez when I was nineteen. She was livin' in the projects I did most of my hustlin out of. I had been seen her before I got the nerve to talk to her. I literally just showed up on her doorstep. I'd never been shy around females but Mercedez had me feeling some type of way. She wasn't just your average hood bitch. She lived in the projects but she wasn't no ghetto girl. She was smart, always working or going to school, and I respected her for that. She had three little boys and they were so well mannered and timid I instantly fell in love with them like I instantly fell in love with her. How could I not, with her honey dipped skin, beautiful hazel eyes, a sharp nose and pouty lips? She was a little on the slim side but I figured if I hit it right that ass would get fat. She wasn't like these other girls that stepped out in bonnets and flip flops, nah, she kept her wig fixed and she was always dressed like she was going somewhere. She was flyy.

Everytime I closed my eyes I went right back down memory lane. The waking hours were the worst because then I couldn't see her, couldn't hear her, touch her, feel her. I stress day and night thinkin' she out there fuckin' with other niggas. I mean, she did every other time a nigga went to jail, so what would stop her now? I was trippin', letting that shit Janice was talking get all up in my head. I knew that Mercedez was really down for a nigga this time. The truth was that everytime Mercedez had stepped out, I had given her a reason to. I'd get locked up and she'd crack the code to my phone and be all up in a nigga messenger seeing me conversate with different females and even makin' plans to see a few. This time was different though. My baby and I were on good terms when I left and I left her no reason to believe I had been disloyal. I kept telling myself I had nothing to worry about. As long as she didn't find out about Krystal everything would be good.

Chapter 21: Mercedez

I was surprised to see Krystal pop up at the storefront after she had been MIA all week. "I hope this means you got my money?" I asked with much attitude. Krystal smirked with pretty red lips and I couldn't deny the bitch was gorgeous. She was mixed with white and creole. She had full red lips and red hair that she had pulled up in a tight bun with chinese bangs. Her nose was perfectly slender and she had natural green eyes that looked like contact lenses. Her light skin was flawless and she stood five feet, six inches with a big butt and small waist and a perfect set of full c cup breasts to match. She appeared taller though in her red stiletto red bottom heels, her open toes showing off her white pedicure that complimented her white manicure. She wore a red pencil skirt and a ruffled white blouse that made her boobs look great. Then, when she smiled at a customer she showed off a perfect set of pearly white teeth like she was modeling in a colgate commercial. For a brief moment a wave of jealousy came over me and I had to check myself because I'm not jealous of no bitch out here. I'm a bad bitch myself but something about her tugged at my insecurities when I was in her presence. She made me want to look in a mirror to see if I looked like perfection too. She followed me to the back of the store to the office and closed the door behind us. I took a seat in the leather chair that sat behind the large cherry oak desk to the right and she sat across from me. "The money?" I asked with an arched eyebrow. I didn't have time to beat around the bush, not when my nigga was locked up in a cell while hers ran free.

"It's in transit," Krystal said, crossing her thick legs and placing her hands over her knee.

"What the fuck does that mean?" I asked. "In transit where?"

"At the bank, there were some issues with the books and we're being audited."

My mouth dropped open in disbelief. "What happened to it being easier to launder through the New Orleans store because it's been established longer than my store here in Hattiesburg? That's the only reason I agreed to let y'all go on with this little plan that I was the last to know about by the way."

Krystal rolled her eyes and I swear I wanted to snatch them right out of her head. "Plans change all the time," she said as if it weren't a big deal. As if we weren't talking about four-hundred thousand dollars. "Anyway it's really not my fault. The girl I hired to balance the books didn't know what she was doing and-"

"Why would you hire an outsider to handle the books?" I cut her off. "Are you fuckin' out of your mind? What did you think was going to happen?"

"Look, the girl is known in N O for doing these kinds of jobs on the black market and honestly this is her first time getting caught up," Krystal explained.

"How fuckin convienient," I snapped and Krystal stood up out of her chair so I stood up too. "Look," I started. "I don't give a fuck what bitch you hired to handle your business, all I care about is the fact that y'all took cash from a muthafucka a week ago and deposited it into your fucked up ass business account and now you claiming the IRS or the bank got my money hemmed up. Seems to me that you and Tragic gone have to cough up some cash and don't tell me y'all ain't got that kind of money because I know better. Y'all might think shit sweet but both of y'all gone have to answer to Solo."

"I don't got to answer to any muthafuckin body," this bitch says, rolling her neck. "When we get it, y'all will get it." She picked up her handbag and tried to walk out the door but as soon as she opened it I pushed it back closed. I pressed the cold steel I had retrieved from my drawer on the small of her back and told her to sit her ass down. I tried being civil with this bird brained bitch but that smart ass mouth of hers had pushed me to my limit. I backed away an inch, giving her room to ease her pretty little ass right back in that seat. I pulled a silencer out of the desk drawer and twisted it onto my gun, really over the bullshit and the games.

"Where all that neck rolling now?"`I asked as Krystal continued to burn a hole through me with her eyes. If looks could kill I'd be one dead bitch.

"If I don't make it to pick up my son from daycare Tragic is going to know something is wrong and where do you think he's going to come look? My location is on," she said smugly. "So whatever plan you conjured up in that pea sized brain of yours, I suggest you reconsider the outcome because clearly you hadn't thought this one through."

She was right, I hadn't thought it through but I just had this sinking feeling that this bitch was playing with me and my money. At this point, I was just acting off impulse. I planned on keeping her here until she decided to tell the truth. Thinking I should probably tie her ass up, I reached for my twelve foot charger cord. But, instead of tying her up I wrapped it around her neck and pulled it tight as she tried to grasp me, swinging her arms wildly behind her in an attempt to stop me from choking the life out of her. This bitch had no idea who she was fucking with; I had killed before for less. Once she passed out I stopped pulling the cords because I wasn't trying to kill her. I just figured a ransom wouldn't be such a bad idea. I would contact Tragic and if he wanted his bitch back *alive* he'd come up off that paper. And the ticket just went up to a quarter million. I pulled out my phone and snapped a photo of an unconscious Krystal and sent it to Tragic. I followed up with a message that said, "If you want yo bitch I need my bread." I knew Tragic wouldn't take a threat lightly and I knew I was playing with fire but what else was I going to do? Solo said to do whatever it takes and shit, I was desperate.

My phone rang and I picked up on the first ring. "Where and what time?" I answered, confidently, folding my arms and taking a seat on my desk.

I heard nothing but laughter on the other end. "Man keep that bitch," Tragic's baritone blared through the phone. "She ain't shit but a dick suckin' hoe anyway. Did you know yo babydaddy fucked my babymomma? Now where and what time was that?" he asked sarcastically. What the fuck did he just say to me?

"What the fuck are you talking about?" I asked, ready to murder this bitch if what he was saying was true. "Who told that lie?"

"Ask that bitch to see her phone. You might want to reconsider what team you on." The call ended.

I spun Krystal around in the swivel chair and slapped her so hard my hand stung. "Bitch, wake up and unlock your phone," I said as she came to.

"What the fuck for?" she asked, slowly coming out of her daze.

"What's the code?" I asked her, hands shaking a bit. That always happened when my nerves got bad.

At first she said nothing but after another hard smack she said, "8599." I looked at her, stunned. I know the fuck Solo's birthday is not the code to this bitches phone. August fifth, nine-teen ninety-nine. "I always knew your ass was crazy," she went on to say. "It's always the quiet ones. Creepy ass bitch."

"Do you have a death wish or something?" I asked, temporarily taking my eyes off of the phone. "And anyway, you're the creepy one having another woman's man's birthday as your pin number. It doesn't get much creepier than that." Placing my attention back on the task at hand I scrolled through her call log and text messages and there wasn't much there. Nothing concerning my man anyway. Then I opened her facebook messenger app. Immediately I recognized his screen name, Solo60 and the messages in there made me sick to my stomach.

Solo60: Wya beautiful

Redbone98: Omw to our spot of course, wya

Solo60: Omw

Redbone98: imy :-(

Solo60: imy more beautiful

Solo60: When you gone cum hop on dis dick

Redbone98: When I get off work. Send me a pic, i miss it lol

Solo60: (dickpic)

Redbone98: I want you to eat this pussy and make me cum

But the message that crushed my soul was *Solo60: I love you*

Redbone98: I love you too

I threw the phone at that bitch's face so hard her nose started bleeding. "So you love him?" I scoffed. This shit was unbelievable. This bitch had some nerve. This the same bitch I let stay in my home when Tragic first went to jail and she lost her section 8 because of the drug raide. This was the same bitch I gave all my name brand hand-me-downs to because she couldn't afford nice shit after Tragic went to jail. This the same bitch I considered to be a close associate (never friend because I don't trust these hoes and with good reason). I bet this whole four-hundred thousand dollar shit was her idea. She probably set him up and he was too blinded by the pussy to filter through the bullshit. Because it never made sense to me in the first place. That bastard was smart because when I went down to the precinct to pick up his property, they gave me everything except for that nigga's phone. I knew he told them not to give it to me because I know for a fact that motherfucker had his phone in his pocket the night they took him in. I wanted to leave his ass in there for being so secretive. I should've known he had something to hide but he was still the father of my kids and even with a broken heart I still felt obligated to get him out of there.

"Look, it's not what it looks like-" Krystal started but I cut her off.

"Oh it's exactly what it looks like. Riddle me this; what could you possibly say to keep me from putting a hollow tip in ya' head right now."

"I can tell you who set Solo up to go to jail and it wasn't Tragic either. But first you have to put down that damn gun down," Krystal said.

I cocked my head and thought for a moment. Did I even care who set him up at this point? Was she just saying something to buy her time? Why did I need her anyway if the ransom was a nogo? She was useless to me now. But this bitch still fucked my man. I felt sick to my stomach just thinking about my man in between another bitch's legs, especially one as beautiful as Krystal. What was wrong with me? Why her? This fucked up revelation was pulling insecurities out of me that I'd tried so hard to bury. I looked at her, wondering why I wasn't beating her ass right now. It's like all of the energy had been sucked out of me and I had none left to give. "So tell me, who was it? Who set Solo up to go to jail?"

"It was Trevor." The words hit me like a ton of bricks because I knew what I did last summer. "He's not dead Mercedez. Solo didn't kill him."

I shook my head and said barely above a whisper, "You're lying." She had to be lying. I watched him bleed out on my kitchen floor. I watched him die. Didn't I?

"I'm telling you the truth. He's alive in a witness protection program. He's helping the feds build a case on Solo. He has full immunity as a witness against him. He's cooperating Mercedez."

I sat down behind my desk in my leather chair, sinking into the cushions as her words were sinking in to me. "So what's your role in all of this? If Solo's so hot, why do the deal we made then? How do I know you're not wearing a wire or trying to set me up too."

"Because if this was a setup the feds would've busted in here the moment you put that gun in my face," she snapped and then stood to her feet. "And as far as the deal, I tried to tell Tragic that fucking with Solo was a bad idea but I couldn't tell him why so I just let the shit play out. I couldn't tell Solo what I knew without incriminating myself so I just tried to protect him as much as I could by warning him about bad moves. Now I need to go get my son. I told you all I know so am I free to go?"

"Protect him huh? How the fuck do you know all this?" I wanted to know.

"Because I'm fucking the lead detective on the case," she admitted and I scoffed. Who wasn't this bitch fucking?

"So where's the money?" I asked, growing impatient with the whole situation.

"Tragic has it," she admitted. "Once you told him Solo was locked up he figured he could flip the cash and have it back before Solo got out. But once he found out about what I've been doing he said fuck Solo. He's going to keep the money Mercedez."

I shook my head and pointed my gun right between her eyes. "He ain't keeping shit because you're gonna help me get it back," I said looking at her cynically. "That is if you want to walk out of here alive. I need some information from you."

Chapter 22: Tragic

I looked down at my phone as it vibrated in my lap to see the 313 area code and I knew who was calling me without the number even being stored in my contacts. I only knew one girl from Detroit, Michigan. I hoped she wasn't calling on behalf of her man again trying to get me to give her the money because it wasn't happening. I've never been the nigga to have to take something from the next nigga but I also never been the nigga to share my bitch. Some might say it's not good to mix business affairs with your personal life but whether you hit a nigga pockets or hit a nigga bitch, it don't get more personal than that. He should've known fucking my bitch was bad for business.

"Yo, what's good Mercedez?"

"Tragic, hey," she said in that soft ass, sexy ass voice of hers. She could work at a XXX call center and get paid for that shit. I bet she could make a nigga bust just by talking if she said the right thing. "I was thinking about what you said about Krystal and Solo fucking around while you were locked up. And I was thinking about leveling the playing field."

My eyebrows shot up and I wondered if she was saying what I thought she was saying. I ain't never been a tit for tat ass nigga, that was hoe shit but I'd be lying if I said shorty didn't have me interested. Tupac played through my speakers, "*Revenge is like the sweetest thing next to gettin' pussy,*" and I smirked. "And how we gone do that?" I said, turning my radio down because she had my full attention now. Just thinking about having that beautiful bronze beauty in my bed had me licking my lips, my dimples showing as I smiled. If a nigga wasn't so dark I swear I'd be blushing. The sound of her voice just did something to me. It was sultry and seductive and it made me want to fuck her.

"Pick me up from the storefront around 7," she instructed me. There was a hint of arrogance in her voice like she just knew I would oblige and I even found that shit sexy.

"Ain't Krystal gone be there?" I asked, knowing Krystal said she would be helping with the storefront all week.

"I'm not worried about her, she knows not to try me," Mercedez said. There it was. That arrogance again. That shit made my dick hard. I love confident women, they are a rare breed. Most women are insecure these days, masking it behind make-up and fancy clothes but Mercedez didn't have to do all that. She did it, and she was beautiful but even without the makeup and fancy clothes she was the definition of beauty. She could teach a class on it because she mastered that shit.

"I ain't worried about her either, I'm thinking about you," I told her. "You know she gone tell yo nigga. I can handle my own but at the same time I don't want to cause you no problems." I knew about her relationship with Solo and their history of domestic violence. The last thing I wanted to do was cause shorty more problems.

She sucked her teeth and said, "I ain't worried about him either." That was all I needed. The green light. Permission. I wondered if she'd keep that same energy if I had to put the nigga in the dirt for fuckin' with her. Because if he put his hands on her over me then it would only be right for me to handle that. "What I am worried about though, and you should be too, is a guy named Trevor."

"Why the fuck would I be worried about a nigga named Trevor?" I asked with a frown. I cradled the phone between my ear and my shoulder as I picked up another stack of bills to count. I'd been counting money at my kitchen table the whole time, never losing count because I know how to multitask.

"From what I'm hearing, he's talking to the feds and your name came up a few times, I think they're trying to build a case on you."

I stopped counting. What the fuck was she talking about? "Run that back," I said, not sure if I'd heard her correctly the first time.

"He got in some trouble last summer and apparently he's trying to snitch his way out of it. I know if he mentioned Solo then you, me and Krystal could all be in trouble too because of the businesses we have together. He knows we clean money at Krystal's spot in New Orleans and if they've been watching us. It's only a matter of time before they gather enough evidence to build a case. The muthafucka just knows too much."

"So what are you saying?" I asked her, my brows dipped in concern. "And how this nigga know so much?"

"I'm saying if you don't want to be indicted on some bullshit we need to find him and shut him up for good. And he ain't no nigga, he a white boy. He knows a lot because I used to keep him around. We used to be best friends."

"Are you tryna help me or are you lookin' out for that nigga Solo?" I asked, the wheels in my brain spinning. "How I know that nigga ain't gone talk."

"You don't," she said honestly. "But if we eliminate the problem he won't have a reason to.

Their whole case is based solely on the testimony of one man who claimed to have penetrated y'all circle and can identify y'all on the stand. All I'm saying is no face-"

"No case," I finished for her. "Say less." I hung up the phone and blew out a breath of frustration. I didn't know how I was supposed to find a white nigga in witness protection on the inside but I knew it had to be done. I don't like loose ends and this Trevor dude was a loose end.

I pulled up on Mercedez at seven as promised. Normally I wouldn't let a female tell me what to do but Mercedez lil pretty ass can boss me around all day. I opened the door to the shop because I thought it'd be rude to just blow the horn so I stepped out like a gentleman and went in to get her. The shop was small, but it was coming together quite nicely. I could tell Krystal had a hand in some of the decorations and I had to admit, she did a great job. I pulled a bouquet of flowers from behind my back when I saw Krystal and walked right by her to give them to Mercedez.

"You got a nigga on some corny shit," I joked, handing her the dozen roses. "But I couldn't step to you empty handed." I licked my lips and grinned as she took the roses and smiled. I could still see her blush red through her honey colored skin.

"Thank you," she said with that million dollar smile of hers. I almost forgot Krystal was in the room until she cleared her throat.

"So I'm just supposed to stand here while you give the next bitch flowers?" She asked with her hands on her hips.

"Watch ya' mouth," Mercedez and I said at the same time and we shared a laugh. I ran my hand over my waves from back to front and pulled up my jeans a little. I didn't like to sag but I always wore them low enough for about an inch of my Sean John boxers to show. I held out my elbow and Mercedez looped her arm through it, waving bye as we walked out of the store. She bumped shoulders with Krystal when she walked past her. It was a petty move on both of their parts because there was plenty enough space for them both to walk around.

"Don't touch me," Krystal said through gritted teeth.

"Don't get touched," Mercedez said curtly.

Krystal came out behind us. She kept her distance though like she knew better than to run up on Mercedez. "So you're just gonna leave with her right in my face?" Krystal asked, her face turning as red as her hair.

I stopped walking with Mercedez and approached Krystal. "Fuckin' right I am," I said. With one finger pointed in her face so close I could've mushed her I said, "Because unlike you, I don't sneak and creep." I'm sure she could see the malice in my eyes because she quickly recoiled. "Now carry yo ass back in that store and stop tryna' make a scene out here," I said, noticing that people on the sidewalk had stopped walking and were staring at us. Leave it to Krystal to be the center of attention, unlike me, I hated extra eyes on me and I never showed out in public. I wasn't a loud dude because real bad boys move in silence. I didn't easily lose my temper because when I did, I probably had to body a muthafucka and I don't leave no witnesses. There were too many people out here and although I could've killed Krystal for her betrayal, I wasn't about to go to jail over no pussy so I kept my cool. I opened the passenger door to my Chevy Tahoe and waited till Mercedez was safely tucked inside and in her seatbelt before I closed the door. I walked to my side and hopped in while Krystal was rolling her neck, moving her hands and cursing me out. Mercedez turned up the radio, clearly ignoring Krystal. I looked at her and smiled. Such a fucking lady. That's what I needed in my life, a real woman and not some dressed up hood rat like Krystal. Mercedez was hood but she knew when to turn that shit off. She wasn't about to get out of line in front of her place of business and I respected her for that. Meanwhile Krystal was throwing a bitch fit like a fuckin toddler. Her ass was so spoiled. She thought just because she was half white that put her on a pedestal or something. She swore she was the shit but that was all a facade. Masked insecurities. I tried to help her with her self esteem by investing in her body because Krystal was done up. It started with her hair, eyelashes and nails and went to nose, lips, and eventually hips. Then she convinced me to buy her a new ass and new titts, all that work and she still couldn't fuck with Mercedez on her worst day. Even with her hair pulled up in a messy bun, no makeup and sweatpants on she was still the shit because even on days like that it was hard to look away from her. Her being dolled up today in her barely there makeup and her all white Ralph Lauren pants suit with red bottom heels was a plus. We pulled off.

I peeped how shorty was looking at my gold watch and my diamond and gold necklaces and I smiled. "We gotta get you some drip love," I said, placing my right hand on her left thigh. Not too skinny, not too thick, she was just right.

"So we headed to the mall then?" she asked. I laughed out loud. Shorty didn't miss a beat. I could already tell she was used to getting her way too. But my jewelry didn't come from no mall, I had a jeweler custom make my shit. I was going to have to upgrade her. I let my hand ease in between her legs and she looked at me with an arched eyebrow. "Oh yeah?" she teased. "So that's how you feel?" I laughed hard at that one because she knew I wasn't the type of nigga to pay for pussy. I could lace her in drip and never lay a finger on her because that's just what type of nigga i am. Shorty was just fine as fuck and I was finding it hard to keep my hands to myself.

Mercedez unbuttoned her pants and pulled the zipper down. "Oh yeah? That's how you feel?" I joked and she laughed. She eased them down just far enough for me to reach my hand in there. I gripped the steering wheel with my left hand as my dick got rock hard. I kept looking back and forth between her and the highway. We were on highway 59 going 75 mph, looking for the next exit so I could find a hotel. Both of our cribs were too far and I couldn't wait too much longer. I didn't want to pull over and fuck her on the side of the road so I gripped the steering wheel harder, trying to find some restraint as my fingers continued to explore her. She reclined her seat a little, letting her head fall back as the wind blew her curls and she closed her eyes, allowing a quiet moan to escape her lips. She licked her lips and rolled her hips as a sensual song played on the radio. Kehlani, *"Could you blame me, for needing you, you're the reason I got a weakness, oh no you drive me crazy, still that's my baby, can't get enough of you, baby it's something that you do".* She grinded on my fingers, first two, then three, in and out as my thumb worked her clit in circles. I was just pulling up to the Hilton when I felt her cream all over my fingers. My whole hand was wet, soaked in her juices and I knew from that moment, this girl was going to be trouble.

   I pulled up at the Hilton and pushed the gear in park. I pulled out my black card and handed it to her. "Go get us the best suite they have available," I told her. She smiled and hopped out of the car. My eyes followed her while she walked with the confidence of a runway model. When she came back with the key we parked on the side of the building and went through the patio door near the pool. It was dark now but the blue water was lit from the pool lights and the bubbles were flowing in the hot tub.

   "Let's get in the jacuzzi," Mercedez suggested but I shook my head no. "Nah i'm good on that love."

"What? Gangstas don't swim?" she asked pulling her shirt over her head. I looked around the pool area and saw that we were the only ones out there, so I let her continue to pull her clothes off. She undressed down to her panties and bra, a red lace set from Victoria Secret's *Pink* collection. "Come on, please?" she asked, backing up deeper into the water. This girl was so damn beautiful. As if I were in a trance, I unbuckled my jeans and started undressing, my eyes never leaving hers. I slipped off my watch and placed it on the table with my keys and cell phone, then I entered the shallow water. "Let's play a game," she suggested. "Truth or Dare?"

I started laughing and said, "Man I ain't played that since junior high."

"Well it should be fun," she said, giggling. "Truth or dare?"

I laughed, shaking my head. This girl had me outside in my drawers, in the middle of a pool, playing truth or dare. "Dare," I said, wondering what she could come up with. I've never backed down to a challenge in my life.

"Okay," she said popping her lips. "I dare you," she put her index finger to her chin. "Tooo…do a backwards flip off the diving board."

"In the deep end?" I asked, not feeling that idea.

"You scared?"

I shook my head and said, "I ain't scared of shit."

She looked at me curiously then tilted her head to the right. "Okay, truth. You can't swim can you?"

I cracked a smile and said, "You got me fucked up love, a nigga can swim it's the backflip shit that I ain't into."

"Uh-huh," she laughed. "You're scared."

"Would you go rock climbing if you couldn't climb rocks?" I asked her.

"Hell no, that's white people shit," she said with the wave of a hand.

"Okay then," I laughed. "I'll let you teach me something one day. But tonight I got other plans." I backed her into a wall them picked her up by her bottom, swinging her legs around my waist. She giggled as I moved her panties to the side while looking around to make sure we didn't have an audience. I pulled my dick out and pushed it deep inside of her.

"Ahhh," she gasped, throwing her head back. "That feels sooo fucking good," She moaned.

I didn't respond with words, I just let my dick do the talking. "Mmm," I groaned, gripping her ass cheeks and pounding into her. The water pressure just made it that much better. After several minutes I felt myself swelling up inside of her and I couldn't hold in my moans anymore. "Ooo"s and "ahhh"s was all you could hear besides the rhythmic splashing of the water. I kissed her passionately as we both came together. I laid my head on her chest and listened to her heartbeat and noticed it matched my own. I looked into her hazel eyes and felt like I could stare into them for hours and get lost in her captivating gaze. For some reason I felt a connection to this girl like I've known her my whole life or perhaps knew her in another life. I was lying when I said I wasn't scared of anything. I was scared of her. The feelings I was developing for her were coming out of nowhere, too hard and too fast and I ain't have no brakes. We dried ourselves with a couple of the complimentary towels folded up on a rack near the door. I retrieved my clothing and followed her sexy ass up to the room, which happened to have a jacuzzi in it. "Well damn," I said, eyeing the luxurious hot tub. "So we was just fuckin' in public for the hype."

She laughed and went to turn on the shower. I dropped my drawers and followed closely behind that ass. It was time for round two.

Chapter 23: Krystal

Reluctantly, I told Mercedez about every stash house Tragic had around the city. I just prayed she'd keep her end of the bargain and split the money because now that Tragic has cut me off, all I have is the money coming in from the shops. I wish Solo was out, he would take care of me or at least make sure I was straight. He always protects the ones he loves.

I met Solo when we were kids, before the babymomma and way before Mercedez. He was my brother, Psycho's, best friend so he used to hang around the house a lot growing up. Solo knew the real me, beneath all this plastic surgery and implants and what not. He's tasted me, been inside of me, hell, he took my virginity. He was my first love and I know I should let go of my past but he's not really just my past. He's ever-present. He's always occupied a place in my heart. We started dating when I was thirteen. I was the only girl in junior high with a highschool boyfriend. I was in eighth grade, my last year of middle school and he was a highschool freshman. Psycho hated the fact that Solo and I had started dating. As a matter of fact, he told Solo he was going to fuck his little sister, just off GP. It wasn't long before general principle turned into Psycho and Jessica shacking up and having babies. When I ended up pregnant myself at the tender age of fifteen my mother moved us to New Orleans with my grandparents, too ashamed of what I'd done to stay in Hattiesburg. Solo never even knew I was pregnant. He still doesn't know my son is his because ever since I moved back to Hattiesburg, Tragic has been a constant in my life. He claimed my son as his own and he took care of us so well that I let him. Solo and Tragic were ike night and day. Tragic wasn't like the average hood nigga. He was a gangster but he knew when to turn that shit off. Before he walked in the house he left his street mentality at the door and became a family man. He wasn't hot headed, he was calculated, playing life like a game of chess. He was strong, there wasn't a weak bone in his chocolate body but he was gentle with me. He was a thug in every sense of the way but he let his vulnerability show to his woman. That gangster mentality was his strength but I was his weakness. At least I used to be before my life blew up over this Solo bullshit. After that stunt Tragic pulled, leaving with Mercedez at the store I said fuck her store and decided to jump on the highway and come see about my own shop. My shop. Tragic had bought it for me for valentines day. Ironically, it was the thing that led me back to my first love, Solo. I was behind the counter, pulling receipts out of the register one day when I heard a knock at the glass door.

"We're closed!" I said without even looking up. When I heard the bells over the door jingle I realized that even though my sign said *CLOSED* I had forgotten to lock the door. That was a bad habit I needed to break. I looked up, annoyed, ready to go the fuck off on whoever this illierate motherfucker was who couldn't read signs. My mouth hung open, but nothing came out. I just stood there looking dumb as Solo approached me with that slick ass smile on his face I fell in love with all those years ago. He stood in front of me, looking fine as fuck with his green eyes like mine, rubbing his goatee. He had a habit of doing that when he was thinking heavy on something. I looked into the eyes of my first love and asked, "What are you doing here?"

He smiled. "Actually, I'm down here on some business shit but a nigga gotta eat and the best pizzaria in New Orleans just so happens to be next door to this shop. I saw you with your head down but I know your physique, I can spot you from a mile away. So I wanted to speak to you, being that we haven't spoken in forever. So this is where you ran off to, all those years ago?"

I nodded, knowing he wanted an explanation but I had none to give. If I told him about our child it would change both of our lives drastically because he'd want to be a part of his son's life and I already had someone in that spot. "How have you been?" I asked, changing the subject.

"I've been missin you shorty," he said seriously. "Come here," he said and like a moth to a flame I gravitated to his arms, knowing that I was crossing the line. I already had a man and he wouldn't appreciate walking in witnessing me hugged up with another nigga. Yet and still, I went, because with his tattooed body, green eyes and goatee, it was hard to resist him. Damn near impossible. So I gave in and wrapped my arms around his neck. He smelled like *Sean John* cologne and I nestled my nose in his neck. I don't know why but a single tear rolled down my cheek and he pulled back and wiped my eyes. He kissed me on my forehead. "I know," was all he said as he pulled me back in. "I know."

No, you don't know, I thought sadly. *You have no idea.* I had wished that I could stay in that moment forever but I knew that I couldn't. I pulled away and he pulled my ass right back in and kissed me again. This time on my lips and with much more passion than before. I parted my lips slightly, allowing his tongue to dance around mine and I felt sparks from my head to my vagina. It was like electricity, the energy was so strong, and our chemistry was undeniable. It was like the motherfuckin fourth of July. I could no longer feel my legs so I was grateful when he picked me up. He knocked everything off the counter top and I wanted to protest in my mind but my heart didn't give a fuck about that shit. Fuck them books, I'd just have to recount later. He pulled off my shirt and laid me on the counter that was cold against my skin. I didn't care. We were about to heat shit up. He pulled my skirt off and pulled me towards him until my ass cheeks were halfway off the counter. He didn't stand too close at first because his dick was long and he wanted to put it in slowly. When he penetrated me my juices flowed instantly as I allowed him to fill me up with his thickness. He looked me in my eyes and talked to me while he fucked me slow. When he said those three little words it was like lightning bolts hit my vagina as he pounded me hard with every word. I. Love. You… It seemed like the more he said it the more I streamed and it felt so good I had to break eye contact to look down and see what the fuck this nigga was doing to me. It felt too good. How could something wrong feel this fucking good? It had to be right. His dick had me questioning the decisions I made to keep my distance from him. How the fuck could I let this nigga go? He grabbed me by the chin and turned my face back to him. His thrusts were so strong the counter shook. Harder. Deeper. Bigger. Deeper. Wider. Deeper. I kept hearing him say, "I love you" but the way he was pounding this pussy I knew this wasn't making love. We were past that. We were straight fucking. I felt him swell up inside of me and the width of him made me cum then seconds later I felt his nut all over my stomach. It felt hot and I swiped it with my index finger and began to suck on it seductively. He smacked me on my ass and I giggled as he picked me up and placed my feet on the hardwood floor. The way he made me feel, there aren't any words to describe it but I will go so far as to say his love is like a drug. Once you've had it, you'll always be feigning for it. Only, I wasn't chasing a first experience high because everytime I'm with that man, his love is more potent than before. How is that even possible? After my encounter with Solo I wanted to be near him, so I convinced Tragic to let me move in with him in Hattiesburg. I didn't even have to sell him on the idea because apparently a friend of his wanted us to expand by making a Hattiesburg store. Imagine my surprise when I walked into the meeting and saw Solo and his *girlfriend* seated at the table. So these were our partners? It really is a small world after fucking all. The girl greeted me with a smile and a handshake and Solo just reached out his hand to shake mine. "Nice to meet you," he said, gazing into my eyes and mesmerizing me with his. A knock at the door forced us out of our little transe and I was grateful for the interruption. My relief quickly turned to grief as I watched a young boy enter into the room and made his way to Solo and the girl. "I can't find her pacifier," the boy said. I was thinking he was talking to the girl but when Solo removed a baby pacifier from his jeans and told the young boy to make sure he washed it off so *his* baby wouldn't get sick, I felt like I was going to faint. How was it that he had a whole fucking family and failed to mention it to me? I gave him a cold glare from across the room and if looks could kill, he'd be one dead motherfucker. The nerve of me right? The girlfriend excused herself to check on the kids and I felt my eyes prickeling, daring to release the hot tears that were brewing behind them and threatening to come out. It had been three weeks, I uprooted my life for him and got hit with a ton of bricks as a welcome. At that point, I hated that I even came back to Hattiesburg at all. Two weeks went by before I heard from Solo again. He had called to take me out of town with him and I obliged because I couldn't help it. I loved this man. "Are you married?" I asked as soon as I was in the car with him.

"No," he had told me."But we live together."

"I know right, with your kids, I see you have your family now, your life is complete. I can't be the girl to come in between that. I won't." Fastforward, years later, I am that girl. Damn.

I was so busy going down memory lane that I almost missed my exit to get off on I-10 towards New Orleans. I planned on staying there a few days at my grandparents to clear my head. Tragic and Mercedez had me fucked up if they thought they were just going to ride off in the sunset and I would be cool with that. They were both using each other to get back at me and to me that was beyond petty- it was *pathetic*. Once thing for sure, two for certain, that little plan Mercedez conjured up wasn't going to fly. I didn' know the intricate details of what she was planning to do but I do know that Tragic ain't no dumb ass nigga. *He's going to find out her true intentions and kill that bitch,* I thought, shaking my head. And when he did, he would come running back to me. Tragic was a good provider and he wasn't just no bad nigga either. He was good looking and charming and his money was so long a bitch didn't want for shit. Truth be told, he was too good for me. He put me on this pedestal that I didn't deserve to be on because his expectations of me were just too damn high. I often felt like I was in competition with random chicks that he knew just because they seemed to have their shit together more than me. I found myself making major changes physically too, just so I could look like those girls he followed on Instagram. I got a nose job, lipo, a lip enhancement, some minor botox, a new set of boobs and an ass full of silicon trying to keep up with them filtered ass hoes and it seemed like he still wasn't truly satisfied with me. It was more like he tolerated me because I'd been down for so long but the love wasn't there. I blamed it on him being a thug, like he just didn't know how to show love but that thuggish shit is what attracted me to him in the first place so I dealt with it. His butter colored Timberland boots, baggy jeans, crisp white tees, low fade and fitted caps and the way he was always rocking a hoodie all appealed to me. His swagger reminded me of Solo but a little more put together and his taste was more expensive. The same went for their personalities. Solo was flashy while Tragic kept a low profile. Tragic was perfect yet I was in love with Solo. However, the fact that Solo never came for me made me question the love he said he had for me. I know we were young but he promised me he would come for me and make me his wife, no matter where I was, he would find me and marry me. Needless to say, he never did.

Chapter 24: Mercedez

I've been hanging out with Tragic for a few weeks now and he has yet to lead me to anything that has to do with the money or the drugs. I was hoping he would take me to the stash houses so I could get familiar with them but he's shown me nothing that has to do with hustling. The only thing he's shown me is a side of him that I've never seen before and I have to admit, I'm liking what I see. It turns out this nigga is a big romantic. From surprise dates to flowers, cards, candy, and expensive jewelry, he's sweeping me off my feet. I'm trying to stay focused because I know I'm on a mission and in order to execute my plan successfully, I need to find out some key information. I already have the addresses to where he keeps the money and the drugs but I need to get on the inside so I'll know what I'm dealing with when I send my guys in there. I don't really trust Krystal but she knows the codes to the safes so I have to cut her in. She's too scared to steal the money herself plus she has no goons to help her pull the shit off so she needs me as much as I need her. Tragic has enough money to make both of us rich. I wonder why Solo was never able to reach the level of success that Tragic has but deep down I know the answer. Tragic doesn't do drugs. If it's not marijuana he's not fucking with it and I respect him for that. You have to be level headed to keep business running smoothly when you're on the level that Tragic is on and you can't make rational decisions when you're high. Solo broke the number one rule: You don't get high on your own supply! Now that I'm away from him I'm starting to realize the amount of influence drugs had on me and after being around Tragic I can never go back to being that girl. I can tell Tragic isn't going for a girl that likes to get high so I'm not even tempted around him, like it's not even a thought. I feel a wave of anger mixed with a little bit of jealousy come over me thinking about Krystal and how she had a nigga that make a bitch wanna strive to do better yet she still came sniffing behind mine. It's crazy how she's fucking with Solo like she wants what I have and now I actually envy her for what her and Tragic had. I know it's supposed to be strictly business but I feel myself falling for him. Or maybe I'm just fed the fuck up with Solo stepping out on me. You heard the song, "When a woman's fed up, there ain't nothing you can do about it, it's like running out of love, and it's too late to talk about it…" *Damn, R.Kelly*, I'm thinking, shaking my head. My phone vibrates on my nightstand. It's a message from Krystal with three different addresses and three six digit numbers next to each of them. "Bingo," I say with a grin and I grab my notepad out of the drawer and write the information down. I text her back, 'I'll go check them out tomorrow night." I lied, knowing damn well I'm going to go check it out right now and send my goons in the early part of the morning, while it's still dark. I don't completely trust Krystal so I had to curve her ass in case she decided to flip on me and tell Tragic everything in a desperate attempt to get him back. I know she still has feelings for him and I just hope she doesn't snitch me out trying to be loyal to a nigga that no longer gives a fuck about her trying to be his ride or die bitch. That's why I have to act fast, plus, according to Krystal the feds are closing in but for all I know that bitch can be working with the feds or lying about the whole thing all together.

"Going somewhere?" Tragic startled me, grabbing me from behind and pulling me to him. He planted a soft kiss on my neck because he knows that's my spot and I wanted to turn around and fuck him since our clothes were already off anyway. Unfortunately, I had shit to do.

"Just to handle some work stuff," I lied. "Business as usual."

He wrapped his strong arms around me and closed the space between us and I melted into him, throwing my head back, allowing it to rest on his shoulder. "I'm tryna make you my business love," he murmured in my ear and I felt his erection on my ass. He caressed my breast and my nipples grew hard instantly. He slid into me from behind before I could object and my juices devoured him. When he pulled out and centered himself on my behind I grew tense. "Just relax," he told me. "I won't hurt you." When he pushed hard dick into my asshole slowly, it hurt like hell and I felt like he was going to rip me apart. I wasn't ready for this, I'd never tried anal sex and it terrified me. "I want you Mercedez," he whispered as he eased himself in. "I want you to be my girl." It seemed like the more he whispered sweet nothings the easier it became to let him in. Once he was all the way in the pain stopped and I started to have multiple orgasms feeling sensations of ecstasy I'd never felt before in my life. He was hitting nerves that I didn't even know existed. He went harder and deeper with every stroke, and at the same time he was gentle and steady with it. I touched my pedicured toes with my manicured hands as the pounding got harder and harder. I was getting wetter and wetter as he slipped his fingers in and out my neatly shaven pussy and the sound of skin slapping against skin filled the room. When I felt him swelling up inside of me I came to a climax and after he figured I was satisfied he pulled out and released himself all over my back. I stood to head to the shower but he collapsed on the bed, pulling me down on top of him. He wrapped those muscular arms around me and held me in his arms until I fell asleep. When I finally woke up Tragic was gone and I remembered I was supposed to be handling that business tonight. Fuck. It's the first of the month and the trap houses are jumping and will be for the next few days. I plan to scope the scene tonight and make my move in a few days when I know the safes will be loaded. When my phone started to vibrate and ring I picked it up without even looking at the number that was calling me, assuming it would be Tragic. "Hello?" I cooed into the phone but when I heard Solo's raspy voice on the other end my smile faded and my stomach dropped as if I had been caught cheating. I quickly reminded myself that he was in jail. He was calling me from a burner phone the guards had snuck in for him. I also reminded myself that I wasn't the cheater, he was, so this was all on him. "First of all, who the fuck you yellin' at?" I snapped before he could even answer, "This my muthafuckin' phone so you either gone respect it or get the fuck off my line!" I pulled the bedsheets over my breast as if he could see me and huffed, "What the fuck do you want anyway? What, is Krystal not holding you down or something?" Although I had known about Krystal weeks ago I never discussed it with Solo, I simply stopped taking his calls.

"Krystal?" he said, sounding confused. "What the fuck she got to do with anything?" Tired of the back and forth before it even began, I decided to shoot it to him straight. I wasn't beat for the bullshit tonight. I had bigger fish to fry.

"I know you've been fucking her and y'all been fuckin' for a minute with your nasty, two-timing ass," I said with a look of disgust etched on my face. I put the phone on speaker and pulled the sheets before I tossed it on the plush king size pillow top mattress.

"Man where is you gettin' all this bullshit from?" he asked, faking sincerity. "I ain't done shit!"

"From the horse's mouth," I replied. "Apparently you've been sneaking around doing all kinds of shit with this bitch. You know you done fucked up right? It's over!" I tossed the dirty sheets into a hamper and went to Tragic's closet to find fresh ones.

"Fuck you then, bitch," he spat into the phone. I stepped out the closet, retrieved my phone off the bed and hit the *end* button, hanging up on him. I didn't have time for Solo's shit. I had work to do and he was just a distraction. I retreated back to the closet and looked on the top shelf to see if there was fresh linen there. When I reached for what looked like a new set of sheets a shoe box came down with it. Some of the contents fell out onto the floor and I picked it up curiously, wondering what the stuff was. It looked like old letters and some of them were stuffed in envelopes addressed to Tragic when he was in prison. I opened one of the letters nosely and began to read. I don't know why a wave of jealousy came over me as I read the romantic words from Krystal. There were pictures of naked women in the box also, one of them Krystal and several other unknown females. I had to admit, they were some bad bitches though. He even had a few of Chassidy's bad built ass in there. I smirked and began putting the contents back in the box thinking somebody as fine as Tragic couldn't help but to be a big ole player. A red envelope stood out and caught my attention. I picked it up and noticed it was addressed to my wife. I slipped the folded sheet of paper out of the envelope and was in awe of the poetic words I was holding in my hands. I didn't know Tragic had a sensitive side to him, he was always so hard. But the words on the paper told a different tale. I sat Indian style, butt naked in the closet, as I read the words. *My dearest and most beautiful wife, the leading lady in my life, I love you more than words can say, I think about you everyday, you restored my hope and faith in love, I know Got sent you from above, i must admit there was a time, when I didn't think you could be mine, because how could someone so precious and pure, love me through the pain that I endure, you wipe my tears and make me smile, we've stood the test of every trial, you are my lover and my best friend, The depth of my love for you has no end. Love at first sight must be true, because I loved you the first time I saw you. Yes, you had me at hello, and now I'll never let you go. I promise to love you and always respect you. I'll always protect you and never neglect you. I saw you in my dreams before this thing even began. I just hope in real life I see you again. Until then, I'll love you through dimensions and worlds afar, just make my dreams come true, whoever you are. I love you.* The poem nearly brought me to tears. A letter to his unknown wife. *I guess Krystal wasn't it or she'd be wifey by now,* I thought with a smirk. I folded the letter neatly and placed it back in the unsealed envelope. I put it back in the box and had to stand on the tip of my toes to put it back on the shelf. I gathered the sheets and made my way back to the bed and spread the fitted sheets at least three times because the corners kept popping back up. As I made the bed, I smiled. Something about being here just felt right and I wonder how could it be alright when the reality of it was so wrong? He wasn't mine. I was using him and planning to rob his ass blind and for the first time I started feeling remorseful. I tried to shake the feeling by jumping in the shower as if I could wash my sins away but the feeling still resonated with me. I was being disloyal. To who though? Solo had already pledged his allegiance to another bitch long before I started this affair. The lines of loyalty were blurred when it came to money, secrets, and sex but to fall in love would be crossing that line altogether. I knew that Tragic was really feeling me so was I being disloyal to him? No, I concluded, because I don't owe him shit. This was all about the money right? So why was I dreading the day that I'd have to end things with him? I would eventually have to leave because I couldn't fathom the thought of building a relationship on lies so I would either have to break things off and follow through with my plan or tell him the truth and take a chance on true love. I knew only fairy tales had happy endings though so I needed to get out my feelings and get in my bag.

   I hopped in the Porsche and didn't even wait for it to warm up, I just threw my seat warmer on and peeled out. The first stop I made was to my house to check on the kids. Although my little cousin was in high school, I didn't want to make it a habit to leave her at home babysitting all the time. She was a teen-aged girl and I knew she had more to do than sit around and babysit. Hell, they weren't her kids, they were mine so before I hit the streets I gave them some mommy time. We sat around the living room table playing Monopoly and eating pizza and I was having a good time with them. Six hours had passed and it was starting to get dark. I put the twins in the bathtub while I stood in the bathroom mirror several times to see if I was rocking the right outfit.   When they got out, I dried them, put on their pajamas and put them in bed. I handed them the remote and rolled my eyes as I heard baby shark for the millionth time. My six and seven year old continued to play board games, both of them competitive just like their father. I slipped my oldest twenty dollars and he said, "thanks mom" without even looking up. His eyes were glued to his phone. I just stood there, shaking my head wondering what kids these days would do without technology. I remember having to go outside and play until the street lights came on. I stepped outside in my black Fendi heels and locked the door behind me. When I turned around to walk to my car a leather glove gripped me so tight around the neck I was unable to scream and I was slammed against the brick wall. I had a bad habit of leaving the house without turning the porch light on and in that moment I regretted my carelessness. The perpetrator stood in front of me and I was shocked to be peering into the eyes of Psycho's dreadheaded ass.

"Psycho what the fuck?" I asked once he released his grip on my throat.

"Two-hundred thousand dollars."

"What?" I asked furrowing my brows. What the fuck was this nigga talkin' about?

"That's the amount that Solo was supposed to be bringing me off that play in New Orleans. I know you snitched on him so you could keep the money and fuck off with that nigga Tragic. Only problem with that is two hundred thousand of that belonged to me!"

I look at the nigga like he's crazy. "I don't know where you're getting this fucked up information from but I did *not* put Solo in jail and I don't know nothing about you gettin two hundred thousand dollars!" I attempted to move around him but he grabbed my arm and slammed me against the brick wall, hard.

"Bitch stop lyin'. Janice told Jessica and Jessica told me," he said through gritted teeth.

I laughed as if I'd just heard the funniest joke ever. He was really coming at me with this clown shit. "So you mean to tell me your source is from two bitches that hate me? I didn't put Solo in jail. Janice is full of shit and Jessica needs her ass kicked for even coming to you with that garbage ass information. It's called *fake news*!"

He released the grip on my arm and closed the space between us. "So how I know it was yo idea to put the dope in some stuffed bears then? I guess that's a lie too. The only problem is y'all stuffed them bears with my dope." He was literally breathing down my neck as the wheels started spinning in my mind. Only Solo could've told him that and if he was talking it had to be because he was talking to the plug. Fuck!

"Solo told me he got the bricks from one of the gang members," I said in defiance. "He wouldn't lie to me."

"What gang member you know sittin' on twenty bricks besides me?" he countered. I grew silent and he said, "Exactly," and backed up off of me. "Look Mercedez, I like you so I don't wanna have to hurt you but you know how the game go. You his number two so the weight falls on you." His dreads hung wildly around his face as he talked, making him look like a lion. "Now what's up with my money?"

I sighed heavily, not wanting to tell him what I was about to tell him. "The guy he was dealing with robbed him. No money, No product. Nothing," I said solemnly.

"So you mean to tell me it's a nigga out there with my dope and my money? Who the fuck is this nigga and where can I find him?"

I could've told him right then exactly what was up. I could've gave him the information on the stash houses and the safes, I could've gave up Tragic. But for some reason I felt like it would be disloyal. I felt a need to protect him because somehow I knew if the shoe was on the other foot, he would protect me too. "I don't know, some nigga from New Orleans I think. I'm not really sure."

Psycho was burning a hole through me with his eyes and I felt like he could see right through my bullshit. He gritted his teeth and said, "Find out!" He turned to walk away but came to a halt as if he had just had an epiphany or something. "Oh yeah," he said. "Tell Solo just cause he in jail don't mean he can't be touched." and with that being said, he back peddled to his Rang Rover and I held my breath until I saw him get in his truck and leave. Although Solo and I are at odds right now, he is still my daughter's father and I don't want anything to happen to him. I needed to hit Psycho with the two hundred thousand in order to protect both Solo and Tragic because it was only a matter of time before he found out Tragic was behind it. This was like dejavu'. How the fuck did I end up owing Psycho's crazy ass? I pulled out my phone. It was time to hit the stash houses and I knew exactly who to call.

Chapter 25: Desmond

When my ex wife called me with a lick, me and my young bloods was ready to roll. A nice lick is exactly what I needed to get back on my feet. It didn't matter how I got it, a come up is a come up and breaking into other people's shit is my specialty. I had three of my lil' vice lord brothers with me, D-Lo, KT, and Ant. All three of them niggas was willing to die behind this shit because this was the type of shit they lived for. Once upon a time I was the same way, eager to do whatever the OG's told me like I didn't have shit to lose and it cost me my marriage. But niggas like Ant still felt like they had shit to prove because they really didn't have shit to lose and D-Lo and KT just didn't give a fuck. I was surrounded by real goons.

I did a countdown, "Three, two, one" and the four of us jumped out the truck and ran up to the spot. We crossed the street in all black attire, rocking black Timberland boots, hoodies, and face masks. We had been watching the house for hours and from what a feign told me for a quick fix, there were usually only one or two people inside this time of night. D-Lo, who wore no mask, knocked on the door with the gun behind his back and started calling out, "Aye Keisha! Bring yo' ass outta there, I know you wit' a nigga!"

    As if on cue, a tall, lanky, light-skinned dude with dreads opened the door with a scowl. "You, got the wrong house my nigga," he said. "Now get the fuck off my door step before I find yo' bitch and fuck her." KT and Ant jumped from opposite sides of the bushes and rushed him back inside. "Whoa! Chill bruh, I don't want yo' bitch; I don't even know her!" He said, struggling with Ant who had him in a head-lock. When the dude reached for his gun KT pistol whipped him and knocked his lil' skinny ass out with the quickness. KT was a real hot headed, ruthless ass nigga. I stay gettin' on his ass about taking minor shit too far and turning it into something major. Tonight, he was off his leash though. I handed D.Lo the cuffs, rope, and duck tape and checked the scene outside to make sure there were no nosey neighbors or witnesses. It was important that we remained unseen because this particular stash house was in the hood on the east side. Our rival gang, the crips, ran this side of town and we were in clear violation of the truce that Psycho and our OG, Buck, had made a couple years ago before Buck got popped and ended up doing time on some Kingpin shit. Getting caught over here tonight would definitely spark a war and that's the last thing I need while on probation but people in the hood are nosey as fuck. It was three o'clock in the morning and niggas still wasn't sleep. Most of the night owls, I like to call them vamps, be up for days off of crystal meth and cocaine. I remember we had to bring KT back off that shit, that nigga had been up for a week straight on ice, no food, no nothing. Only thing he was interested in was rolling the glass dick between his lips. It wasn't until he got too high and started a fire while trying to smoke the meth that he seemed to snap back into reality. The firemen got there just in time to save his daughter and wife from the flames. Unfortunately, they had already died from the smoke inhalation. The guilt of that night ate his ass up because it was then that he realized he had been choosing drugs over his family for quite some time now. He checked himself into a rehabilitation center and got cleaned up and when he came out he was back to his old self, only more murderous than before.

KT continued to point the gun at the man's head while Ant and D.Lo tore the house up looking for the stash. The man was bloody and beaten very badly for refusing to tell where the guns, money, and drugs were. His head hung to his chest as he appeared to be slipping in and out of consciousness. "Man let's just kill this nigga," KT said, his trigger finger itchy.

"Chill yo trigger happy ass the fuck out nigga, we ain't come for all that," Ant said.

"What, we came for all this?" KT said, motioning to the damn near lifeless man. "Niggas got guns and scared to use them. Well I ain't." *POP!* KT shot the man, the force of the bullet knocking him over in his chair.

Before Ant could say anything to KT, D-Lo called out, "Yo, it's a dark ass staircase over here!"

I instructed Ant to turn on his flashlight as we made our way towards D.Lo. Ant flashed the light and saw two niggas walking up the steps letting off rounds from their own guns. Ant and I emptied the clips on them niggas, causing one of them to fly backwards down the stairs. When i saw the other man fall too,I walked down to the bodies and shot both of them in the head just for good measure. When I heard Ant groaning I quickly ascended the steps and what I saw made my eyes mist. Ant had been hit, three shots to the chest to be specific. "No, nooo, Ant," I said, rushing over to him. "We need to get him to a hospital," I said, knowing that there was no use. He was already dead. D-Lo and KT pulled me away from Ant's lifeless body .

D-Lo said, "Look, I know shit is fucked up but we on a mission so we gotta keep it moving. All those gun shots I know twelve gone be pullin up in a minute. Let's get out of here."

I looked at him like he's lost his mind. "Nigga this is your brother and my best friend! We can't just leave him here like this," I protested.

D-Lo scowled. "Nigga fuck that shit, i'm not tryna go to jail, so let's go!"

I closed Ant's eyes and released him and stood up in my blood stained shirt. "We ain't leaving till we get what we came for, what the fuck you sayin'?" I took the keys I'd taken from one of them niggas and descened the staircase. After three tries and three different keys we finally hit the jack pot. There was money wrapped in thousand dollar bands on a table that sat in the middle of the damn near empty room. KT shot out the surveillance camera and we bagged the money, along with the bricks of cocaine we had found hidden in the wall, just like Mercedez said there would be. Duffle bags full, we got out of there just in time because as soon as we hit da corner a dark blue Suburban pulled up in the driveway. I pushed the petal to the metal and hauled ass till I got to the interstate. The car ride was silent. What should have been a sweet victory now put a sour taste in my mouth because the money wasn't worth losing a brother. "We shouldn't've left him there," I finally spoke.

D.Lo gritted his teeth in frustration. "I told you, there was nothing we could do for him-"

"I know, I know," I cut him off. "That ain't my angle. I'm sayin, when them crip niggas find three of their soldiers dead with a VL layin' there next to them they gone know it was us who hit 'em."

"What, we supposed to be scared now?" KT chimed in. "It's too late to be scared."

D.Lo opened his mouth to speak but didn't say anything. I noticed and asked him to spit it out.

"It's just your wife is bad news bruh. Not only did we lose Ant tonight tryin' to help her, we also sparked a war that shouldn't even be happening."

"So what you sayin'?" I asked, ready to defend the only woman I've ever truly loved.

"I'm sayin' that tryin' to help that girl always have and always will land you in a world of trouble Des. All this is for her and for what so she can break bread with the next nigga? Bread that you put in work for."

"You don't even know what you talkin' about," I said but my mind was racing. What if D.Lo was right? What if Mercedez had set me up? She never had before but the truth of the matter was I didn't know what she would do while she was with that crip nigga Solo. We pulled up to D.Lo's babymomma's house and once we were safely inside we counted the paper and I gave D.Lo and KT their cut. I gave Ant's cut to D.Lo because that was his brother. I waited until I was back in the car to call Mercedez and give her a run down on the events of the night.

"Damn Ant," she said solemnly "I should've never sent you over there like that. This one's on me."

"No, I'm a grown ass man, Ant was too. We could've all said no but you know like I know them niggas was sittin' around waitin' on their next come up. It was just a matter of time..." his voice trailed off.

"It could've been you," she said softly and I knew that she was tearing up. "I don't know what I would do without you Desmond."

"Yeah well it wasn't me. I'd do anything for you Mercedez, I'd die for you, I fuckin' love you. I love the shit out of you," I admitted.

"I know," she said sniffling. "I love you too." I knew she meant it but I also knew she meant it in a different way than I did when I said it to her. Mercedez loved me, no doubt, but she had fallen out of love with me a long time ago and we both knew that.

"I dropped the stash off at ya' crib, in the garage," I told her.

"Thanks Des, I owe you one," she said. "Look, now might not be a good time to ask you this but there's another stash house-"

"Say less," I said and then ended the call. I got on the highway with my estranged wife on my mind. I remembered when we first met. She was at a party Ant was having for his birthday. Her and Ant used to fuck around until that night when she learned she wasn't the only bitch at the party he was fucking. She was leaving and I followed her outside and down the stairs that led to the parking lot. Before she could pull off I found myself knocking at her window. "I don't know what's goin' on between you and that nigga but I wanna fuck wit' you the long way shorty," I told her, licking my lips. "It's not only because you're the baddest chick at the party but you're the prettiest, funniest, smartest most down to earth girl I've ever met. You dope as fuck. That nigga is a fuckin fool for fuckin' over you."

"It's cool," she had said. "I've only known him for a couple of months, it was nothing serious."

"Look I don't give a fuck how long you been knowin' that nigga and like I said, I don't know what you and that nigga had goin but you can dead that shit right now , you fuckin' wit' me now, so get out the car and let's go have a good time, together."

Her smile was as bright as the stars in the sky that night. We went back to the party together and had been inseparable since that night. Not only was she my girlfriend, she was like my best friend. We got fucked up together, drinking and smoking till we passed out, doing gangsta shit like robbing stores like we were bonnie and clyde or some shit, we just didn't give a fuck. When she got pregnant and shit got real, shit started to change between us. There was no more partying, the good times were replaced with mood swings and arguing because I wasn't maturing fast enough for her. It seemed as if Mercedez had matured over night into this beautiful mother and housewife and I just couldn't get my shit together. Despite our problems, the love was real so when i asked her to marry me, against her better judgment she said yes. Less than a year later I landed my black ass in jail and needless to say, Mercedez was gone with the wind. It wasn't even that long before she had moved on. When I got out we had tried to make shit work but I gave up when I realized she wasn't just cheating- she had given her heart to another nigga. So I moved on. I never stopped loving her though, despite the fact that we both had children outside our marriage. Imagine waking up and going to sleep next to a woman that you could never give your whole heart to because you were still in love with someone else. The shit sucks. I'd give anything to have my family back, to go home, because to me home is wherever she is. I'd lay my life on the line for her if it ever came to that, everytime.

    Lost in my thoughts, I wasn't paying attention to my surroundings. I was bending the block towards my crib when I halted the car to a stop. Posted up in front of my apartment building were three cars that I instantly recognized as the crips. Trying to back up before they noticed me, I fucked around and hit a parked car, causing the alarm to go off. Immediately the blue chevy that was first in line took off in my direction. I tried to make a u-turn to try to go the other way but was blocked in by a grey, old school van that slid it's door open and out jumped three men in blue bandanna face masks all pointing their guns at me. I had never been religious before but I tried my best to recite the Lord's prayer but before I could say "Amen" they had sent me to my maker.

Thirty-six bullets hit my car, at least sixteen bullets hit me; two to the head, four to the chest, and ten more to various parts of my body. I coughed up blood, trying hard to catch my breath but it was like I was drowning in my own blood and I couldn't come up for air. Finally, I got tired and gave up the ghost.

Chapter 26: Mercedez

I tried calling Des at least ten times and each time his phone went to voicemail. I was irritated as fuck, knowing that a job like this should have been taken more seriously. Growing more and more restless by the minute, I finally got up, grabbed my keys and headed over to Des's crib to see what was up, praying the whole time that he hadn't got locked up or shot up. For him to not answer my calls was an immediate red flag because Des would never not pick up for me. It didn't matter what he had going on or who he was around, that nigga was picking up for me everytime. I noticed the yellow tape and flashing lights as soon as I turned on Des's street and my heart sank to the pit of my stomach. First, I noticed the cop cars lined up outside his apartment. Then, I noticed Desmond's car wedged awkwardly between two other cars and I immediately knew there must have been some kind of accident. As I got closer, I saw the bullet holes and my worst fear became my reality. When I saw a body covered with a blood stained white sheet being wheeled towards an ambulance, my heart began to race and thud loudly in my chest. Tears stung my eyes and blurred my vision. I climbed beneath the tape and hurriedly made my way to the ambulance while two officers made an attempt to try to hold me back.

"Ma'am, this is a crime scene," one of them said with a thick, country accent.

"That is my husband's car, is he on the stretcher?" I asked, looking back and forth between the two officers, who weren't answering me fast enough. Impatient with no time to wait, I moved around the officers and sprinted towards the ambulance, getting there just in time to pull back the sheet. I heard the officers yelling at me as the sound of sirens wailed in the background. I tried my best to breathe. It felt like the air was stuck in my chest and I just couldn't exhale. When I finally did it came out in a shrilling scream, "Nooooo!" was all that could escape my lips. A female officer who was looking on empathetically wrapped her arms around me and stroked my hair soothingly. "What happened?" I managed to ask after sniffling and wiping my nose with the wrists of my sweater.

"Your husband was gunned down in his car tonight and right now we don't have any suspects," she answered.

"We're going to need you to come down for questioning," a white detective stepped in and said, handing me his card. I sucked my teeth. I had no rap for these pigs. Noting my apprehension, the detective smirked and walked away. But not before making a smart ass remark. "You sure know how to pick them, don't you Mrs. Jackson?" I lunged at him but the lady cop intervened and steered me away from the scene. She suggested I try to get some rest before coming down to the station for questioning and advised me to seek legal counsel.

"For what?" I asked, bewildered. "I didn't do anything." When she told me that being young and black and the fact that my name had come up in another case more than likely made me a suspect, I appreciated her keeping it real with me and wished her a goodnight.

"You be safe," was all she said before we departed. I went home feeling like the biggest piece of shit on the planet. I had set my sons' father up to be killed by sending him on a suicide mission.

Tonight was supposed to be a big win for me but the loss of Desmond Jackson was a heavy price to pay. All this money and drugs…I would trade it all for Des. As I put on a pot of coffee, the wheels in my brain started spinning. I wondered if it was Tragic who had called the hit. I wanted to call him up and see what the business was but I also didn't want to look suspicious so I decided not to. Instead, I called Krystal. It was time to come up with another plan.

"The guy I sent to the trap was killed," I told her, trying to suppress the emotion in my voice. "He was my husband," I said softly as a salty tear rolled down my face and bounced off my lips.

Krystal gasped, "Oh my God. What the hell happened? This was supposed to be a robbery only, nobody was supposed to get hurt," she stammered. "If we had stuck to the plan and hit the houses tomorrow I could've made sure it was clear for him to go in!"

"Well as you can see, tomorrow isn't promised," I said sarcastically "It's time for a plan B. This time I'll do it myself," I said, ready to pop off at any nigga that could've potentially popped Des. At first this was business. Now it was personal.

"That's a stupid decision," Krystal warned. "They're going to be on their shit now since this shit happened."

"I know," I acknowledged. "But I'm at a point where I just don't give a fuck."

"Yeah, well if you get caught slipping don't think that nigga won't dead you. Good pussy don't give you no pass when it comes to his money." I knew she was right. I couldn't throw the rock and hide my hand this time. By showing my cards I'll be exposing my hand for free yet at the same time it will cost Tragic everything. If I was to be honest with myself, I really didn't want to do anything to hurt Tragic on any kind of level because he had been so good to me. Or was he just a beautiful distraction? What did I really want at the end of the day? *Who* did I really want? I kept telling myself I was sticking around for the money and playing Tragic close as part of a plan but I'd be lying if I said I wasn't constantly in my head over whether or not I should dismantle the plan altogether and ride off into the sunset with this nigga. Ahmad motherfuckin' Williams, also known as Tragic, had somehow found a place in my heart and it didn't feel like he was moving anytime soon. I had fallen in love with a street king. The dilemma was that while I had been playing him close just to get to the money, I had managed to get to his heart. But had I gotten close enough for him to forgive me if he were to ever find out the truth about my early intentions? I could say fuck him and just get the money and bounce or I could risk it all for love. I was sure we were in love but was it too new to withstand the test of trial? What if I said fuck the money and put all my cards on the table just to be rejected or even worse, killed in the end? Was loving this man, this one, beautifully sculpted, chocolate god of a man worth it? Once I got the money, what would I do anyway? Run off with Solo? I didn't think so. That was a chapter of my life I was sure was closing, whether Tragic was in the picture or not. Krystal could have him as far as I was concerned. He could shift all that pain and inflict it on her ass and not me. For some reason I thought having the girls would've changed Solo but that couldn't be further from the truth. The truth is, having a baby by a nigga won't change how he treat you or how he feel about you. Instead of getting what you expect, whatever you accept is what you're going to get. I let Solo fuck me over so many times that just doing right by me wouldn't quite satisfy. I wanted a nigga that loved me too much to fuck over me in the first place. Tragic had been nothing but good to me, yet here I was contemplating on whether or not I should fuck over him. Solo didn't deserve me but that didn't mean that I deserved Tragic. I might as well pull off the heist because once he finds out who I really am he won't want to be with me anyway. So I might as well get paid and get the fuck on because happy endings only happened in fairytales. I fucked up and fell in love but I had to forget about that shit if I was going to win. I planned to rob Tragic and take over the streets. In order to be a queen pin I was going to have to take out the kingpin by any means necessary. "I just don't want to see anyone else get hurt," Krystal was saying. The truth was that I didn't want that either but at this point I was all in. It was double or nothing. "Just be careful," she warned before hanging up.

@   My phone beeped and I looked at an incoming message from Tragic. *Tragic: Wya gorgeous?* I smiled involuntarily. The effect this man had on me was uncanny. Butterflies fluttered in my stomach at just the thought of him thinking of me. My smile faded as I thought of what I had to do next. *My iphone: Omw to wherever you are. Tragic: I have to pick up tonight. I'll catch up with you later.* I frowned. He wasn't supposed to pick up the cash from the trap houses till midnight tomorrow. Krystal was right, he was on his shit tonight because the first house got hit. If that was the case, I had to make my move tonight. *My iphone: wya? I can ride with you, if that's cool.* There was no immediate response, then he finally texted me back. *Tragic: yeah you can ride. Matter fact, you can drive, come pick me up from 4th and Main. My iphone: omw* I got up and jumped in some blue jeans and slid in my leather boots. I snagged a plain white fitted tee with the word *Dior* printed on it off the hanger and pulled it over my chest. I threw on some silver hoops and put on some eye liner and lipstick, grabbed my purse, and was out the door in less than ten minutes. Since my car was junky with toys and carseats, I grabbed Solo's keys and hopped in the infinit. During the long drive across town I tried to think of any and every other way to get the money without Tragic knowing it was me. With Des being dead I no longer had shooters in my corner ready to ride for me on shit like this, so I had to be careful. I tried to catch the tears welling up in my eyes at the thought of Desmond before they ruined my makeup. I felt morally obligated to finish what we started and get rich quick or else Desmond would have died in vain. Tragic had enough bricks and cash to make me a wealthy woman for certain, I just couldn't help but wonder what it would be like to sit next to him on his throne as the first lady of the streets instead.

    I pull up at the 4th and Main street store just like Tragic told me to, but as I look around, I see no sign of him. In fact, the parking lot is empty except for me and an old drunk singing by the door, probably ready to harass people for change. I called Tragic's phone back to back and each time it went to voicemail after the first ring. I waited for a few minutes but after the drunk started knocking on my window I reluctantly pulled the fuck off. Now what type of shit was this? He had me drive all the way over there just to stand me up? "I guess he got another bitch to drive him around for the night," I mumbled to myself. There I was, thinking he was different from Solo but as it turned out, all men were the same. At least that's how it was starting to feel like. I wasn't tripping though, that just made it easier to do what I had to do.

Chapter 27: Solo

    I walked in the zone full of every bit of two hundred inmates, yelling, gambling, fighting, and horseplaying. It was a fucking Jungle and to top it off, it was the middle of June so it was hotter than a muthafucka in the south mississippi regional jail. I was transferred here a couple of months after I got locked up and it was a far cry from the county. From the jump I had all types of dudes asking me what I am and which set I was claiming. "You a gangster G?" "You a vice lord B?" I told them niggas, "Nah, I'm crippin'. Rollin' sixty." When one of them replied, "It's a couple of yo' homies in here," I knew that I was outnumbered which meant I had to tread lightly. When I learned there were only four crips on the zone I knew we weren't running shit so the first few nights I didn't get any sleep. I would stay awake till morning, watching my surroundings and after breakfast I would rest. When I finally got a phone pin number the first thing I did was call to check on my girl but each time I tried I didn't get an answer. There were only seven phones, the ViceLord's had two, the Gangstas had three and there were two civilian phones. It was like I came from crip city to some foreign bullshit. They handle a nigga so fucked up in here, I just stay out the way. Now, with it being my first time here, I ain't accept shit from nobody, not wanting to be in debt to anyone and I damn sure didn't give them country ass niggas shit. I basically just stayed to myself, worked out, sold cigarettes and did my own thing. The shit is crazy, the penitentiary is just like the streets, full of hustlers, smokers, and broke ass niggas. I was different though, far from your average hood nigga. My whole lingo and the way that I carried myself was different so I moved differently. Muthafuckas respected me and I ain't have no problems. One of the niggas I grew up with on the block had the nerve to tell me I changed. My response was, "What the fuck muthafucka I'm just supposed to stay the same?" For real, you live, you learn, and you grow, life is all about evolution. So if a nigga from ten years ago saw me ten years today and I'm still the same nigga, I might as well be dead. I try not to assume people are in the same place in life as they were the last time I saw them because we're supposed to change. I don't know what type of time that lil nigga was on so I ain't have no kick it for him, crippin' or not. We were just two regular muthafuckas up in this joint anyway. When I got back to my rack after getting no answer from Mercedez again, I immediately noticed the white envelope that sat in the middle of my bed. I looked around until I spotted one of the guards and saw that he was passing out mail. Curious as to who would be reaching out to me and hoping it was my girl I quickly picked up the envelope and flipped it over. I frowned in confusion. I hadn't talked to this girl since I been locked up and out of nowhere I get a letter? Disappointed that it wasn't Mercedez, I almost threw the shit away but curiosity lead me to see what the girl had to say. *Dear Solo, I'm surprised I haven't heard from you. Usually when you go to jail is when you be hittin me up the most. But you weren't fuckin with me the few months before you left so I get it. I just wanted to let u kno that if da reason ur not in touch w/me is because of ya lil girlfriend then she got u out here lookin stupid. She's fuckin my nigga on some tit for tat shit bc he found out about us & told her. That money he owed u, he probably gave it to her because they've been riding around town makin moves like they Bonnie and Clyde or sum shit. In case this is all news to u and u haven't heard from her, this is why. I put some money on ya commissary books too so u won't have to ask them niggas in there for a damn thing bc I kno it's different than county jail & I kno how u are. Anyway, now that u kno what's up I hope 2 b hearing from u soon. I put some money on my phone so u can call me anytime. Love, A&F, Krystal. P.S. We need to talk about SciFi. He's not dead and he's coming for you. Call me ASAP!* My jaws clenched so tight I thought my teeth would break. I crumbled up the paper and slung it against the wall.

"Bad news there bruh?" I turned around and was shocked to see my nigga KT standing before me. KT was my long time friend, we'd been rockin' since the sand box. Even though KT ended up getting down for Vice Lord, at the end of the day there was a mutual understanding and respect for brotherhood. We were friends before all this gang shit popped off so no matter what set we claimed, there existed a safe space between the two of us. That was my nigga.

"Damn, what's up bro?" I asked, shaking hands and embracing him in a quick half hug. "I hate that you in here but it is good to see a familiar face in this muthafucka."

"Likewise," KT said, flashing his gold grill with a smile. "I only sat in the county for two weeks before they hurried up and snatched me off the zone. Guess I was causing too much hell."

I shook my head and chuckled. "What the fuck they pick you up on?" I wanted to know.

"All man," KT said, his left hand rubbing the top of his head. "They threw me in here on that violation of probation bullshit after I refused to talk. Had a nigga in the interrogation room for hours."

"Interrogation room?" I questioned. "For what?"

"For murder," KT said and my eyebrows shot up in surprise. "Them crip niggas killed my homeboy, my VL brother, my bestfiend," he said solemnly. "They killed Desmond."

I shook my head in disbelief. I mean, me and dude ain't always see eye to eye but I wouldn't wish death on nobody. We may have had our differences but over all Desmond was a good dude that was just into some bad shit. "What he was tryna' rob somebody?" I guessed, knowing what line of business Desmond was in.

KT nodded his head but didn't say anything at first. Then, after a brief moment of silence between us he finally spoke up. "Yo' babymomma went too far this time bruh." I stared at him hard, jaws clenched. "I don't wanna say it's her fault because I know she didn't mean for shit to go down like that but all this bullshit stemmed from what she had going on." I used my right hand to rub my goatee between my tattooed fingers. KT followed me to my rack where he sat down and told me what all he knew was facts because I didn't give a fuck about what the streets was saying. Everybody would tell the same story with a different twist, their own version of what happened based on a few loose facts and their opinion. I wanted the true story. The more KT talked the more heated I became. By the time he was through I was fuming. Knowing how quick I could go from zero to one hundred, KT tried to calm me down by rationalizing the story on Mercedez's behalf. "I mean, she was probably just fuckin' wit' bruh so she could figure out how to rob him the whole time. She said the nigga owe you two hunned racks. I don't just see her rockin' wit da opps for no good reason bro."

"Say bruh, I know you love Mercedez like a sister and y'all done been through some shit together but you don't know her like you think you know her. So, don't try to sugar coat shit cuz it is what it is."

"I'm just sayin," KT went on to defend her anyway. "I know Mercedez be havin' some crazy ass ideas and she don't always think shit through but you know like I do her intentions are always good. This time shit just got out of hand. I bet this whole Tragic shit was about gettin' to the money, nothing more, nothing less."

"And she had to fuck the nigga to do that?" I scoffed. "Get the fuck outta here with that bullshit KT, Mercedez on some get-back shit. Out there doin' that thot ass shit bruh."

"She must've found out about you and Krystal," KT said. "Because I can't see you lettin' another bitch come in between y'all but I told you Krystal was trouble."

"Krystal's aight, it's not her fault"

"The bitch is bad news bruh. Period. Always have been and always will be."

"How the fuck you gone say what somebody will be?" I asked.

"Aw, come on man admit it. You just got a soft spot for red-heads." I chuckled at that. "I'm for real bruh, this the same broad that had you wrapped around her fingers in school just to leave you fucked up in the head when she ghosted yo ass. Anyway, I can't believe you was still fuckin' with ole girl, I thought you and Mercedez was on good terms."

"We were," I said solemnly. "This Krystal shit happened last year when Tragic was still locked up. I broke that shit off before the nigga even got out because I went back home. The bitch just can't let go, no matter how many times I tell her it's over and I have a family. She don't give a fuck about none of that shit. She want a nigga home life fucked up so I can be free to be with her. But it's not her fault. I have to take some responsibility for her feelings because I kept leading her on for a while."

"Okay, Dr.Phil, even if all that's true," KT said, "Mercedez love yo ass, she'll come around."

I scoffed. "Nah, she can stay laid up with Tragic black ass. Sound like she givin' that nigga hell. Better him than me." The words tasted salty coming out of my mouth. Truth was, I wanted my girl back. How could she just leave me in here to die? Because that's what it felt like. I was dying a little bit more daily without her. Sneaking around with Krystal was wrong but the shit Mercedez was doing was straight foul. She cut me deep this time and I can't lie, the shit hurt. It hurt like hell. She won't even answer the phone for a nigga so I can explain. She was hurt. She had every right to be. Krystal wasn't just your average jump off, the bitch was bad and boujee and to make it worse, I had history with her. If I was honest with myself, I'd even say that I still had feelings for her. Is it possible to love two women at the same time? Did she have real feelings for Tragic? I mean, she had did her thing before when I was locked up in the past that she think I don't know about but the truth was I didn't give a fuck about it because I know the hand I played in that. I had her smiling in the same bitches face that I would drop her off then double back and fuck with. I know I was wrong, but I was young and dumb. I'm wiser now and I've been in here long enough to realize who and what was important to me and who and what is just a distraction. I had to stop fucking up my future by flirting with my past. Krystal was in my past. If I had to choose between her and Mercedez it would be Mercedez everytime. I could forgive my girl for fuckin' with another nigga because I know what I did pushed her into his arms but she was gone have to wrap that shit up before I handled it myself. Just cause I'm locked up don't mean a nigga can't be touched. Then this bitch ass white boy, Trevor, back from the dead and shit. I don't know how this muthafucka still breathing but I had to bring a stop to that asap.

The next morning when shift changed, I went and hollered at the guard, an old school lady that used to run with Janice and asked her to get the 411 on SciFi. Mary had all kinds of connections on both sides of the law, she only worked at the prison as a pastime. Not my idea of a good time but she got paid big money to smuggle almost anything an inmate could ask for without getting caught. When she came back, what she told me blew my mind. Not only was the mothafucka alive, he wasn't even in the witness protection program yet. Her job was to make sure he never made it there. It would be hard because Trevor was in a maximum security prison on money laundering charges waiting for his trial date because he couldn't afford to bond out. Because the case he was building against me was directly related to his charges, he would have to testify against me. Without his testimony the case was dead. Apparently, he would be passing through this facility to get processed at the top of the week. My job was to make sure he never made it out alive.

 The following week came and Trevor arrived at the jail just as expected. I purposefully got into a fight that day so that I would get sent down to the hole, a tiny cell in the basement that had no cameras so no one would see me coming or going. At a quarter till three the lights went out and the cell doors were unlocked because they were electronic. It would take twenty minutes for the generator to kick in so the minute she had the lights cut off, Mary led me out of my cell and up to the holding cell Trevor was in. He didn't even see it coming. I snapped his neck so fast he didn't have time to scream before hitting the cement floor, his skull cracking on impact. By the time the lights came back on I was back in the hole, stretched out on the metal bed like I'd never left. I slept good that night knowing I'd just saved my own life by ending his.

Chapter 28: Tragic

When I saw Mercedez pull up in a dark blue Infiniti I instantly changed my mind about riding off with her. She wasn't about to have me up in another nigga's car, that just wasn't my style. I passed the blunt back to my lil' homie Skoot and told him to take me to my car. We were backed in at the house that sat directly across the street from the corner store. Skoot nodded his head and pulled off, passing right by Mercedez's silly ass. I saw she still had a few things to learn about me. When she called I sent her to voicemail, not wanting the distraction. One of my stash houses had just got hit and I wasn't in the mood to entertain no female noway. Don't get me wrong, Mercedez was good people and all but at the same time, fucking off with her was what was keeping me away from my business lately. If I wouldn't've been so caught up in this girl and what she had going on, I would've been able to focus more on my own shit and this bullshit robbery might not have ever happened in the first place. I made it to my car and after sending Mercedez to voicemail for the third time a text popped up on my screen. *Mercedez: We need to talk. 2057*

Highland square. 911. What the fuck? I jumped in my Tesla and ran through every stop sign till I made it to the highway. I looked at the message again, to make sure I read it correctly, in disbelief. Highland square is the location I keep all my money at. It's the second stash spot but I never told this girl that so how the fuck is she telling me to meet her there? The only bitch that ever stepped foot in that spot was Krystal. "Fuck!" I yell, banging my fist on the steering wheel. As soon as I get there I see the Infiniti parked outside and I pull up behind her and blow the horn. I'm thinking she gone get out of her car and jump in mine but then I see her exit the house, posting up on the front porch. I got out my car and slammed the door so hard I thought the window was going to shatter.

"Let's talk inside," she says, turning toward the front door but I quickly spun her around by the shoulders.

"Nah, we gone talk right here," I said, not trusting the situation. I didn't know what the fuck this girl had going on but she just didn't know, I was two seconds off her ass, and I didn't hit women. There was no way I was following her inside and risk possibly running into an ambush.

"Fine," she said, slapping my hand off her shoulder. She took a seat on the concrete stoop and pulled out a box of Newport shorts. She lit a cigarette before speaking. "I guess you're wondering why we're here. Well you don't have anything to worry about; we're alone."

"Fuck you mean we alone? What happened to my men?" I asked.

"They're fine. I sent them away."

I scoffed in disbelief. "And they just listened to you without gettin' at me first?"

"Oh they called, but you didn't answer," she said, montioning to my phone. I looked at the screen and saw that I had two missed calls besides hers. "You'd be surprised what these thirsty ass niggas will do for a bitch when they think they got a shot at some pussy," she said matter of factly. I frowned at that. I didn't like the idea of no nigga thinking he had a chance with no bitch that I was fuckin'. Noticing my screw face, Mercedez laughed. "Not with me crazy, they left with a couple of my homegirls. I nodded, making a mental note to put a bullet in both of them niggas skull for not using their brain. "The feds are planning to raid this spot, my people sent me the address. I have some friends downtown that don't want to see me locked up but I'm a direct link to you so unless we do something, it's likely that I'll end up behind bars. We need to load up all this money and dope and get it the fuck out now. I got an empty storage unit in the suburbs that we can use until we figure out our next move."

I raised an eyebrow, wondering where all this, "we,we,we," was coming from because I didn't remember her telling me she could speak french. "Hold up Mercedez, you not calling the shots here. First I'mma need you to tell me everything you know so I can make a hypothesis on what the next move should be."

"I just told you everything I know," she said, motioning towards the house. "So make your next move your best move." I followed her inside. Her heels clicked and clacked against the hardwood floor beneath our feet. I didn't like being told what to do but at the same time I wasn't sure what the fuck to do yet, I just needed to stay out of jail so loading the money and product up and moving it to the suburbs seemed like the best possible solution at the time. I agreed to load everything up in her trunk and back seat for her to take to the storage. She said if we were on the radar, my car was hot so it didn't make sense for me to transport it myself. It took us about thirty minutes to load it all up. As soon as I slammed the trunk closed we heard sirens drawing nearer by the second so I high-tailed it behind Mercedez who was headed to the suburbs. A little over an hour later I stepped out of my car and noticed just how ducked off we really were from the city. You could kill a muthafucka and take the body out here and no one would probably find it for weeks. We were past the suburbs. We were in the country. As soon as Mercedez stepped out of the car her phone started ringing. After rummaging through her Birkin bag for a minute, she found the phone and placed it to her ear. I didn't know who was on the line but they gave Mercedez some news that brought her to her knees. I rushed to her side, trying to catch her as she collapsed to the ground. "No, No, Noooo!" she was wailing. "God no!" I asked her what was wrong and what she told me made my heart sink. It was her little cousin. Apparently, her twins had been abducted from their bedroom in the middle of the night. I hugged her tight in an attempt to comfort her as the panic set in but she pushed me off of her and demanded that we go join the search for the girls immediately. Once we were inside the car I peeled off as fast as I could. Her phone started ringing and when she saw it was a private number she quickly swiped right to answer it. "Who is this?" she asked desperately. A distorted voice that sounded like it was slowed down by a computer app came through the phone's speaker phone. The caller was demanding two hundred and fifty thousand dollars and we had seventy two hours to get it. The kidnapper warned her not to go to the police or the girls would be killed. I wanted for the mufuckas that were behind this to die. The money wasn't an issue, I would give her whatever she needed to bring her daughters home safely. It was then I realized just how hard I was rockin' with shorty. She had come into my life and had a nigga nose wide open. She made it easy to forget about my ex, like I really hadn't thought of Krystal unil last night when she was hittin' my line back to back on some bug-a-boo shit, Just then, her name and picture flashed across my screen and again, I sent it to voicemail. I had some serious shit going on and I had to focus on the situation at hand. Mercedez was now crying hysterically into my shoulder and I knew I needed to be her knight in shining armor on this one so I clicked Krystal's crazy ass to voicemail again, then shoved the phone in my pocket. Looking back and forth between her and the road, I tried to wipe away her tears but to no avail, her solem cries were like a stream flowing from a river, endless. I grabbed her left shoulder with my right hand and shook her gently. I then grabbed her chin and tilted her head up , forcing her to look me in the eyes.

"Do you trust me?" I asked her as the tears spilled over on to my wrist and down to my elbow. She nodded. "I'm going to handle this shit for you and kill the muthafuckas that's behind it," I said, trying to reassure her. "I got you," I said, kissing her soft, pouty lips, her nose and her forehead.

The next two days crept by slowly as we waited for the phone to ring. I had Mercedez and the kids come and stay with me so I could keep a close eye on them. I wasn't about to let them get snatched up on my watch so I gladly welcomed them into my home.

"Eat love," I urged her, holding a grilled turkey sandwich from Newk's in front of her. She shook her head no and slowly pushed my hand back down. She just sat there looking out into empty space. Dark circles had formed under her eyes that were swollen from crying. I sighed. "At least drink somethin' then." I placed the straw between her lips and she obliged. I felt my phone vibrating in my jeans but I waited for her to finish the smoothie before I averted my attention. When I finally looked at the number I frowned. It was Krystal again. She had really been blowing a nigga up these past couple of days and I was starting to wonder what the hell was up with her all of a sudden because she hadn't been on my dick this much since I put her ass on ice for cheating. I was about to just block her damn number when a text came through. *We need to talk, don't trust Mercedez, call me.* I laughed dismissively, thinking, is that what this was about- she's jealous of my lady? I kissed Mercedez on her head and told her I would be back. I had two goons at the door, Lil' Skoot and another nigga. They wasn't letting nobody in or out. If she needed anything all she had to do was call me. I had been spending more time in the streets for the past couple of days trying to ease my anxiety and at the same time give Mercedez and her kids the space they needed. My condo was much safer so going back to her house wasn't even an option.

I filled a suitcase up with two hundred and fifty thousand dollars and put it in the trunk of my car. I wanted to be ready when the call came to get the twins back. Paying the money wasn't exactly a part of my plan, it was a last resort. I planned to get the suitcase back but just in case I made sure every dollar was in there. Getting the lil' shorties back was well worth the money. Against my better judgment I picked up the phone and called Krystal. "What's good?" I asked when she picked up on the first ring.

"Is she around you?"

"No," I said, growing impatient with her bullshit already.

"Good."

"What's this about K?"

"Meet me at our spot. We need to talk *now,*" she said. Before I could convince myself why I shouldn't give a fuck I was headed to the resuraunt, *Nannie Mac's*. It was where we first hung out together, like a semi-first date or something. I guess it was curiosity that drove me over there because other than that I had no desire to be in this girl's presence. It wasn't always like that. Once upon a time I adored Krystal. She used to be the Bonnie to my Clyde out here in these streets. When we met we fell in love instantly. She was what you would call a bad bitch because she had her own shit and she didn't need no nigga. A crazy ass redhead from New Orleans that stole my heart, I never thought our love would end. I was blind enough to believe I was the nigga for her when in fact, another nigga held the keys to her heart. I did some investigating on the matter and come to find out her and the nigga Solo were like distant lovers or some shit. They had this romantic ass back story from growing up together to being each other's first love. They had a whole life in Hattiesburg together when the whole time I thought I was bringing the bitch here from New Orleans to start a new life and she already had one. Why nobody told me this shit before was beyond me, I know I'm not the friendliest muthafucka breathing but I'm approachable. The phone started ringing through my car speaker and I saw lil' Skoot's number go across the screen in the digital dash board. "What's up?" I answered.

"Yo, Tragic, I got somethin' to tell you and you ain't gone like it," Skoots voice came through my speakers

I scowled, not wanting to hear anymore bad news. I hoped it had nothing to do with Mercedez.

They were supposed to be watching her! "Spit it out."

"I just had to rough up one of them lil' young niggas you got on the block."

I frowned. "For what?"

"For selling that shit to the wrong girl." My heart dropped and I knew who he was referring to before he even spoke her name. "It's Satajiah," Skoot confirmed in a low tone. "She out here on a binge again man, I can tell she been up for a few days." I shook my head as he continued. "She went off on me, called me all kind of bitch ass niggas but I still scooped her little ass up and put her in the car. I locked her in there while I stepped out to call you. What you want me to do?" I blew out a breath, exasperated. I'd been through this so many times with this girl that I'd lost count. Satajiah was a full blown meth attic. I'd tried to save her so many times, take her off the streets and get her cleaned up. But you know how the saying goes, "You can lead a horse to the water but you can't make him drink." I loved Satajiah with all my heart; besides my mother, I'd never loved a girl more than I did her but she was testing my gangsta. I'll air out the block before I sit back and let them niggas serve her. It was a catch twenty two because I was the one flooding the blocks with the dope.

"Take her to the pent house," I ordered. "Keep her there until I get there. I don't care if it take three days for me to get there, do not let her out of your sight."

"Say less," Skoot said. "But what you want me to do about the nigga that was servin' her?"

"Finish him," I said coldly. "I told them niggas not to serve her and he did anyway. Let him be an example to the rest of them niggas and whoever else go against my word." I ended the call. I wasn't usually a violent mufucka but I'd body any nigga that hindered Satajiah's sobriety. I had already lost my father to crack when I was a kid so I'd be damned if I lost my sister to drugs too. My mother had washed her hands with both of them a long time ago so I was all my baby sister had. How she got strung out on drugs so bad wasn't exactly clear to me but I knew it had a lot to do with that nigga Deon she met at Tennessee State. My sister left Mississippi as an intelligent, beautiful, and driven young woman who was enthusiastic about life and came back a full blown drug attic. She seemingly gave up on life because she was slowly killing herself as if she didn't have anything to live for. I tried helping her so many times but like a moth to a flame she'd gravitate back to the streets every time. Satajiah was what you'd call a binge smoker. She'd be clean for weeks, months even, then out the blue go on a smoking binge getting high for days. I'd find her, clean her up and help her get back on track but after a while she would always go back. It may seem pointless but I'm never going to give up on her. I run my hand over my waves, something I tended to do when i was thinking then continued to weave in and out of traffic, heading towards Nannie Mac's.

Chapter 29: Krystal

Before leaving the house to go meet Tragic, I run back upstairs to check on the two little girls I have tied up in my bedroom. Two wooden chairs sat back to back in the middle of the plush room and Mercedez's twin brats sat in them, whimpering like little puppies. I pulled the duck tape off their mouths. The room was soundproof anyway. One of my side hustles was being an Only Fans porn star and my neighbors started to complain about all the noise so I soundproofed the entire top floor. "Now," I said, squatting down so I could be at eye level with the girls. "You have nothing to worry about. Everything will turn out just fine. I'm not going to hurt you. Do you understand?" Both girls nodded their heads.

"But I want to go *ho-ome*," one wined.

"Our mommy is going to be worried about us," said the other.

I marveled at how well they spoke at three years old. "Well as soon as your mommy delivers my package you guys are free to go. But for tonight, you are here with us." They both dropped their chins to their tiny little chests and tears streamed down one of their faces. The other seemed tougher than her sister. She seemed braver with thicker skin, like at just three years old, life had hardened her. Then again, with Mercedez as a mother there wasn't no telling what the girl had seen or been through. I know Mercedez had a history with drugs and had not always been the great mother she claims to be. Reminds me of my own mother. She used to be too high to give a fuck about what was going on with me. That's probably why I got pregnant at the age of thirteen. I know I broke my father's heart with that one. I was his only girl and even though we didn't live with each other, our bond was unbreakable. He died of congestive heart failure a few days after he found out I was pregnant. I think I broke his heart.

The loud voice behind me boomed and snapped me back to the present. "Why the fuck would you untie them?" he barked. I turned around and faced my brother.

"Because they're harmless and hungry. I'm going over to Nannie Mac's to get them some food. They haven't had a meal since we took them two days ago!" I was down with the kidnapping but I wasn't about to starve them to death. We needed them alive if we wanted to get the money.

Psycho scoffed. "Why the fuck you so worried about these little mufuckas anyway? We just using they asses for bait. They are the meal!" He started chuckling but I didn't see shit funny. I wasn't down for killing no little kids. We're supposed to be in this for the money, nothing more, nothing less. That two hundred k was sill on the table and I wanted my piece of the pie . Matter fact, I want the whole pie! I seriously doubted Mercedez was going to hold up her end of the bargain and pay me anyway because I haven't heard from her since she called and said she was going with plan b. Well this is plan c. So even if her plan b worked it would come back to me. Psycho was the muscle of my operation, I included him because the work came from Psycho and it was on consignment so he still hasn't been paid. I know my brother is ruthless and will do whatever it takes to make that bitch pay. He don't care if it's women or children- nobody's safe!

On the ride to Nannie Mac's I tried to come up with the words to say to seduce Tragic back into my arms by convincing him that Mercedez is no good for him. One thing about Tragic, if you're his girl his money is our money and i needed my money back. There wasn't no telling how long Solo would be locked up and I wasn't about to be out here broke. I'd convince Tragic to leave

Mercedez because that rat doesn't deserve the kind of love or money he has to give. I figured I had a shot. After all, this man really loved me at one point. And if I can just let Solo go I can learn to love him too. I crank up my Mercedes Benz and head towards fourth street where the restaurant is, anticipating this reunion with my estranged boyfriend. It's funny how your life can be going one way and with a blink of the eye everything changes. I was tired of rolling with the punches. It was time I dominated life and started calling the shots.

When I saw the Denali pull up in front of the restaurant, I straightened out my black, silk blouse and ran my fingers along my edges to make sure my hair was still intact. I had on Levi' jeans and a pair of black Dior slip-on heels. When he walked in, I was taken aback a little at first. *Damn, I don't remember him being this damn fine*, I thought. He was sexy as fuck. He had on black jeans, a crisp white tee, black *Timberland* boots, and, bling everywhere. From his ear to his neck, to his wrist and his fingers Tragic was drippin' in diamonds. I felt my juices start to flow, causing my panties to moisten. At that moment I started to daydream about his chocolate toned skin all over my vanilla toned body and I realized how much I missed him. I stood to greet him, flinging my arms around his neck and giving him a quick peck on the cheek.

"What's good ma?" he asked, pulling his fitted baseball cap low over his eyes. I hated when he did that because it made him hard to read. I needed to know where his head was at and know how he was reacting to my words so I'd know what angle to take.

"Hey Ahmad, how have you been?" I asked him sincerely.

"I've been good, what's good with you? You said you got somethin' to tell me, what's up?"

"It's about Mercedez," I started.

"Of course it is."

"You don't know her how you think you know her."

"How you know what I think?" I asked rhetorically.

"I'm just saying, she's been playing you the whole time."

He laughed. "Playin' me how, like how you was playing me when you was fuckin' dude?"

I rolled my eyes. "This isn't about him. I'm really tryna look out for you."

He scoffed. "Oh, like you were looking out for me by telling me straight up you was a fuckin hoe?"

"This isn't about me either."

He smiled at that. "Isn't it always about you though?" He asked, leaning in. *You* were supposed to be my bitch. *You* got caught cheating. *You* was out here suckin' dick while I was locked up. *You* the one sittin' up here hatin' on my new lady."

"Your new lady?" I asked with an arched eyebrow.

Ignoring me he said, "And whatever you think you bout to roll up in here and tell me about her, save that shit and tell me why you here without my son. Where is he?"

"He spent the weekend with my brother and his babymomma, is that a problem?"

"Hell yeah it's a problem! My son don't need to be around that toxic ass shit they be on, you can bring him to me."

"That's his uncle and his biological aunt, they have a right to be around him."

"Fuck that, that's my son. I raised him. You can be a hoe all you want and hop from dick to dick but you won't be taking my son with you. I'll go to court and have him taken from you."

I dropped my mouth incredulously, in shock at the fact he was actually speaking to me like this. The nigga got some new pussy and now he wanna act brand new? I was going to warn him about his new piece of ass he was laying up with and knock the bitch he thought so highly of off her pedestal. I wanted to burst that bubble so damn bad.I wanted to warn him about how dangerous this girl really was but the way he was talking to me and looking at me disgustingly made me change my mind. While he's worried about taking my child, I hope that bitch takes him for everything he got! He sounded like he was going to give her the two hundred and fifty grand and when he did it was all going to me anyway. So I win either way. I smirked and grabbed my Louis Vuitton clutch. "Well I guess we're done here," I said.

"We been done," was his response. He pushed his chair back and stood up to leave.

I grabbed his arm. "Wait," I pleaded. I started rummaging through my purse until I found a picture of me and him that I printed through facebook Portal. "At least let me give you this so you can remember at one point in time, we were in love." He yanked his arm back, taking the picture without even taking so much as a glance at it and walked out. I shook my head in disbelief then got up from the table and approached the counter to order the girls' food. I couldn't believe Tragic came at me like that. And to think, I was going to help his black ass by telling him what the real deal was with Mercedez. Now, he was going to have to find out for himself what type of snake ass bitch he was dealing with. He can sleep with the enemy all he wants, my payday is coming regardless.

While I'm waiting on my food I get a collect call from Solo. I press 1 to accept the charges then I hear his voice on the other end. "Hello?"

"Hey," I say with a smile. "How are you?"

I can hear the pain in his voice when he says, "My girls have been kidnapped," and it makes me sick to my stomach. A lump forms in my throat and I struggle to think of the right words to say. To be honest, I hadn't even thought about how my plan might affect him.

"Kidnapped?" I say, trying to sound surprised. "Oh my God, by whom?"

"By a broke ass ma'fucka that wants a ransom. Have you talked to Tragic? I need that money now more than ever. I'm confined within these walls so my resources are limited. I feel so fuckin' helpless," he sulked.

"No, he doesn't fuck with me anymore since he's been around Mercedez," I said. "But knowing Ahmad, he's going to give her the money to get them back, that's just what type of nigga he is."

"It ain't like it's a muthafuckin hand out, that shit belongs to me! That's why I need to hurry up and get the fuck out of here." I could hear the pain in his voice and hated that I was the cause of it. I had to be careful to make sure my identity as the kidnapper remained anonymous or Solo would never forgive me.

    I paid for my food, grabbed the bags, and managed to cradle the phone between my ear and my shoulder. "So what's going on with that?" I asked, using my butt to push the restaurant door open so I could exit . "What is your lawyer saying?" I had hired a lawyer to help him beat the case.

    "They working on getting the new charges dropped but I might have to sit this violation of probation out."

    "Well just be patient, it will work itself out. And as for your little girls, I'll pray that they make it home safe and sound." We said our goodbyes and exchanged "I love you"s before hanging up.

    When I got back to the house, the smell of kush filled my nostrils as soon as I opened the door. Psycho was passed out on my couch, blunt in hand. I took his blunt with me to my room so I could smoke before I ate. When I made it to my bedroom, the girls were hurled up in a corner, holding each other as they slept. A pang of guilt hit my stomach and I asked myself, "What the fuck are you doing?" I've done some crazy shit in my life but I think I may have gone too far this time. "Girls," I say loudly enough to stir them out of their sleep. "Come eat," I instructed them. Slowly, they made their way over to me. I handed them both a bag filled with burgers, fries, and cookies and then I sat on my bed with my own food. In less than twenty-four hours I'd be a quarter million richer but at what cost? I took Solo's little girls and once I delivered them back to their mother I could never be around them again without them knowing me as their kidnapper. How was I supposed to have a serious future with their father without crossing paths with them at some point or another. I needed to spin the narrative in my favor. "Twins," I say, getting their attention. "I want to help you get home and away from the bad guy that took you away from your mommy. But if I help you, you must promise one thing; that you'll never tell ANYONE I was here. If you do, the bad man will come and take you again. Do you understand?" They nodded their heads in response and I heaved a heavy sigh of relief. I sparked my blunt and took a few puffs. Before I knew it, I was out like a light. The girls, not knowing what to do, also climbed in the bed and fell asleep too. Tomorrow was the big day that would hopefully work in everyone's favor.

Chapter 29: Mercedez

    I was extremely grateful for Tragic taking me and the kids in and making sure we were safe, sound, and secure. I didn't know what I would've done without him being there for me like he had been the past couple of days. He opened up his home, his heart, and his wallet and I would be forever indebted to him for that. I never really had a plan when I convinced him to move his money to my storage, I was just free styling and going with the flow, trying to make my next move my best move. I'll be the first to admit that I never think a plan all the way through. I'm glad I didn't though because as sweet as he'd been to me, I would've been playing myself if I had robbed him. Two hundred and fifty dollars seemed so futile now, compared to the lives of my twins. It left me wondering why I was going so hard for the cash in the first place. People are either naturally greedy or the spirit of mammon is a common spirit in these last days we're living in. What other explanation was there for somebody demanding that much money from someone with six kids? I wondered who was behind this bullshit. Everybody was suspect as far as i was concerned. And that number, that ransom was significant because I didn't believe in coincidences. The streets were talking, everybody thought I had the quarter mill when in reality I ain't have shit. I knew Tragic was only giving me the money because it was rightfully Solo's in the first place. He acted like his intentions were pure, but I knew better.

I heard a knock at the door and I peered through the peephole and saw Tragic standing there with a low cap and a hoodie. I didn't have to see his eyes to know if it was him, I knew his style. No one that I knew had swagger like him. His whole demeanor screamed money and any other day that would have made my panties wet but today was not the day for all that. "Where've you been?" I asked him, latching all the deadbolts back into place.

"In the streets," he said, pulling me in his arms. My nostrils are filled with Tom Ford cologne and I bury my face in the nape of his neck. Because of him in less than twelve hours I would have my twins back. I owed him everything for that. Regardless of his reason. I tilted my head up and kissed him with so much passion I surprised myself. A part of me wanted to love this man, to be *in* love with this man but the logical part of me knew that I'd screwed up so bad that it wouldn't be possible. In order to do that, I would have to confess and come clean with my intentions from the start if I wanted to be genuine with him. On the contrary, what he doesn't know can't hurt him, right? I try to push the notion out of my head but still I found myself following him into the master bathroom, gazing at him as he undressed for a shower. He nodded his head back, motioning for me to come join him. "It'll make you feel better," he said. I walked in slowly and pulled off my clothes. I stepped into the steaming shower with him and allowed the warm water to hit my body. He picked up my Olay liquid soap and squeezed some onto a sponge. He then proceeded to wash me from the neck down, not leaving one spot untouched. I stood beneath the sprayer allowing the soap to wash off my body. I had to admit, it did make me feel a little better. Wanting to return the favor, I took his washcloth out of his hand and squeezed some Old Spice soap on it. As I washed him he held his head down, letting the water run over his head and he placed both hands on the wall.

"What's wrong?" I asked, noticing the tension in his back.

He held his head up and allowed the water to rinse the soap off of his strong, muscular body. "Nothing I can't handle love," he answered. "What's the word about the case and the feds and shit, I know it didn't just go away."

"Oh my god," I said. "I've been so worried about my own shit that I forgot to tell you that the shit really did go away. At least for now."

His thick eyebrows shot up in surprise. "How is that?"

"Trevor is dead Aamahd. The case died with him." Tragic gave me a skeptical look and I placed my hands on his broad shoulders. "It's over." He grabbed me by my waist and turned me around, bending me over. I felt him enter me from behind and my breath caught in my throat. My eyes closed and I moaned as he pumped in and out of me, plunging so deep it felt like he was in my stomach while he pounded me over and over. There was a loud smacking sound as my skin hit his and the water splashed in between us. I turned wetter than the water as he quickly brought me to my climax, causing me to feel an orgasmic high. When I felt him swelling up inside of me I turned around and dropped to my knees and swallowed the dick as he pushed in and out of my throat. His nut tasted sweet so I swallowed it, allowing him to relieve every drop of semen in my mouth. When we were finished we washed again before we turned the water off and stepped out of the shower. I was exhausted, realizing I hadn't slept in almost three days. I checked on the kids then went and laid in Tragic's king size bed and as soon as my head hit the pillow I started to drift off to sleep. When I awoke, the clock read 6:53 am. I decided to let Tragic sleep while I took the kids to school. Not sure where i put my keys, I opted to take the Denali instead. Although I had never driven his truck before, I was sure he wouldn't mind me using it to run the kids to school, so I slipped on my slippers and his robe and quietly eased out the door with the kids behind me.

"Mom, can I sit in the front seat?" my middle son asked me.

"No way," my oldest son said. "I'm the oldest, I should get to ride in the front."

"I wasn't talking to you. I was talking to mom!"

My oldest son, ignoring my middle son, pushed past him and stood at the front passenger door.

"Hey! No fair!"

"Don't push your brother like that," I said, unlocking the doors.

My baby boy slipped past them both and jumped in the front seat, saying "Ah-hah!" sticking his tongue out mockingly while my oldest pretended to punch him,

"Cut it out!" I warned them as I hopped in the driver seat. The baby boy handed me a stack of what looked like junk mail to make room for him to sit. "Thanks," I said, grabbing the stack to throw it in the garbage can. As I was walking, a picture slipped out and landed upside down on my feet. I bent down to pick it up and read the words, "Forever Mines" with a heart around it. I knew it was none of my business but my curiosity weighed in and caused me to flip the picture over. My breath caught in my throat as I stared at a photo of Tragic and Krystal half naked on a boat holding half filled wine glasses up and smiling side by side, their free arms wrapped around each other. The picture had yesterday's date on it and I know the picture wasn't taken yesterday so that meant it was printed yesterday. I quickly grew envious and before I knew it, I had ripped the picture in two halves, then four quarters, then six parts, crumbling their smug little faces piece by piece. The lying ass nigga was probably with her yesterday while he was telling me he was in the streets. I didn't know where the sudden wave of jealousy came from, Tragic wasn't my man and at the same time, he wasn't hers either. I wasn't exactly feeling the fact that he still had pictures of her anyway, posted up in his ride like he missed her or some shit. And here I was feeling bad for plotting on his ass when in reality he deserved that shit. How could he claim to care deeply for me when I'm finding pictures of him and his ex in his truck like he's been riding around missing her? I wasn't trippin', I'd use that nigga to get my kids back and then turn around and rob his ass like I was supposed to from the start. I was tired of these niggas playing with my heart like a toy, it was about to be game over!

Chapter 30: Tragic

I walked out of Nannie Mac's looking for a trash can to throw this old ass picture in. I only glanced at it, not wanting to look at it too long and be reminded of the times I had with her. Those days were long gone. After looking around for a garbage can and not spotting one, I got in my truck, photo in hand, and threw it on top of some junk mail. I'd been intending to throw the mail out anyway and I could send that picture right with it. I was doing a hundred on the freeway, nodding my head back and forth to Drake's latest hit, anticipating getting back home to my queen and taking a shower because I'd been out in the streets all day. When I got home I jumped in the shower with my lady and we made love beneath the water. I was feeling emotions for her I'd never felt for anyone before, like she could be my future wife. We smoked a blunt and chilled till we fell asleep. I hadn't had a good night's sleep in days. It felt good to be sleeping with a real woman and not no gold digging little girl who threw fits and jumped to vain conclusions, accusing me of whatever she thought I was doing when I was away from her. Mercedez didn't mind a nigga being in the streets as long as I came home with a bag my boo was straight. That's why I vowed to keep it a hundred with her like she's been with me. When all this is over I plan on telling her exactly how I feel about her.

I woke up to the sound of keys jingling in the door and I wonder where she'd been this early in the morning. She looked distressed when she came into the room without even greeting me. "Well damn, I know I slept with you last night but can a nigga at least get a "good morning"?" I frowned, not liking the "fuck you" vibes she was giving off. At first she had me wondering if I'd done something wrong for her to be giving me the cold shoulder but then, I chalked it up to her being stressed about the twins.

"The exchange is at noon," she finally said. "Are you ready to head that way?"

"Yeah," I said getting out the bed and slipping on my boxers. "It's going to take us two hours to make it to State Line and we still have to find the exact location. Any idea why they want to do this on Alabama's border?"

"I don't know," she said plopping down on the bed. When I leaned in to kiss her she abruptly jumped back up leaving my lips hanging in the air.

What was that all about? I wondered but decided not to speak on it. She had enough on her mind as it was and I didn't want to add more stress. We got dressed without saying much and the ride there was filled with an awkward silence. I wanted to talk to her about the status of our relationship while we had the opportunity but now didn't seem like the right timing. She didn't seem like she was in the mood for love. *Love??* I was shocked at my own thoughts. The L word had never been in my vocabulary before, at least not in that context. I knew I had strong feelings for her but was it really *love*? It must've been what love felt like. Waking up and going to sleep in each other's arms, making love every chance we got and constantly wanting to be in each other's presence? Wanting to share your truths with them and keep no secrets from them? Being with someone who made you feel like your life began with them and somehow nothing or no one before them mattered? I thought about Krystal and how I had been simply passing time with her because with her, I felt none of those things. Suddenly I remembered the picture she'd given me the day before and I realized I hadn't thrown it away because the junk mail was still sitting on the dash. I wanted to find it and burn it because I had no intention of going down memory lane with Krystal and I didn't want Mercedez to find it and get the impression that I was missing her or something. I had no plans of haunting my present with my past. The GPS came through the speakers, "in one mile your destination will be on the right." I frowned, noticing there wasn't a building in sight. "The fuck they on, some wild wild west, mexican stand off type shit?" I ask with a frown. Mercedez didn't respond; she simply shrugged her shoulders. Fed up with her shitty attitude I decided to say something to her about it. "You wanna tell me how long you gone keep the attitude?"

"You wanna tell me why you're keeping pictures of your ex?' she shot back. Damn, she had found Krystal's photo. So that's what this is about.

"Look, I can explain," I started but she wasn't about to let me finish.

"Then on top of that, you riding around with the shit so that makes me not trust you because now I'm questioning if you're really in the streets or are you laid up somewhere with a bitch because the picture was printed yesterday, so you can't say it's old," she huffed, folding her arms across her chest.

Knowing she's used to being cheated on, I try to choose my words wisely, not wanting to sound like I thought she was damaged goods. "You've been hurt before but I'm not the nigga to hurt you. I'm not him." She glared at me until the GPS announced we had arrived at our destination. I looked up to see we were in front of an abandoned school building. It looked creepy as fuck. Half the roof was torn, one side was partially burned off and the entire frame leaned a little from years of weatherization. I immediately grew angry knowing the twins were somewhere in that hell hole. "Make the call," I instructed her and she nodded her head in response. She pulled her cell phone out of her purse and noticed she had no connection out here. "Use my phone," I said, tossing her my iphone. When she placed the call, the auto-tune voice started to give her specific instructions. They wanted her to walk inside with the money and take the stairs to the basement. Then she was to open the door and drop the money in the middle of the floor. There, she would find a note telling her where to get the kids. I scowled when they said "Come alone!". "Hell no," I protested. I didn't like the sound of none of that shit.

"Look," Mercedez said, taking my hands. "We have to do this the way they tell us to ensure that we get the kids back safely. Let's not be difficult and just get this over with." Her voice was shaky and I could see the fear in her eyes and I knew she was right. The last thing we wanted was for them to do something to the kids. This was something she had to do alone. I popped open the glove compartment and pulled out a small .38 caliber pistol. I made sure it was loaded with one in the chamber before I handed it to her.

"Put that in your pocket," I told her, then I opened up the console and pulled out a chrome .22. "Put that in your boot." She tucked them away like I told her. "Let off a shot if anything goes wrong and I'm coming in." I gave her a kiss and then she opened the door to get out of the car. She looked at me like she was feeling indifferent, like she was unsure of something but she said nothing as she walked away. About five minutes go by and there's no sign of Mercedez or the twins. After another five minutes I heard the shot fired. I hopped out the car and took off towards the building. When I reach the door I see the kids running down a flight of stairs. I rushed in to get them and carried them both out in my arms. I didn't stop running until I reached the car. I locked them in and told them not to move, that I'll be right back with their mommy. "Mercedez!" I yelled, calling out for her and all the while praying that nothing had happened to her. I eased up the steps with my back against the wall, holding my gun up, ready for action. When I stumbled across Psycho's lifeless body I was confused like a muthafucka. What the fuck was he doing there? It couldn't have been him behind the kidnapping all along, could it? Bitch ass nigga. When I called out to Mercedez and heard no answer my heart started pounding in my chest. Please God, don't let nothing have happened to my girl. I checked every room on the top floor except for the last one on the left. I crept that way, mentally trying to prepare myself for what I would possibly find. I pushed open the door and found myself staring down the barrel of the same .38 I had just given to Mercedez. She held the gun shakily as she pointed the other at a smiling Krystal. "What the fuck?" I asked, looking back and forth between the two of them. I thought about slapping the .38 out of Mercedez's hand because she was so unsteady with the gun but then I figured I'd get hit with the .22 if I tried that. Suddenly I hear police sirens far off in the background. "Do somebody want to tell me what the fuck is going on here?" I asked them.

"You tell me," Mercedez said. "Because according to her I'm the only one that's in the dark. So please, shed light on this situation. You were leaving me to go back to this bitch?"

"Tell her baby," Krystal said with her hands up. "Tell her how you're done with her and how you knew she was using you! Tell her where you were yesterday." She looked at Mercedez. "He wasn't even going to give you the ransom money, I had to beg on your behalf, not because I give a fuck about you or your kids, I just wanted the money." She looked back at me. "Tell her what you told me yesterday."

"Yeah, please, tell me baby," Mercedez said to me mockingly.

"Bitch, are you fuckin' serious right now?" I growled at Krystal. I looked at Mercedez. "She's lying."

"You want to be with her so bad that it was fuck me and my kids huh?" Mercedez asked with tears in her eyes. "You want her so bad, go on over there and stand next to her so you two silly muthafuckas can die together." She waved the gun in Krystal's direction and I knocked it out of her hand, not realizing I was making it look like I was trying to protect Krystal. However, I was already planning to knock it out her hand, it had nothing to do with Krystal. I just wanted the gun out of Mercedez's possession. Krystal turned to run but Mercedez quickly retrieved the other gun I had given her from her boot. When the .22 went off, Krystal's body dropped with a loud thud. The bullet went straight through her back. By the time Mercedez looked back at me I had my own gun pointed at her. We were at a standoff, only I had the bigger, more powerful gun. I steadied the glock 9, aiming it right between her eyes.

"You wouldn't," she said and I let off my shot without hesitation. I aimed with precision so I didn't miss my target. She screamed because that bullet barely missed her head.

"That was a warning," I told her. "Next one's going in your skull." I expected her to start crying and pleading for her life as I went around the room collecting guns, all the while still aiming the 9mm at her. But she did neither.

Instead she put her hands on her hips and said with a neck roll, "So it's fuck me and my kids? Fuck you nigga."

"What the fuck you want from me?" I asked. "If that's the case, was she telling the truth about you just using me?"

Her silence spoke volumes.

"You were playing me anyway," she finally said. I saw the picture in your truck. You fucking love her. Or should I say *loved*?"

I looked at Krystal's bloody body and frowned. "Are you serious? She gave that picture to me yesterday when I went to see her-" I kicked myself, knowing I had said the wrong thing.

Mercedez's face twisted up and she said, "So you did go see her? I should've known you were a liar but I pegged you as different. I sure hope it was worth it."

Frustrated, I started rubbing my head with my free hand. "Man…" my voice trailed off as Krystal started to move around and moan. Mercedez walked right up to that bitch, knelt down, and spit on her. She was about to shoot her again until I grabbed her by the wrists. "What the fuck?" I exclaimed.

"What?" Mercedez asked, looking at me with a vindictive look in her eyes. "The bitch talk too much."

"We don't have time for this shit, your kids are probably terrified," I said truthfully. "Fuck Krystal, she can die slow. I'm mad she didn't get a chance to tell you the truth, that she called *me* yesterday with something important to tell me about you! She gave me that picture and I took it to throw the shit in the trash but once I made it home to you I forgot all about the picture because that's the kind of effect you have on me. When I'm near you, all I see is you; all I want is you." Her eyes began to mist as mine pleaded with hers. "Look baby, I know you not used to a man treating you right but like I told you, I'm not the bad guy. Matter fact, fuck what I told you, what have I shown you? I'm not the bad guy, if anything I'm your knight in shining armor."

"I don't need saving," she said as a single tear escaped from her eye. All I wanted to do in that moment was hold her. This beautiful woman was standing in front of me allowing her wall to come down. My beautiful woman. I lowered my weapon, tucked it behind my back and reached out for her hand, motioning for her to give me the gun. "You can blow my head off or hand me the gun but you better do something quick because we gotta get outta her before the cops come. She tucked the gun in her back pocket and rushed into my arms. The sirens were getting closer so we had to make a break for it. We ran down the steps and rushed out the door and to the truck. I fumbled with the keys until I got to the car remote, opened the back door and threw the duffle bag full of cash in. We flew out of there like a bat out of hell. I could see the blue lights in my rearview but the faster I went, the further we grew apart until I was sure they were not after us. Once I got to the highway, I slowed down to seventy-five miles per hour, not wanting to bring any unnecessary heat to our vehicle. As I watched Mercedez reunite with the twins my heart began to swell with joy. It was the epitome of love in its purest form. I wondered if my son, Krystal's son, missed me like that. I looked over at Mercedez and wondered if she knew that the boy I had been raising was actually Solo's son. I was so busy looking at her that I didn't notice that the car in front of me had come to a complete stop. We crashed into the car violently and both of our vehicles slid on the black ice on the road. The other vehicle hit a pole and instantly blew up while ours flipped over twice and landed upside down against a tree on the side of the road. I was completely thrown out of the truck onto the pavement. I could hear the kids crying and I was relieved when I saw them in the truck and not on the road or the woods. "Mercedez!" I called out but got no response. My legs felt like they were on fire and I was suddenly in excruciating pain as I used my arm and elbow to crawl back to the truck to get to Mercedez. I could see the airbag but I couldn't see her face and my anxiety went from zero to one hundred. "MERCEDEZ!" I hollered out in a panic. My adrenaline must've been pumping because somehow I found the strength to get on my feet and rush towards the truck with glass sticking out of my legs but I didn't feel a thing anymore. All I felt was distress in wondering if my woman was okay. The girls were hysterical by now because their mother wasn't responding. Not only that, they were upside down in the truck. Luckily their seatbelts were on. I managed to get both girls out through the back window and gave them a quick once over to make sure they weren't bleeding anywhere. After I was sure they were fine I placed them on their feet, side by side and got back down to help Mercedez. She was slumped under the airbag with a huge gash on the side of her head and she was unresponsive. I shook her head until her eyes fluttered and she mumbled something incoherent. When her eyes finally came into focus and she became consciously aware of the scene around her she immediately started searching for the girls. "They're fine," I reassured her and helped her ease out of the truck. "Find your purse and get your phone and dial 911," I told her once I helped her on her feet. "You need medical attention."

"I think my arm is broke," she said, holding her elbow like she was in pain.

Suddenly, I didn't feel too good anymore. I guess the adrenaline ran out because all the pain came rushing back and my head was pounding with a headache.

"Oh my God, Aahmad, your head!" Mercedez exclaimed frantically, and for the first time I noticed the moisture trickling down my forehead. I wiped my forehead from what I thought was sweat but was actually blood and winced in pain at Mercedez's touch. That's when I started to feel woozy and I collapsed on the grass. "Tragic!" I heard Mercedez's voice but I didn't see her. As a matter of fact, I didn't see anything but darkness as I was slipping in and out of consciousness. The last thing I heard was ambulance sirens before I saw a bright, white light in the midst of the darkness. It seemed so close and yet so far away. When they say your life flashes before your eyes before you die, it really does because all I could see was scenes of my life from adolescence up until now playing in the background as I gravitated towards the light. That's when I saw someone I never thought I'd see again, my grandma.

"What are you doing here?" I asked her, not comprehending the fact that she was dead.

"I'm here to take you home baby," she said and she grabbed my hand as we continued to walk down memory lane on the way to the light.

Chapter 31: Solo

I walked out of the jailhouse grateful to be breathing fresh air again. One hour a day outside was not enough when you're couped up with a bunch of niggas all day. I wrapped my arms around my momma and she hugged me tight. "Thank you God, so it's really over?" she asked with a look of uncertainty.

I looked at her with a sly grin. "You see me out don't you? The witness got himself killed. And, you know what they say, no face-"

"No case," she smiled, showing her gold tooth, slapping hands with me. We both chuckled, relieved that SciFi's snitching ass was dead. My probation officer let me go back on papers when the charges didn't stick so besides being on probation I was a free man.

"I thought you were gone have the girls with you?" I asked as I hopped in the passenger side of my mother's green Honda Civic. "What, they at the house?" I was anxious to see my daughters for some reason. My mom cranked up the car and we pulled away from the precinct."

"Yeah, they at the house with John and Sug," she said.

"What's goin on with Mercedez? Was she doin' alright?"

Janice grimaced at the mere mention of that girl's name. Damn, she really couldn't stand her. I just shook my head. I didn't give a fuck about Janice's feelings towards Mercedez, she was the mother of my kids and that was never going to change. I wished she would just give the girl a chance, especially considering that terrible accident that put her in the hospital with a fractured arm and head trauma. The internal bleeding was so severe that once she fell asleep that night in the hospital she had slipped into a coma. A lady that Janice knew from The department of human services (DHS) had contacted my mother as the girl's next of kin at the hospital due to the fact that I was incarcerated and Mercedez's mother lived way in Michigan. "As far as I know, she hasn't come out of it yet," Janice was saying. "You know the doctors are saying there's a chance that girl might not come out of it at all."

I furrowed my brows. "Yeah, you'd like that, wouldn't you?" I asked sarcastically.

"Hmmph," Janice huffed. "Now that'll be too much like right."

"You be on that bullshit," I said, shaking my head.

"How?" Janice asked. "You was in jail while she was out here fuckin' out of both pants legs, had my grandbabies ridin' around with yo' homeboy at that! It's no wonder they asses ended up in a accident, you know God don't like ugly," she tried to reason. "And he ain't too fond of pretty either,"

"Watch the road," I said as a car blared its horn at us. I took the blunt she was trying to light and sparked it myself. "And anyway, I told you ma, this one's on me. I'm the one that cheated on her first with Krystal."

Janice's eyes grew large. "You know they found that girl in Stateline in an abandoned building. Somebody shot her and left her for dead!" I looked out the window wearily, not really wanting to talk about Krystal. She had been the root of my problem and the beginning to a series of bad events. "They say the bullet went through her back and punctured her lungs. "It's a wonder she's still living," Janice was saying.

"Yeah, the bullet hit a nerve in her spine, paralyzing her from the waist down. You call that living?" We pulled up to a red light and a jeep with four young cats pulled up next to us. They wore loud chains and dread locs and had their radio turned all the way up. They were shirtless with endless tattoos and they all wore gold and platinum grills in their mouths. A thick cloud of smoke came from all sides and hovered over them like a storm cloud. I smiled, remembering when I was that young and wild. I wasn't no old nigga but life had taken its toll on me and forced me to grow up. These lil' niggas was wildin' and probably didn't give a fuck about nothing but pussy, money, and drugs, in that order. They took off as soon as the light turned green and before they were less than a quarter mile down the road, a police car had crept up on them and threw their blue lights on. *Better them than me,* I thought with a smirk, shaking my head. That was a perfect example of why I no longer craved the streets. Trouble wasn't exactly enticing anymore. I'd rather get a nine to five and be a square before I get locked up again. What I longed for now was love. Agape' love, the kind you could only get from a family. One day my daughters will be old enough to date and I want them to be able to say they want a man just like their daddy. I wanted to be the father they knew at home, not the man they heard about in the streets. I wanted their relationship with me to be different from the one I had with my pops. My dad left my mom when I was just five years old. Even at that young age I was still able to process a lot of shit. My pops was getting money. He often stayed out late nights and he and my momma used to fight about that every night he came in late. She would prepare these big meals and run him a bath only for the water to go cold and his seat left empty at the dinner table. My momma would fuss and gripe about it but he would pay her ass no mind because he knew he was the one putting food on the table, until one day he stopped and my momma's food stamps were our only source. It was like the money train had stopped and the ass whippings started. He would beat her, steal her money and stay out all night, sometimes for days and come home broke. It got to the point that we had to move out of our house and into the projects and that was when Janice found out that he was smoking the crack he used to sell. Dealers would chase him home and my momma would have to give them whatever money she had to keep them from killing him. When he overdosed and died, the ass whippings didn't stop, they just trickled down to me and my siblings but mostly me. It was like my own momma hated me because she took most of her anger out on me. I guess because I looked like the man, I don't know, I still don't know what the fuck her problem was. I know she had issues though because she went from one man beating her to the next. Abusive relationships were a pattern for her. I guess that trickled down to me too. I wanted to break the cycle though, I wanted things to work out differently for my kids, that's why I was so hell bent on making things work with my kids mother. Ashley was a lost cause because I wasn't beat for being with no junky but Mercedez was different. She never allowed a substance to totally consume her and take over her life unless that substance was love. She was the epitome of love.

My girls jumped into my arms as soon as I walked through the door. "Daddy!" They sang in unison as I swooped all three of them into my arms at one time. They smelled like *Blue Magic* hair grease and baby lotion. "Granny curled my hair," one of the twins said, pulling on the hair rollers in her long, thick hair. "We ate spaghetti and meatballs," the other one said. "I got an A on my science project," my oldest said, smiling. Then, one of the twins asked, "Where is mommy and Chwa-gic?" The oldest one nudged her and smiled embarrassingly. My jaws clenched tightly. This bitch had my daughters asking me where the next nigga was at.

"Who want some ice cream and cookies," Janice intervened as I stood there, blood boiling. I was finally home and the only thing they worried about is this bitch ass nigga? I watched the girls indulge in their ice cream party as I thought about vengeance on Tragic. Murderous thoughts invaded my mind. The accident should've killed him but I guess God showed mercy and spared that nigga his life. I, on the other hand would show no mercy and spare no milliceous act to put that nigga six feet under. I grabbed my mother's keys and decided it was time to take a trip to Forrest General Hospital. Tragic was there and I would make sure he never made it out. Not only that; Mercedez was in there and I needed to lay eyes on her to make sure she was okay. As mad at her as I was I still couldn't bring myself to wish no harm on her. How could I? She was the mother of my kids and we had been together forever. For as long as I could remember, she had been my girl, my ride or die, my down ass bitch who would put a nigga in the dirt for me. She had to be my soulmate because I couldn't imagine living life without her. Even after she crushed my soul by fucking with the opps I didn't want to be with nobody but her. But, our world had been shaken up like a snow globe. My only hope was that when the pieces fall into place, we fall together.

    I pulled into the hospital parking garage and parked on level four to get to room 402. As I made my way to her room, I tried to pull my thoughts together and find the words to say to her in hopes that she would hear me. The doctors said that there was still brain activity so there was a strong possibility that even in a coma, she could hear me. It may even trigger a response. As I entered the hospital room where the love of my life lay bandaged and hooked up to respirators and IV's, a lump formed in my throat and my eyes started to mist. Nothing could have prepared me to see her like this. I fought back tears as I walked over to her and knelt at her bedside, grabbing her hand and kissing it gently. "Hey beautiful," I said, clasping both her hands in mine. "It's me. I'm sorry I haven't been here, but I'm here now." My heart skipped a beat when her hand squeezed mine and then my heart nearly stopped beating when her hand gripped mine hard as her body started convulsing violently and foam seeped from the side of her mouth. The monitors started beeping like crazy and the lights flipped on as doctors flooded the room. "What's happening?" I asked the nurse in a panic.

    "She's having a seizure!" The nurse said, pushing me out of the room. "You'll have to wait out here," she said and slammed the door. I pressed my hands against the door and my forehead on the glass as I tried to see what was happening on the other side. "We're losing her!" One of the doctor's said, The nurse closed the curtain over the window and I couldn't make out what was going on. A few minutes later it grew eerily quiet in the room and I heard the doctor say, "Time of death, 3:47 pm." That's when my entire world went black.

I jumped up, panting and sweating, my heart feeling like it was beating out of my chest. I looked around the dark room, confused. I pulled out my phone to turn on the flash light so I could find a light switch and I noticed it was 3:47 am. I searched the wall until I found a switch and flicked it upwards causing the overhead lights to come on. When I looked across the room and saw Mercedez laying peacefully in the bed I was really confused. Her IV was beeping and her heart monitor was active. Then, in walked the nurse that had put me out of the room. "What happened?" I asked. "Is she okay?"

"Yeah, her fluids are just low. I'm here to change out her iV bag," she explained with a smile. I frowned. "Are you okay sir?" she asked, picking up on my uneasiness.

"Huh? Yeah," I answered, rubbing my hands over my face. "Just a bad dream I guess."

"Or more like a nightmare," she smiled again. "You're sweating. I'll bring you a cold soda. Coke or Sprite?"

"Coke," I said, walking over to Mercedez's bedside. "Thanks doc."

"Don't mention it," she said as she closed the door behind her.

The next morning a nurse tech entered the room to get vitals on Mercedez. While taking her blood pressure she informed me that Sunday morning visitation hours hadn't started yet and I was not supposed to be allowed to stay all night last night.

"I'm not goin' nowhere," I said boldly. "I gotta be here when she wake up."

"That could be weeks," the tech said objectively.

I shot her a cold look and said through clinched teeth, "I'm not leaving until she wakes up."

The tech just stared at me like she was standing her ground so I pulled out a wad of cash and peeled off five one hundred dollar bills. "This ought to cover my keep," I said with arrogance because I knew she would take the money. When money talks, bullshit walks.

She grabbed the cash quickly and said, "Well I guess we can make accomodations due to the severity of the situation."

I thought so, bitch, i thought bitterly but all I said was, "Thank you," as the young tech giddily left the room. Now, it was time to go get rid of Tragic. I planned on putting a hollow tip through his fuckin' brain. I knew the chances of me getting to him early on a sunday morning without being noticed would be easier than monday through saturday when the hospital was busiest. I called the front desk and got the room number for Aahmad Williams, Tragic's government name and discovered he was just four doors down. I peeked out of the room and scanned the hall. *This'll be easier than I thought,* I thought to myself, seeing the hall was completely empty. I closed the door to Mercedez's room and pulled the silencer out of my pocket. I attached it to the gun smoothly, shoved it on my waist, and when the coast was clear I darted to room 407. The curtains were closed and all of the lights were off in the room except for the lamp over the headboard of the bed. Tragic lay there, seeming to be resting peacefully. I was about to disturb the fuckin' peace and lay his ass to rest forever. Just as I raised my gun to shoot him his eyes flew open and scared the shit out of me. I was startled because I didn't expect him to be awake. Tragic's eyes grew large when he saw me aim right for his head. His fingers scrammed desperately in search of his call light to alert the nurse's station but it was out of reach. He had on a neck brace so he couldn't move his head to look for it. "I been wantin' to do this for a long time," I said, my trigger finger itchy. I cocked the gun back but before I could shoot the commotion outside made me stop and check the hall again.

"She's awake!" I heard someone say and I watched them go into Mercedez's room. All of a sudden I didn't care about Tragic or shooting him for that matter; all I wanted to do was go out there and see about my girl.

"This wasn't no tit for tat shit," I heard Tragic say behind me. "I love her."

"What nigga?" I asked, not believing what I just heard. Love? I fucked his bitch then he fucked mine. That's as tit for tat as it gets. Love how? I turned around slowly. "You just told me you love my bitch?"

Tragic, who now had his own gun pointed at me said, "You should've killed me when you had the chance."

"And you better kill me while you have the chance, "I warned him.

"If we weren't in this hospital your ass would be dead right now," he said in an icy tone.

I raised my hands and backed up slowly. "Till we meet again," I said with a sly smile.

"Till we meet again," Tragic agreed. I turned around and walked out of his room as murderous thoughts invaded my mind.

Epilogue: Mercedez

I was shocked to see Solo enter my hospital room. I didn't even know he was out of jail. How long had I been in a coma? I didn't know how much he knew about what happened but I'm sure if he heard it from Janice 99% of it was bullshit. The hospital social services representative informed me that's where my girls were. I had no idea how they reached her; she wasn't on my emergency contact list. Solo waited for the staff to clear the room before he spoke. "Long time, no see."

"Yeah, tell me about it," I said with a small smile but he wasn't smiling at all.

"No, you tell me about it. Why you have that snake ass nigga around my kids? Who was driving when y'all wrecked?"

"I was," I lied, not wanting to place blame on Tragic for anything. If it wasn't for Tragic we wouldn't have two of our kids so I wished he would get off his back because he had no idea... "And you don't have a right to question me. We're not together. But oh, since your bitch is dead, you want to come back to me?" I wanted to bust his bubble and tell him so bad how it was Krystal that kidnapped our kids but that revelation would only lead to a long line of questions which could connect me to her murder and I didn't trust him with that information. He might try to get back at me for leaving him and snitch me out. I don't put nothing past him. Besides, I didn't want to hear him bitch and gripe once I explained the whole situation that he was going to over-react to anyway. Some things were better left unsaid.

"What you talking about Mercedez? What bitch is dead?" he asked me looking puzzled.

I smiled, figuring he hadn't heard about Krystal. I know the police were on the scene so I know they discovered her and her brother's bodies. It had to have been on the news. A double homicide? The Hattiesburg Patriot would eat that up. "So, you haven't heard about Krystal? The bitch is dead. She got shot."

Solo laughed and now it was my turn to look confused. "Damn baby, I forgot you been in a coma for two weeks. That girl didn't die from that shit. She's at Hattiesburg Health & Rehab learning how to walk again." The color must've drained from my face because Solo asked, "Are you okay? You look like you just seen a ghost or somethin'."

"You've been to see her?" I asked, already knowing the answer.

"Yes," Solo admitted. "When I heard what happened I went to check on her. But, what's it to you? You got a whole other nigga."

He was right, I didn't have the right to be concerned but I wasn't tripping on him seeing her, I was wanting to know if she told him what happened. "Did she tell you what happened?" He shook his. "She must've written a statement," I said. If the police found her I was sure that they pressed her for information although there wasn't much she could say without incriminating herself.

"Nah, she says she can't remember. She has temporary amnesia from shock or some shit. Apparently that's her body's response to trauma," Solo explained.

"Temporary?" I probed. "So she'll eventually remember?"

"Maybe," Solo said, eyeing me curiously. "Why are you so distraught?"

"Distraught?" I laughed. "Someone's been reading books in prison," I joked.

"Fuck you bruh," Solo laughed.

"How'd you get out anyway?" I asked. "I thought your P O violated you?"

"They had to let me go when them bullshit ass charges didn't stick," he said, shoving his hands in his pockets. That was something he did when he was telling a lie. I wondered if Detective Miller helped him. I eyed him curiously with an arched eyebrow but decided not to press the issue. I had enough dirt on my own front porch, no need to be sweeping around his.

"So, where are you staying, with Janice?" I asked nosely.

"Why does it matter, shit I can't come home can I?"

"We're not there yet," I said, speaking on the status of our relationship. "You need to figure your shit out like I need time to figure out mine."

"Fuck that, I'm not about to sit around and wait for him to fuck up so you can come back to me. You made your choice and I got options."

"You *been* having options, that's the problem. But I'm going to make it easy for you and eliminate myself as an option," I said, trying not to get in my feelings.

"Go head then Mercedez. You been wanting to do that shit anyway. I should've never tried to turn yo hoe ass into a housewife in the first place."

"Get the fuck out of my room!" I exclaimed just as a nurse technician was entering the room. She looked back and forth at the two of us and asked if everything was okay. "Yes, he was just leaving," I said, my eyes never leaving his.

"Bye then, bitch," he said, slamming the door on his way out. I was beyond embarrassed.

"Do you want me to call security?" the young black girl asked sympathetically.

"It's not necessary," I assured her.

"Are you sure? I can make it to where he can't come back. Stress is unhealthy. He has your blood pressure sky high," she said, looking at the monitor. "That can hinder the recovery process and even cause you to go into remission."

"In that case, yes, you can make it to where he isn't allowed back in here. That would be great," I said, finally looking at her. She was absolutely, drop dead gorgeous. She had lemon colored skin with slanted blue eyes. She had high cheekbones, plump lips and a diamond stud nose ring on the right side of her pointy nose. Her hair was cut in golden layers that fell on her shoulder and her eyelashes were naturally long with a hint of mascara. Her thick eyebrows were arched and her dark brown eyeliner matched the lip liner she wore with a touch of lip gloss. Her red scrubs made her skin look radiant and fitted her tiny waist, big hips and bigger boobs to perfection. Her Nike VaporMax gave her an inch so she looked 5'7" instead of 5'6". She was definitely a bad bitch and she carried herself like she knew it too.

"I'll take care of it," she said, giving me a tight lipped, sympathetic smile.

"Thank you…" my voice trailed off, realizing I didn't know her name.

"Anastasia," she said, extending her hand. "My friends call me Asia."

I shook her hand with a smile. "How long do I have to be here?" I asked seriously.

"Just a few more days, long enough for them to run some tests and scans and make sure your lab work is okay. If everything comes back okay you can be out of here as early as wednesday."

"I have one more question," I stopped her before she left out. "The guy that came in with me in the accident, is he okay?"

"There's only so much I can say without violating HIPPA rights but I will say this, he's doing just fine."

"Can you take me to see him?" I asked buoyantly.

"You really shouldn't be out of the-" Asia started but someone cut her off.

"She's not going nowhere. I'm right here love," Tragic's voice boomed from behind her.

Anastasia turned around and clasped her hands over her mouth and said, "Oh, how sweet. He brought flowers!"

Tragic wheeled himself in the wheelchair with one hand and held a bouquet of giant Hibiscus Exotic Coral flowers in the other. My heart skipped a beat. It always did that when he entered the room. Even in a wheelchair with a bandaged head, he was still the most beautiful species of a man I had ever seen. "Look at you," I said, getting choked up. I hated to see him injured like that but at the same time I was relieved to be seeing him at all.

"I tried to push him but he insisted on doing it himself," a young, mexican guy with tan scrubs on said with a heavy accent.

"I keep tellin' this nigga I ain't handicapped," Tragic said and we all laughed.

"Yeah, he's wheeled himself over here everyday since y'all have been here," the Mexican revealed. "He was talking to you like you could actually hear him or something,"

"Cut it out man," Tragic said, waving his hand over his head with a smile.

"What? It's true," the guy said, dodging a playful slap from Anastasia.

"We're going to leave you two alone and give y'all some privacy," Anastasia said, grabbing the Mexican by the arm. "Let's go Gabriel," she said to him.

"Speak for yourself princess, I'm a sucker for romance," Gabriel joked and we all shared a laugh. "Nah, it's time for me to clock out anyway. I'm done cleaning for the day." He stood in front of Tragic. "Later dude," he said, slapping hands with him.

"Alright my guy," Tragic said back.

Anastasia and Gabriel cleared the room and Tragic and I were alone. He looked at me so intensely it felt as if he could see through my soul. His gaze seemed to capture me and I couldn't look away. My breath grew shallow and I could feel my body responding to his captivating energy. Not wanting to jump on him and fuck him right there in the hospital, I decided to speak to break the spell he had on me. "Where'd you get the flowers?" I asked, reaching for the bouquet. "And how'd you know they were my favorite?"

"The gift shop, and a lucky guess," he said, handing them to me. "They looked like the same flowers you saw at wal-mart that time we were out of town and you said you would get them if they had the same plant in Hattiesburg." I inhaled their scent as I closed my eyes, basking in the moment. I imagined I was in a field on a spring day instead of in a hospital bed. I could almost feel the sunshine. When I opened my eyes, Tragic had opened the curtains allowing the light to illuminate the room. I admired the beautiful bouquet because it was even prettier in the sunlight. When I commented on how pretty they were, his response was, "not as pretty as you," licking his lips and I blushed. A compliment from him made me feel like the words he said about me were really true. I mean, I already knew I was pretty but for him to acknowledge it made me feel... I don't know...*extra* pretty or something. This man was so sweet and so good to me. Suddenly, I felt a pang of guilt for the way I was treating him the day of the accident and I felt like I should come clean about everything. If I was going to build something solid with this man, the foundation couldn't be rocky, built on lies. A foundation with cracks wouldn't weather a storm and everything we built would come crashing down because it had nothing to stand on in the first place. Living like that, any straw could break the camel's back.

"Tragic I-"

"Shhh," he said, at my bedside now. He fisted my hair and pulled me into the sweetest most gentle kiss I'd ever experienced. "You don't have to explain," he said, resting his forehead on mine. Some things are better left unsaid and what's understood-"

"Doesn't need to be explained," I said, finishing a phrase he used often.

"That's right love," he said with a kiss to my forehead this time. "You could use a toothbrush," he smirked and my face flushed with embarrassment. "I'm just playin' woman, come here," he said, pulling my chin to his. After allowing our tongues to dance with each other, Tragic pulled back. "I've been thinking," he said, looking me in the eyes. "I'm getting out of here today after I do my last round of physical therapy and I want to take you and the kids home with me....for good."

My eyebrows shot up in surprise. "You want me to move in with you?"

"You can keep your place for you to have your own space. But, I want you to come home to me at night. You and the kids."

"To your bachelor pad?"

"Fuck it, we can buy a house then. Whatever it takes to make this dream a reality. Our reality."

"You're serious aren't you?" I asked.

"Hell yeah I'm serious," he answered. "I've been doing a lot of thinking since I've been here sorting out what's important and what's not. And I discovered you're important to me Mercedez. You and the kids are a priority."

"I don't know what to say," I said, a bit flustered. When we went to stay with Tragic it was only supposed to be for a few days, I never intended to make it a permanent thing.

"You're my queen," Tragic was saying. "And I'ma need you to help run my new empire."

"Your new empire? What are you talking about Tragic?" I asked curiously.

He lowered his voice and propped his elbow up on the bed as he spoke. "I'm about to flood the streets with the purest cocaine they've seen since the eighties," Tragic revealed.

"You got a new plug?" I asked him, thinking about how I killed the old one. I shook the images out of my mind and listened intently as Tragic explained.

"The nigga Gabriel gone open the pipe line," he said grinning.

I frowned in confusion. "The mexican?" He nodded his head still smiling. "The *janitor* mexican?" I asked just to be sure.

"That nigga only got this hospital gig as a front for his soon to be n-laws. They think he's the regional manager over the maintenance department for the hospital and a few of its clinics. If they knew he was a drug dealer they would never approve of the marriage and wouldn't allow their daughter to go through with the wedding. The thing is, the marriage is only a front for immigration in order to get his visa. He's paying the girl big bucks to play along because if her parents found out they would probably call ICE themselves and have him sent back to Mexico."

"Wow," I said, shaking my head.

"Now," Tragic continued. "Gabe has an uncle named Lorenzo who's bringing the coke, pills, and fentanyl in from Mexico and it just so happens that Lorenzo needs a new distro."

"What happened to the last one?" I asked skeptically. "Did he get caught?"

"He overdosed on fentanyl," Tragic said disdainfully. "I don't know when these niggas gone learn you don't get high off ya own supply."

"So when do you meet Lorenzo?" I asked, trying to gather all the facts.

"As soon as I get the fuck up out of here. We graduated to the big leagues baby, we moving on up like George and Weezy. We only dealing with heavy weight now, by the truck loads. Supreme clientele only."

"I like the sound of that," I admitted. "Less heat, more money, more powder and more power. Sounds like a plan," I said with a grin. "You'll be the king of the streets."

"And you gone be my queen, thunder thighs," he said, slapping me on my thigh playfully. "If you think these bitches envied you before, wait till you boss up on 'em,"

"Oooh, you ain't lyin'," I laughed, ready to get out and level up on them hoes.

They say money is the root of all evil but that's not entirely true. It's the *love* of money that's the root of all evil. It doesn't matter what color you are, black, white, mexican, we all chase that one common color: green. Those who don't have it will envy those that do and envy is the onset of corruption. Envy opens the door to jealousy, pride, hate, greed, and evil doings. So you see, money isn't the problem. It's the broke muthafuckas who don't got it that you have to watch out for. They'll attempt to try to fuck your whole world up to get what you have, but they never will because it wasn't theirs to begin with. What's for me is for me so I envy no man, these bitches envy me. And if you thought this was the end of my story, it's just beginning. I'll be getting one of the hottest new authors out here, *T McB* to tell my story. So find out what happens next in *Envy II : For the love of money!* Coming soon to book store near you!

Sneak Peek @ Envy II: For the love of money

She weaved in and out of mid-day traffic on the Biloxi, Mississippi streets with the precision of a Nascar driver. She had less than fifteen minutes to make it down Pass road to the church to stop him from making the biggest mistake of his life. Plenty of vehicles blared their horns and the drivers yelled obscenities at her as she ignored every stop sign and red light, trying desperately to make it to the chapel in time. She never even took the time to glance in her rearview mirrors, if she had, she would have noticed the black on black Cadillac Escalade that was following close behind her. The car came to a screeching halt in front of the grand sized church. She hopped out in a hurry, not bothering to find a parking space and ran up the church steps two at a time. She wasn't dressed for the occasion wearing no shoes and tattered clothing but she came bursting through the sanctuary doors anyway, causing all of the guests to look at her and began whispering amongst each other in their seats. The preacher quit talking and all eyes were on her as she made her way down the aisle.

"Anastastia?" Gabriel asked with a look of confusion and mixed emotions plaguing his face. What was she doing here? After she didn't show up last night and sent the message insisting he move on with his life without her and with Mariah, he never thought he'd see her again. He looked her up and down wondering what the hell happened to her and why she was looking so disheveled. This was uncharacteristic of Anastasia because normally you couldn't catch her not dressed to perfection from head to toe. Besides the fact that she was busting up his wedding something was definitely wrong.

"What is the meaning of this?" Mariah asked, glaring at Anastasia. If looks could kill Anastasia would have dropped dead right there in the middle of the aisle.

"Oh, you know exactly what the meaning of this is," Anastasia said through gritted teeth.

"What are you doing?" Gabriel asked her.

"I'm stopping you from making the biggest mistake of your life," Anastasia said to Gabriel. "You can't go on with this wedding. I love you Gabriel Gonzales and I can't let you marry her."

"Okay girl, speak yo' truth or forever hold yo' peace!" Mercedez yelled from the bride's maid side of the alter. A few people laughed at that.

"I don't understand," Gabriel said.

"It was Mariah! I was on my way to you last night and she and her men took me and-" she stopped talking when she saw the red light dancing around his heart. "GABRIEL MOVE!" she darted in front of him just in time for the bullet to miss him but hit her instead. She collapsed in his arms as the blood seeped from her back. The crowd gasped and scrambled frantically for cover or an exit. It was pure pandemonium in the sanctuary.

"No, no, No! Asia!" Gabriel cried, scooping her up in his arms.

"I love you," she whispered, looking him in his eyes.

"Shhh," Gabriel tried to hush her so she could preserve her strength. Tears fell relentlessly from his eyes as he held the only girl he had ever truly loved and now he knew she did love him too. She had taken a bullet for him. She sacrificed herself for him. She was the epitome of true love.

"Let me see her, I'm a doctor!" an older, Jamaican lady said just as more gunshots rang out.

POW POW POW! Tragic let off three shots towards the balcony where the sniper had been spotted. One out of the three bullets hit the sniper in the shoulder. Tragic took off towards the steps that led to the balcony only to get up there and find the shooter was gone. He had jumped…

Made in the USA
Columbia, SC
27 November 2023